P9-DUF-122

CLAYTON COMMUNITY
LIBRARY FOUNDATION

Collateral Damage

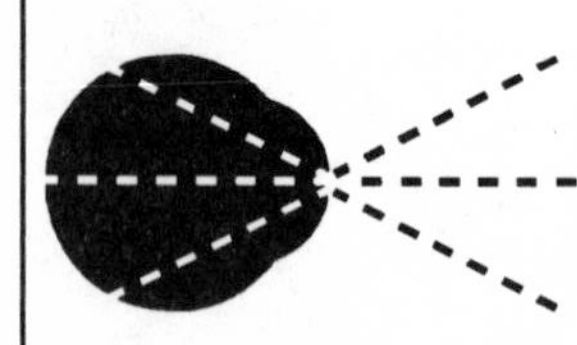

This Large Print Book carries the
Seal of Approval of N.A.V.H.

Collateral Damage

Fern Michaels

WHEELER PUBLISHING
A part of Gale, Cengage Learning

Detroit • New York • San Francisco • New Haven, Conn • Waterville, Maine • London

Sisterhood Series.
Wheeler Publishing, a part of Gale, Cengage Learning.

Wheeler Publishing Large Print Hardcover.
The text of this Large Print edition is unabridged.
Other aspects of the book may vary from the original edition.
Set in 16 pt. Plantin.
Printed on permanent paper.

LIBRARY OF CONGRESS CATALOGING-IN-PUBLICATION DATA

Michaels, Fern.
Collateral damage / by Fern Michaels.
p. cm. — (Sisterhood) (Rules of the game)
ISBN-13: 978-1-59722-775-9 (alk. paper)
ISBN-10: 1-59722-775-7 (alk. paper)
1. Female friendship—Fiction. 2. Large type books. I. Title.
PS3563.I27C65 2008
813'.54—dc22 2008022158

Published in 2008 in arrangement with Kensington Books, an imprint of Kensington Publishing Corp.

Printed in the United States of America
1 2 3 4 5 6 7 12 11 10 09 08

Chapter 1

Her name was Erin Powell, and she was almost perfect. She was beautiful, intelligent, kind, generous, and had a megawatt smile. *Almost perfect* because there was no such thing as "perfect." Or so said her mother. She was also considered the best of the best. She knew it, and so did the man standing in front of her. The others . . . They knew it, too, but would never admit it out loud. She'd told herself so many times over the years that no man would *ever* admit a woman could best him in *anything.*

Special Agent Erin Powell had graduated first in her class at the FBI Academy. She'd taken first place in the gun trials, first place in the endurance trials, first place in the triathalon, first place in *everything.* She didn't get any special medals or awards. What she got were scorn, snide remarks, and a gallon of grease to put on her sneakers to outrun all the lascivious agents hot on her trail. She knew the male agents had a pool going on as to who would get into her bed first. Like that was ever going to happen.

Erin Powell wasn't the name on her birth certificate. Her mother had named her Honey Sweet because she was such a little honey when she was born, all pink and beautiful, just the way a baby was supposed to be. And the reason her mother thought she was perfect was because she had all her toes and fingers, not to mention a full crop of curly hair. A trifecta for a newborn. Her parents were true romantics. She'd changed her name to Erin the day she turned twenty-one because even then she knew she wanted to be an FBI agent. Who in their right mind would ever take an agent seriously with a name like Honey Sweet? No one, that's who.

She'd done everything she could to join in, to try to belong, simply to fit in, but she was met with belligerence and hostility — forget those sensitivity classes. She'd even gone so far as to attend a retirement party with her colleagues and somehow managed to drink them under the table and still remain standing, much to their chagrin. She'd been sick for four days afterward, and to this day never drank more than one glass of wine. That, she'd heard through the grapevine, was the biggest thing that they held against her. Stupid, stupid, stupid. From that point on, she'd focused on her career and tuned them all out. She told herself over and over, at least a million times, that she didn't want *them* watching her back. She'd watch her own back, thank you very much.

She'd hoped for more in this career of hers, but it hadn't happened. For the most part she put in her time and went home at night to read procedure manuals and write her dissertation. She wondered how she would feel when she was finally, after all these years, addressed as Dr. Powell. Where would she fit in at the Bureau then? Her gut told her it would be worse. Maybe it was time to move into the private sector.

Erin looked up when the man standing in front of her cleared his throat. Finally, he was going to get to the reason she'd been summoned to this private room along with five of her colleagues. They thought *they* were the best of the best. Her insides started to quiver with laughter when she thought about how the vigilantes had escaped their clutches and left them standing there, looking like the fools they were. *Cocky, sanctimonious bastards.*

"Something funny, Agent Powell?" Elias

Cummings, the head of the FBI, asked quietly.

"No, sir," Erin said. She liked Elias Cummings. She'd been told by the women in the office when he stepped up to the plate that he was a fair man, a learned man, a man who knew and took his job seriously. If he didn't approve of women in the Bureau, he never let it show. She liked his grandfatherly looks, the twinkle in his eyes. He had a sense of humor about everything except the Bureau, and that's the way it was supposed to be. She wasn't sure he knew anything about her other than her name and Social Security number, so she couldn't help but wonder why she was standing here in this hallowed room with what the Bureau considered its other top agents.

Elias Cummings motioned for all six agents to take seats. They obliged, their eyes on the director and the six colored folders in his hands. They all knew something was up, something important. Erin could see the questions in her fellow agents' eyes as they wondered why *she* was here.

Cummings addressed Erin first as he opened her file. His eyes were thoughtful as he skimmed through her performance evaluations. He didn't look at her until he got to the background check report. There was no twinkle in his eye when he asked her why she hadn't informed the Bureau that she knew several members of the vigilantes.

"I beg your pardon, sir. Would you mind clarifying the question?"

"It says right here," Cummings said, waving a sheet of paper in the air, "that you grew up with Barbara Rutledge, Myra Rutledge's daughter, and Nikki Quinn, Myra Rutledge's adopted daughter. Nikki Quinn is a member of the vigilantes, as is Myra Rutledge."

"That was twenty years ago, sir. We were children, we played together. We were friends. We stayed in touch for a while, but we got on with our lives. I did go to Barbara's funeral, and I cried the way everyone else cried. She was too young to die. Nikki, Barbara, and their mother came to see me when I graduated from the Academy. They gave me a lovely pearl necklace. When I bought a house, Nikki's law firm handled the closing. After a while the Christmas cards stopped, and we lost touch. I'm sure that's all in your file . . . *sir.*"

Erin could hear the five agents sitting around in a half circle snickering. Well, maybe not all five were snickering, but she knew Doug and Joe were. Somehow, some way, she was going to make them pay for those snickers. Her nerve endings started to twitch as she wondered if there was any way for Director Cummings to know how she had secretly rooted for the vigilantes the day they were arraigned in court and how her fist shot in the air when she'd heard they'd gotten away. Was there any way for the director to know she followed their missions with joy in her heart? *Impossible!* She let her elation show only in the privacy of her own little cottage, which she shared with a big old cat named Dancer.

"It is, Agent Powell. So, what you're telling me is you've had no contact with the infamous vigilantes?"

Erin's nerve endings screamed. "Yes, sir, that's what I'm telling you." The silence in the room thundered in her ears. Was she being set up for something here?

"In the interests of clarification, you have not contacted them, and they have not contacted you. Is that right?"

"Yes, sir, that is right. With all due respect, sir, why are you asking me these questions? I'm sure there are hundreds of people who knew and have interacted with the members of the vigilantes in the past. Are you questioning them, or is it just me?" she asked coldly, her eyes flashing with anger.

"You're a federal agent, Agent Powell.

That puts you front and center. The others you speak of are too numerous to count, but rest assured we are talking to everyone we can find. Someone is helping those women, and I believe there is a mole right here in this building who is helping them. I'm not saying it's you, Agent Powell. Having said that, I am appointing the six of you in this room as a special task force to apprehend the women known as the vigilantes. You, Agent Powell, will use whatever you know about Myra Rutledge and Nikki Quinn, to figure out a way to catch them. I want you to do everything possible to figure out where they are and how to get them somewhere we can arrest them."

Erin's heart fluttered wildly in her chest. She knew the director was watching her carefully, waiting for her to respond. Of all the stupid, dumb luck, for her to pull a case like this. Suddenly the private sector was looking better and better. But for now, she couldn't refuse. She felt her body go ramrod straight. "How would you suggest I go about doing this, Director?" She couldn't resist a sarcastic shot of, "So far no one else in the FBI has had any success in capturing them, and when we've tried they made us look like fools. And, sir, while I am attempting to do as you request, what will my colleagues be doing?" This last was asked coldly and boldly, leaving nothing to the director's imagination.

Erin's sarcasm was not lost on Director Cummings. "They'll be your backup, Agent Powell. You are to apprise them of every movement, every detail the moment it occurs. Are we all clear on this?"

Six heads nodded in unison.

"Good. That means we're all on the same page. A room has been set up on the fifth floor for your use. Althea Cook is being assigned to you for the length of this special investigation. I hope there are no questions."

"Excuse me, sir, I have a lot of questions," Erin said, her head buzzing with wondering what she was expected to do.

"If you have questions, Agent Powell, you don't belong in this job. Treat it like any other case. Start at the bottom and work upward. Use your colleagues' expertise. I thought it was understood that you, Agent Powell, are in charge of this task force. And, let me make something else crystal clear. I want no tattling. If any of you agents have a beef, if your feelings get hurt, if you don't like your assignments, take it up with your boss, and for now Agent Powell is your boss. She and she alone will report to me in a timely manner, which in this case means once a day."

Erin was so stunned she was suddenly speechless. Finally, after all these years, she was the agent in charge. All of the yahoos standing behind her were going to have to take her orders, do what she said, when she said it. Oh, yeah!

As was the rule, the agents waited until Director Cummings exited the room before they moved or uttered a word. Erin was prepared for the storm that would no doubt erupt the moment the door closed. But nothing happened — which worried her.

Erin looked down at the Mickey Mouse watch on her wrist. A gift from Myra Rutledge when she graduated from the FBI Academy. It had been a joke at the time and was followed by the exquisite string of pearls, but she loved the watch with the big hands and equally big numbers even more than she did the pearls, and she wore it every day. There was no need for anyone to know where the watch had come from.

Erin allowed herself a few moments of pure victory. She eyed the men, who wore angry looks and were waiting for her orders. She played it for all it was worth. It was her due, pure and simple. She looked at her watch again. Then she took a few seconds to look the men up and down until they grew uncomfortable.

"Since it's almost lunchtime, gentlemen, let's decide what we want. Joe, today you get the honors. I'll take a pastrami on rye with two pickles. Two. Not one. Two. Write it down, Joe. Then I want it entered in the new logbook I'm going to set up."

Joe Landos was a buff, good-looking, sandy-haired six foot-four guy with a beacon smile who cheated on his wife left and right, then bragged about it. Landos nodded, his eyes spitting sparks.

"Doug, I want you to go with Joe to help him carry lunch. Oh, I'd like some coffee. Light. No sugar. Tell me you understand this order."

Doug Parks was also buff, and tanned, thanks to a tanning bed. He had an atrocious combover that was laughable. He called himself a bachelor, divorced twice with three kids. He showered at the Bureau and on many occasions slept in one of the rooms they reserved for all-nighters. Right now he was an unhappy camper, and he let it show. Erin watched as he bit down on his lip to stop one of the hateful comments that were his trademark. Somehow he managed to spit out the words, "I understand."

"Charlie, you, Bert, and Pete come with

me. We need to set up our workroom. We'll need some extra phones, a fax, and a copy machine. I don't want to overwork Althea. She is, after all, a woman, and you guys know how delicate we females are."

Charlie Akers grinned. Charlie was seasoned, a good agent who went by the book. He was in his fifties with a sweet wife, who was a wonderful homemaker, and two kids in college. A man who loved his family and his job. She'd never heard a derogatory remark come out of his mouth.

Pete Mangello was near retirement and a grandfather to seven girls. He was someone you could count on to do his share and never complain. He was known to partner with Charlie, and Erin knew for a fact that they were also social friends. Neither one would give her any trouble. Joe and Doug would try to throw monkey wrenches into the case, not caring about the end result. Sending them for lunch was her first shout of authority. She made a mental note to ride their asses till they were scraped raw. She was up at bat, and it was a whole new ball game.

The fifth man and her favorite agent, looked at her, his eyes full of questions, but he didn't say a word. He simply waited.

Erin smiled. There was a time when she

seriously thought about dating Bert Navarro, but something told her to keep the situation the way it was. And she had listened to her own advice, which didn't mean she couldn't enjoy his company. He was Cummings's number-one man, and for the director to lend him out was not only the highest compliment he could pay her, it was telling her Cummings had faith in her abilities. She looked around at the others as they waited for her next words. "Bert, you're my number one."

"Okay, boss. Just tell me what you want me to do."

"Right now, give Joe your lunch order, then you and I are going to map out a little strategy, which we will share with the others."

Landos shot Navarro a look of pure hatred that was outdone only by the more intense glare he shot in her direction. Erin smiled and made shooing motions with her hands to get the two lunch runners to move.

Right now, the score was one–zip. But she was the umpire.

CHAPTER 2

It was a chilly day even though the sun was bright and golden with more than a hint of autumn in the air. The gorgeous canopy of colored leaves overhead attested to the fact that October was coming to a close on Big Pine Mountain in North Carolina. At the stroke of midnight it would be All Hallows' Eve, and there still wasn't a pumpkin or scarecrow in sight.

A light breeze whispered through the trees stirring the brilliant gold and bronze leaves. They whirled and twirled with abandon as Annie de Silva and Myra collected them from the blanket they'd spread for a light picnic lunch. They were waiting for the girls to finish their ten-mile run.

Annie sniffed at the deep aroma from the pungent pines the mountain was known for. "I just love the smell of pine. It reminds me of Christmas when I was a little girl, and the house was full of evergreens."

Myra thought Annie sounded sad, which was not at all like Annie. Normally she bubbled and babbled nonstop. Myra raised her eyebrows in question but then only nodded.

"What do you think it will be like up here when the snow comes, Myra?"

Myra thought about the question for a moment. "I imagine it will be just like it was in McLean, Virginia, Annie. The only difference will be our outlook. And we won't be able to drive anywhere. By the same token, there isn't anywhere to go. There are snowmobiles here so we can spin about the mountain if we want to. I'm thinking it's going to be bitter cold up here, and we won't want to go anywhere. There's a lot to be said for roaring fires, good food, wonderful books, and listening to music. We have good friends here and, best of all, Annie, no matter what anyone says, we have made a difference in a lot of people's lives. All for the better. Are you getting homesick?"

"Sometimes," Annie answered honestly.

"Memories are wonderful, but sometimes they become our worst enemies." Myra leaned closer and whispered because she knew even a low-voiced comment carried over the mountain. "Supplies came in this morning, and if I'm not mistaken, I saw a whole crate of pumpkins being unloaded. I think Charles has a surprise for us, and that's why he arranged this little picnic. He wanted us out of the way. I think he's going to decorate the porch the way Nikki and Barbara did our porch back home when they were girls. Then I think he's going to make pumpkin pies, pumpkin bread, and pumpkin soup for dinner tomorrow night. You a betting woman, Annie?"

"Nope. It's a sucker's bet, Myra. I saw those pumpkins, too, and was wondering what they were for. I hope he saves a few so we can carve them. I think the girls need a little diversion. How is it that we lucked out on avoiding that ten-mile run?"

Myra smiled. "I told Charles we'd do the time on the treadmill later this afternoon. Now, if we suddenly get too busy . . . oh, well."

Annie laughed. "Things have been quiet lately. Why do you suppose that is? Surely there are people out there who need our help." She let the words hang in the air to await her friend's response, since Myra had the inside track with Charles Martin.

"Oh, there are, Annie. Charles has stacks and stacks of requests for our help both here and abroad. But each request, while it comes with a huge payout to us, isn't always feasible. First and foremost is our safety. It's not the actual mission itself but the planning, the getting in and getting away safely. I think," she whispered again, "something is up. Charles received a call when he was packing up the picnic basket. He walked away out of earshot to talk. His whole body language changed when it came in. I think we're about to go back into business. I could be wrong but I don't think so."

Annie clapped her hands. "Ooh, ooh, that sounds exciting. I'm up for whatever it is. How about you, Myra?"

Myra smiled as she opened the picnic basket. "You know what, Annie, I am. Like you said, it's been exceptionally quiet of late and . . . I hear the girls!"

Both women turned to one of the many paths leading down the mountain. The young women bounded into the clearing, whooping and hollering and, to Myra's and Annie's chagrin, barely breaking a sweat. They plopped down on the blanket, all of them reaching for the frosty bottles of water.

"I can eat the entire contents of that basket," Kathryn said as she swigged at the water. Kathryn Lucas had an enormous love of eating and a stomach that could handle any kind of food twenty-four hours a day. "What are we having? Please don't tell me cheese and crackers."

The others groaned at the prospect of cheese and crackers.

Annie clucked her tongue. "Shame on all of you. A picnic is a picnic. That means fried chicken, without the skin, of course, hard-boiled eggs, potato salad, melon and kiwi, sugarless sweet tea, and sugarless brownies. Charles said you can each have two. You know how he is about desserts."

"That's because we're sweet as honey as it is," Isabelle Flanders said, giggling.

At Isabelle's words, Myra looked over at Nikki, who was staring back at her. Both women had strange looks on their faces.

"What? Why are you two looking at each other like that?" Alexis Thorne asked in a jittery-sounding voice.

Myra shook her head and reached up to catch a golden leaf that was sailing downward in the soft breeze. She looked at it for a moment before she replied. "It's what Isabelle said, that we're sweet as honey. A long time ago, when my daughters were young, they had a friend named Honey Sweet. She used to live on a neighboring farm, and because it was too far to walk, her mother would drop her off to play. They rode the school bus together."

"We stayed friends for a long time," Nikki

said, picking up on the story. "We went away to different colleges but stayed in touch with letters, calls, and cards on birthdays and Christmas. We lost track of each other after a while, but Honey sent us an invitation to her graduation. Myra and I both went. She graduated first in her class at the . . . at the FBI Academy!"

The women reared up as one. "What?" they chorused.

Myra's eyes filled up. She ignored the outburst. "Honey came to Barbara's funeral. She cried so hard. There was no consoling her."

"Honey changed her name, from Honey Sweet to Erin Powell the day she turned twenty-one," Nikki said. "She said when she joined the FBI no one would take a woman with the name Honey Sweet seriously. She's Erin Powell now. When we were little, we all had these imaginary friends, and Honey's was Erin Powell. The name didn't surprise me at all. I haven't heard from her in years and years. I don't even know if she still works for the FBI. I do know she got her master's degree and was planning on getting her doctorate. We laughed about how Barb and I would then have to call her Dr. Powell. I wonder where she is these days. Have you heard anything, Myra?"

Nikki asked.

"No, dear, I haven't heard a thing from her in years."

The others started to jabber all at once. The questions all ran together. "Does she know who you are these days? Are you saying she didn't give you up to the fibbies? Whose side is she on? Why didn't you ever tell us you knew someone inside the FBI?"

Lawyer that she was, Nikki responded, "Because it isn't pertinent to us. That was long ago, another life. Honey was a loyal friend. The three of us were like sisters. Old friendships are treasured. That's the best answer I can give you. If any of you are thinking that Honey would spill her guts about us, think again."

"Nikki's right," Myra said.

A sudden gust of wind whipped through the clearing, sending down a shower of golden leaves that the women tried to catch. The overpowering scent from the pine trees rushed about them at the same time.

Ever suspicious, Kathryn demanded to know if the Honey Sweet connection meant anything in their current position. She reached for a thickly coated chicken leg and bit into it.

"I don't see how a memory can mean anything at this time. Isabelle said we were sweet as honey, and that triggered a memory Myra and I shared with you. End of story," Nikki said. "I will say this, though. Knowing Honey the way I do, I'm sure she rooted for us every step of the way. FBI or not."

"I agree," Myra said. "Now, let's eat this wonderful food Charles prepared for us. The rule is we have to eat it all and take back an empty basket."

The women fell to it until the hamper was empty. As they munched and chewed, they talked about the glorious fall colors, the ten-mile run, and what lay ahead of them for the rest of the day.

When it came time to clean up and fold the blanket, Annie called for silence. "I got a call a little earlier, actually it came through at 8:10. It looks like my offer to buy the *Post* is going to be accepted. Not to worry, ownership is buried so deep it will take years before anyone can figure it out. I was told there's another week or so of paperwork to go through, after which the paper is ours. Say something, ladies."

As one, the women whooped and hollered out congratulations, their shouts ringing down and around the mountain.

"This is a good thing?" Alexis asked.

"Oh, yeah," Nikki said.

"Now you can really kick some ass, Annie," Kathryn said. "Are you going to be hands-on behind the scenes? What are you going to write for your first op-ed piece?"

"That's down the road. Right now I have to think about how I'm going to tell Charles. I'm a little nervous about 'fessing up to that," Annie said.

Tiny Yoko Akia waved one of her arms. "Do not give it another thought, Annie. I think Sir Charles already knows and is not saying anything so as not to spoil your surprise when he says, 'And what else is new, Annie?' "

The women burst out laughing, even Annie.

"Time to head up to the Big House. Charles wants us to gather in the dining room at four o'clock. Today is Tuesday, so that means there might be mail. I for one can't wait for the Christmas Neiman Marcus catalog," Isabelle said.

"That came out in July. Where were you, Isabelle?" Alexis laughed.

The camaraderie was evident as the women trooped up the incline to the open area surrounding the compound. Murphy and Grady, Kathryn and Alexis's dogs, raced up to the women, barking furiously.

Murphy nudged Kathryn's leg as he tried to head her off in another direction. Knowing the big shepherd wanted her to see something, she followed him, the others trailing along.

"Oh!" was the collective comment as the women looked at the object of Murphy's angst. A huge scarecrow was settled comfortably on one of the Adirondack chairs, which was surrounded by bales of hay and pumpkins. Spiderwebs with black silk spiders stretched across the entire porch. A huge, furry stuffed black cat sat perched on the windowsill. White-sheeted ghosts, hung from wires suspended from the roof of the porch, swayed in the breeze.

The women clapped their hands in delight as they remembered their youth and similar displays at their own homes.

Myra waved her arms around. "I guess I was right after all. And that has to mean we're having all things pumpkin for dinner tomorrow. Come along, girls, we have to thank Charles for this wonderful display."

The dining room was a symphony of delightful smells. Cinnamon, nutmeg, baking bread, and baked apples. Even though they'd just finished eating, the women's mouths started to water at what was to come for the dinner hour.

Charles emerged from the kitchen wearing a snowy white apron, with flour on his hands and a smudge on his nose. "Ah, your timing is perfect, ladies. I just made fresh coffee. My pies and bread are baking. The leg of lamb is ready to go in the oven when they come out. So, give me five minutes to freshen up, then I have news for you."

The women, glowing from being outdoors, were effusive in their praise of Charles's efforts on the porch. He smiled and thanked them, adding, "I saved seven pumpkins that you can carve this evening so you'll have them ready for Halloween tomorrow."

Yoko set the picnic hamper on the counter and joined the girls at the table. Annie was setting out cups and saucers and the sugar substitute into a small cut glass bowl. One of Charles's theories was that something one didn't like was more palatable when served in something pretty to the eye. No one had the heart to tell him his sugar substitute sucked and that they all kept packets of real sugar in their pockets.

Charles was as good as his word and took his place at the table in the allotted five minutes. He carried a small yellow folder that he slid onto the table. He waited until Annie poured the coffee. His eyes were like a hawk's as he watched to see if any of his girls would try to sneak real sugar into their coffee. When he was certain everyone was obeying the rules, he opened the folder.

"I had a call this morning from Bert Navarro. Director Cummings of the FBI has appointed a special task force of six agents. Yes, I know that his predecessor tried to do the same thing, and we all know what happened to him. This is different. Cummings has hauled out what he considers his secret weapon in his war to catch the vigilantes. His secret weapon is a young woman named Erin Powell aka Honey Sweet."

Myra bolted upright in her chair. "We were just talking about Honey while we picnicked. Nikki and I were explaining to the others how we knew her, and how we haven't seen or heard from her in years."

"Well, if she has her way, you're going to be hearing from her soon. This all happened a few hours ago. Bert is on loan to Ms. Powell. As you know, he's Cummings's number one. Now Ms. Powell has made him *her* number one. He is not enamored of two of the agents assigned to this particular task force. Supposedly the group is comprised of the best of the best.

"According to Bert, Cummings appointed Powell lead agent and her orders are to use what firsthand knowledge she has about you and Nikki from her past relationship with you to figure out where you are and a way to get you where you can be arrested.

"Bert said when he gets home this evening, he will send the other agents' dossiers so we can see what we're dealing with. As I mentioned, he's very concerned about two of the agents — that's Joe Landos and Doug Parks. Charlie Akers and Pete Mangello are okay guys and will work with Powell, whereas the other two will work against her. That's all I have at the moment. Now would be a good time to talk this up."

Nikki shrugged. "Honey will never give us up even if she knew something to give up. Shoot, I keep calling her Honey, and I should be calling her Erin. What do you think, Myra?"

Myra's voice was thoughtful. "At first blush, I agree with you, Nikki. But we haven't seen or heard from Hon . . . Erin in many years. She might now be a dedicated agent, and this would put her at the top if she could bring us in. We are, after all, breaking the law. She's sworn to uphold the law. Right now, the best thing we have going for us is Bert, who has the inside track. If we're lucky, we can stay one step ahead of the task force."

"Should we be worried about this?" Annie asked.

Charles looked around the table. "We all

need to be very worried. I never thought I would say that, but I'm saying it now."

"I'm not buying into it," Nikki said. "In her heart, Erin is one of us. You can take that to the bank. Chalk it up to my gut instinct, Charles."

Charles's face wore a serious expression when he said, "I hope those words don't come back to bite your cheeks, Nikki."

"Ass, Charles. Say 'ass,' and it will carry more weight," Kathryn admonished.

Charles allowed a tight smile to stretch his lips. "Consider it said, my dear."

"Well, this is a pretty kettle of fish," Annie said, smacking her hands together.

"Are you aware that kettles of fish *smell,* Annie?" Nikki asked.

"Uh-huh."

Chapter 3

As Bert Navarro packed up his briefcase, he looked down at his watch to check the time. It was 6:45 P.M. Time to hustle to Harry Wong's *dojo.* There were times when he resented the fact that he had to take Harry's training, but it was an FBI edict, and he was glad he wouldn't have to come up with a lie to Erin Powell. Jack Emery would be there, and they could talk openly.

There was outrage in Erin's voice when she barked, "You're leaving? We haven't even started!"

"Look, Erin, I learned a long time ago that if you don't keep reasonable hours, stick to your routine to the best of your ability, this job will dump you over the edge. By the way, those are the words of every director who's sat on the throne. You picked my brain, there is nothing more I can do here tonight. I've been here since five thirty this morning. That means I've been here thirteen hours, and thirteen is an unlucky number, so I'm out of here."

Bert snapped the lock on his briefcase. "You should go home, too. Kick back and think about what exactly you want this team to do. You must still be reeling from the way it was all dumped on you. There are going to be a lot of eyes on you, Erin. You don't want to make a mistake right out of the gate. I've headed up six different task forces, and it's going to drain your blood, so be prepared. My advice, regardless of whether you want it or not, is to plan, delegate, execute, and be careful around Joe and Doug. Develop a set of eyes in the back of your head. Those two play for keeps."

Erin brushed back the hair from her forehead. She knew that what Bert was saying was true, but she was caught up in an adrenaline rush. She frowned. "Are you trying to tell me something, Bert?"

"Actually, I am. Watch your back."

Erin felt her stomach juices start to kick up as she looked at the wild disarray on her desk. "I hate it when people talk around something, Bert. If you know something, tell me what it is. I like things out in the open. If you're harboring any ill feelings because Cummings appointed me to lead this task force, spit them out right now so we can lay them to rest. I know you're Cummings's right hand, and you're probably looking at this as a demotion of some kind. I didn't ask for this assignment, but I'm stuck with it. If I'd had a choice, I would have turned it down."

Bert looked at the beautiful woman sitting behind her desk. He knew how hard she'd worked, how good she was, and he knew about the pool the guys had going on her. At that moment he felt sorry for her. God, if she only knew what a thankless job she had ahead of her.

"You know what, Erin, you're way off base. I'm happy to work here with you. Working with Cummings can be a real pain in the ass at times. The truth is sometimes I feel like the Bureau is wasting my time, and there are times when I actually feel guilty taking a paycheck for shuffling papers. I'm a field agent, and that's where I belong. This will give me a chance to get out there and do something. I don't resent you at all. But to answer your question, what I'm trying to say is that Doug and Joe are not team players. Oh, they work well together because they're birds of a feather, but they want all the glory for themselves. Both of them are damn fine agents. I can't take that away from them, but they do have their own agendas. I've watched them over the years and know their style, so just be on your guard and tread lightly, or they'll find ways to sabotage you every chance they get."

Bert reached for his jacket and slipped it on. "The only thing they heard the director say is that you have a history with two of the vigilantes. That's what they're going to go on. Trust me on this."

"What about you, Bert? What do you think about my history with Myra and Nikki?" Her voice sounded so bitter that Bert winced.

"Personally? I think that history belongs in the past, where it's lying right now. If you can make that history work for you, go for it. See ya in the morning." He wondered if it was good or bad advice. Probably a little of both.

Outside in the corridor, Bert heaved a huge sigh as he sprinted down the long hallway to the elevator.

Fifteen minutes later, he blasted through the doors of Wong's *dojo* to attend a class of two, Jack Emery and himself. The *dojo* was the perfect place to talk. He knew for a fact that good old Harry had his quarters swept for listening devices three times a day. He knew it because he'd provided the equipment.

Harry Wong was the number-two martial arts expert in the world, and he trained local law enforcement, the agents from both the FBI and the CIA. The instruction was mandatory, and woe to any officer who tried to blow it off. Harry Wong took no prisoners. There were more black and brown belts in the District, thanks to Harry, than there were cars on Pennsylvania Avenue. Harry was the best.

The moment Bert stepped out of the dressing room, he said, "Gather round, boys, I have news. Big news!"

When Bert finished his tale, Jack Emery looked off into the distance and said, "Oh, shit!"

"Here we go again," Harry said. "Jack and I were just talking yesterday about how quiet it was of late."

"What's your take on Powell, Bert?" Jack asked. "I've never heard of her."

"No reason for you to have heard of her. She's not a secret weapon of any kind. She's good. And she looks good, which is a strike against her. She tries to play down her looks and body, but, man, it's there for the world to see. She's probably smarter than this whole new task force put together. Her creds are super. The guys resent her, that's the bottom line. By rights, if you go by seniority, either Mangello or Akers should have gotten the job. Too old, is my opinion. Landos and Parks are glory hounds. They perform but are not detail-oriented. Cummings pulled her out of the bull pen because of her history with Myra and Nikki.

"This goes no further, guys. Cummings offered me the job with Powell as my number one. I turned him down flat, said I would quit first. I'm sure you understand why. He likes me, so he agreed to go with Powell. In other words, I'm his snitch. Hey, look sharp here, you two. It's a win-win for us."

Jack nibbled on his thumb. "How good is she, Bert?"

"She's not just good, she's *good.* She's a detail person, a nitpicker, a plodder. She doesn't miss a trick. She's thorough; nothing gets by her. Her gender is what's kept her under wraps. Yeah, yeah, in this time of women's rights, it shouldn't be happening. But it is and does. She sucks it up. My personal opinion is I think she's at odds with herself right now. She hasn't come to terms yet with what's expected of her. And, yeah, before you ask me, she could be turned. I think. Look, we just have to wait and see."

"Guess we aren't going to train tonight," Harry said.

"If you want, Harry, I can wipe up the floor with you after I send Charles some stuff that he's waiting for." Bert walked back into the changing room to get his sat phone. Harry's laughter followed him. On his best day, Bert couldn't lay a glove on the instructor.

Jack sat down in the middle of the mat and hugged his knees. "I think this damn well sucks, Harry."

Harry sat down and contemplated his bare toes. "You know what, Jack, you're right. The last guy that tried that special task force shit is still picking the fiberglass out of his ass and reclining in prison. Do you think this is going to be any different?"

"Yeah, Harry, this is going to be way different."

Harry continued to contemplate his toes, which were like steel pistons. He looked glum.

Jack Emery looked even more glum.

Back at the Hoover Building, Erin Powell looked around at the cluttered empty office. Empty of employees. Maybe Bert was right, and she should go home. Maybe she should stay and make notes. Maybe she should get some dinner. She suddenly remembered she'd had nothing today but a gallon of coffee. Her stomach was protesting. Maybe she could pick up something on the way home, open a good bottle of wine, and slide into the Jacuzzi and relax. Relax? How was she going to turn off her mind? That wasn't going to happen, and she knew it. She also knew she would just be spinning her wheels if she stayed here.

Erin got up and glanced once again at the stack of cartons that represented everything that was known about the vigilantes. A stack of colored folders looked like they were going to topple to the floor any minute. She straightened them and realized what a daunting task lay ahead of her. Was she up to the job? More important, did she even want the damn job? Maybe if she'd seen it coming, she would have turned it down, resigned, and her decision to go into the private sector would have been that much easier. And while she looked for a new job, she could finish her dissertation and get on with her life. *Why in hell didn't I do that?*

"Because you're stupid, that's why," she muttered. "And because you're vain and want to show up Landos and Parks."

Wondering if the temperature had

dropped, Erin reached for her jacket. She'd been in the hermetically sealed building since six thirty that morning. So Bert beat her to work by an hour. So what? She glanced at the Mickey Mouse watch and smiled the way she always smiled when she looked at it. A memory she had no intention of destroying.

On her way down in the elevator, Erin thought about Nikki and what a wonderful friend she'd been. She'd known how Erin had scrimped and saved for the down payment on her little house, and so hadn't charged for her legal services. Nikki had even sent her a housewarming present. Erin had loved Nikki and Barbara like sisters. When Barbara died, Erin went into a tailspin. It had left her sleepless and a nervous wreck for months. She still teared up when she thought of her old childhood friend.

And there was Mrs. Rutledge. A second mother, to be sure. Myra had always hugged and kissed her when she went to the farm. Myra treated her the same way she had treated her own daughter and her adopted daughter, Nikki. A wonderful, kind, generous lady who helped others and never let it be known.

Outside in the blustery October air, Erin walked to where she'd parked her car. She shivered in the dark night. She climbed behind the wheel, started the engine, then clicked on the heater. She waited until warm air spewed from the vents before shifting into DRIVE. At that hour she could make it out to Arlington in thirty minutes if she was lucky. She would stop at Donatelli's to pick up some Italian, and maybe some breakfast rolls while she was at it.

Her eyes on the road, she realized leaving the building was a wise choice. She was bone tired. Her thoughts drifted back to Myra and Nikki. How could she turn on them? How could she be the one to bring them to justice? Both of them must have searched their souls before they embarked on such a path. If only she could sit down and talk to them.

Erin's eyes filled with tears.

This was not what she wanted in her quest to move forward at the Bureau. "I should just up and quit," she mumbled to herself. "I don't owe Cummings or the other agents the time of day. I know in my gut they're going to screw me over somehow, some way, in their search for the vigilantes. I don't have to let them use me unless I want to let them use me. And I do *not* want that," she continued to mutter and mumble to herself.

Erin swiped at the tears dripping down

her cheeks. If she'd been more alert, less tearful, she might have seen Joe Landos in the car that was following her, but she was so wrapped up in her own misery that she missed it.

CHAPTER 4

Charles brought the after-dinner meeting to order with a raised hand. The women immediately seated themselves at the long oak table, abandoning their lively discussion on aromatherapy and the use of scented candles in the art of seduction.

"Girls! Girls! I think that's more than I need to know for the moment."

The women giggled, then sobered when their fearless leader held up a sheaf of papers.

Always the most verbal of the group, Kathryn Lucas blurted, "Is that our next mission you're holding in your hand?"

Charles gave his shoulders an elegant shrug. "It depends on all of you. At this time let me say it is a very serious request for your services. It will be extremely . . . uh . . . dicey if you accept."

"We get off on dicey, Charles. Tell us the good stuff. What's the payoff for us?"

Annie asked.

"More important, where?" Nikki demanded. "Location, location, location. Whatever it is, the location will be the deciding factor."

Charles looked from one to the other of his chicks. That's how he sometimes thought of them, and knew it worked for them as well, because his beloved Myra had told him the girls often compared him to a mother hen. She'd hastened to add that it was a good thing, and he should be flattered. A rooster, yes, a mother hen . . . Sometimes it made him anxious, like right now. "Right back to your old stomping grounds, girls. Washington, D.C."

Yoko Akia squealed in pleasure. Going back to Washington meant she would get to see Harry Wong. It didn't matter how dangerous or dicey it was. Love was where it was as far as she was concerned.

Kathryn beamed. Bert Navarro was in Washington.

Nikki positively glowed with the thought of returning to the nation's capital because that's where her fiancé, Jack Emery, lived.

Myra, Annie, Alexis, and Isabelle just smiled because, as Charles said, it was their stomping grounds. They knew the city and the surrounding areas better than any tour guide did.

Myra fingered the pearls at her neck. "I believe, dear, that's a resounding *yes* as far as the location goes. Who is it that requires our services?"

Annie leaned into the table. "What's in it for us?" she asked again.

"I'm working on that, Annie. The politician hasn't been born that I trust, so can we put that on the shelf for the moment until I explain the mission and what it entails?"

The women nodded.

"But before I get to the business at hand, I have a question of my own. It goes without saying that if we aren't up front with each other, and if there is no trust, we can't succeed. So, is there anything I should know that you haven't told me? Bear in mind that, as Kathryn has pointed out on many occasions, there is very little I do not know when it comes to all of you."

Somehow or other the women all managed to stare at Charles with blank expressions. Only Annie squirmed in her chair. When she was certain the others weren't going to speak, she said, "All right, Charles. I was . . . We were going to tell you, but I wanted to wait to see if things . . . you know, worked out. It looks like it will, so here it is.

I made a bid to buy the *Post.* Yes, yes, I know I'm a fugitive, but I have people . . . Well, let's just say money talks and bullshit walks." Annie frowned. "Did I say that right, Kathryn?"

Kathryn nodded, grinning from ear to ear.

Annie focused on Charles's stern features. "It appears that my bid is going to be accepted, which means the paper will be owned by all of us girls. Next year is an election year. The *Post* is a very powerful paper, as you well know. They can dig from now to eternity, and they won't come up with the true ownership unless we want that to happen. I thought, Charles, you would try to stop me. We voted, and we all agreed this was a good thing."

"This might sound like a silly question, Annie, but why didn't you talk to me about it and at least try to convince me if you thought that was the case?"

"Because I thought you would try to derail it all. We all thought . . . Well, we thought you wouldn't think it was a good idea," Annie said without missing a beat. Her mood and voice turned sour. "You're going to do that right now, aren't you?"

Charles looked around the long table again. Then he looked at his beloved Myra, who looked absolutely fierce. He knew a revolt was imminent if he gave the wrong answer. He smiled. "I thought it was a smashing idea. Had you come to me in the beginning I could have saved you a lot of angst. I knew what you were planning even before you did. Remember now, I have four sets of ears and two sets of eyes. I believe that is Isabelle's assessment of me."

"You agree!" Annie said. She looked so astounded, Charles found himself laughing heartily.

"But of course. However, I was joking a moment ago. Jack Emery told me what you were planning. No, he did not breach your trust. At the time he didn't know it was supposed to be a secret."

Still smiling, Charles said, "While I mean no disrespect to your . . . uh . . . people, Annie, they are babes in the woods when it comes to something like this. I took the liberty of stepping in on your behalf and had *my people* make it happen. If I do say so myself, I got you a magnificent deal, Annie. And you're right about something else, too. True ownership will never see the light of day."

Annie looked nervous. "I haven't looked at my bottom line in a while. I won't be destitute, will I?"

"Good Lord, no! You have enough money

left to buy several small countries, some islands, and a couple of oceans — not to mention all the real estate in Manhattan. Translated at last count I believe your net worth was something like 140 billion dollars. Just so we're on the same page, that's your net worth *after* the money necessary to buy the *Post* is excluded."

The gasp from the table made Charles smile.

"Does that make Annie a trillionaire?" Kathryn asked, awe in her expression.

Charles winced. "No. It takes a thousand billion to make a trillion. I think," he said, a frown building on his face. "If you absolutely need to know, I'll check. I don't normally work with such large numbers."

Alexis leaned across the table. "Where did you get all that money, Annie?"

Annie looked embarrassed. Her friends were looking at her differently, and she didn't like what she was seeing. Suddenly she felt sick. What if they turned on her because she wasn't like them?

"My husband inherited most of it. Spanish land, that kind of thing. He . . . he came from royalty. Oil. Way back when, he was into all things electronic. He . . . he loved gadgets. When my family died, I stopped caring about it all. Is this going to make a difference with all of you?" Her eyes wet with glistening tears, she looked so pitiful that the others bolted from their chairs to crowd around her.

"Absolutely not! . . . Never! . . . Shame on you for even thinking such a thing . . ." The women babbled as they hugged and squeezed the newest member of the Sisterhood. Annie beamed her pleasure as she wiped at her eyes. They were her family, and if they were okay with her wealth, then everything in her world was as right as it could be. Nothing else mattered but this new family of hers, Charles included.

Charles sighed. "Ladies, can we get back to work here?"

Myra reached over to squeeze Annie's hand. The tense moment had come and gone.

"But before we get to the business at hand, I want to share something with all of you." When he was confident he had the women's attention, Charles continued. "As you know, Bert Navarro, the newest recruit to our group, has been loaned by his boss, FBI Director Cummings, to a special task force headed up by Erin Powell. We discussed this earlier, but what I didn't share with you was that Bert also told me that Cummings was summoned to the White

House for a breakfast meeting. Bert was not privy to what transpired at that meeting. Moreover, for some strange reason, Cummings decided not only to keep his number one in the dark about what went on at the meeting, but he didn't even tell Bert that there had been such a meeting. Bert only found out about it by accident.

"Bert said that has never happened before. And after he asked Cummings about the meeting and got no response, he was suddenly transferred to Powell. Whatever is going on must be serious, and Bert is not afraid to admit he's worried.

"As you all know, the former acting head of the FBI, Mitch Riley, tried doing the same thing Director Cummings is doing by appointing a task force. That was unsuccessful, thanks to all of you.

"Several days before the meeting at the White House took place, a request came into the special message board I use with some of my operatives. It's not necessary to tell you how many people the request came through until it reached me, but suffice it to say, there were many. It seems that the brother of the president's chief of staff is closely tied to the Republican National Committee's fund-raising operation. Everyone is out there scurrying to raise money, as you know. Elections are expensive, and sufficient funds can be the difference between the success or failure of a campaign.

"Three weeks ago something happened. Perhaps I should say 'allegedly happened' because I haven't been able to pin it down. The master list with the names of well-heeled people willing to hold fund-raisers and the Republican Party's major contributors was stolen somehow. It appears that all the personal information was then sold to an identity theft ring. So far this information has been contained, but Washington is Washington, and the town leaks like a sieve. All those wealthy contributors, all those Wall Street people, are suddenly running scared. Supposedly bank accounts have been emptied, the dossiers the committee kept are going to be made public. Secrets will come out. If it isn't stopped, the candidates for president could go down the tubes. At the moment, the coffers are as dry as the Mojave. Is this all true? I have no idea. It's what I've been told, but as I said, the politician hasn't yet been born that I would believe."

Annie slammed her hand down on the table. "This is the third time I'm asking. What do we get out of this?"

Charles straightened his shoulders before

he spoke. "A presidential pardon for you all."

The women gasped.

Annie spoke again. "And who promised this presidential pardon?"

"The president's chief of staff, Daniel Winters. Do I believe him? I told you earlier that when you deal with politicians, it's the luck of the draw. Personally, I don't believe he can deliver on the promise, but that is only my opinion."

Nikki shifted her reading glasses higher on her nose. "If you don't believe him, why should we? What if something goes wrong?" Lawyer that she was, she said, "I want to see something in writing with the presidential seal at the bottom."

The women all agreed with Nikki.

"There's more, I can see it on your face," Alexis said. "Tell us."

"This morning a second message arrived on the message board. This one came from the head of the fund-raising operation for the overwhelming front-runner among the contenders for the Democratic Party's nominee in next year's presidential election. It came via a third party, probably twice removed. The same thing happened to them that happened to the Republicans, their donor lists were stolen. All that personal information is out there floating around. The Democratic campaign's head honcho didn't say this, but the Republicans did. People are being blackmailed, so I have to assume the Democrats will be blackmailed also. If it's even true.

"Now, here is the interesting part. It appears that the heads of both the DNC and the RNC were seen together talking in hushed whispers. Archenemies that they supposedly are, my people found that just slightly short of amazing. Personally, I think it's just a PR move on both their parts. Think Watergate and Deep Throat. The meeting took place at the foot of the Washington Monument at two o'clock in the morning — while the city slept. If you're keeping track of the timeline, it happened night before last."

"What are the Democrats promising?" Yoko asked.

"In a manner of speaking, nothing. We can negotiate with them, but there won't be a presidential seal at the bottom of the agreement. The way it stands now, the COS is the one doing the promising. But like I said, I don't trust anyone in Washington. It's pretty hard to beat out an incumbent. Having said all that, I am going to post a message on my board and say you are taking the request under advisement. That will give you time to think it through for a few days. I don't want you rushing into a decision. I will further state what we require in the way of assurances.

"We can adjourn now, ladies, and retire to the dining room for an after-dinner snack, including my famous Margaritas, to be personally served by yours truly."

"Sounds like a plan," Kathryn said as she led the women out of the Big House to the outdoor compound.

The dark night was exceptionally cool, with the trees rustling overhead. Grady and Murphy appeared out of the darkness and barked a greeting. A golden orange moon, which had been full a few days ago, glowed high in the sky.

"I just knew that something weird was going to happen this week. Things happen when there's a full moon," Alexis said quietly. "All the crazies come out to cause trouble. Emergency rooms fill up for some reason. I read that once in the *Post*."

"Speaking of the *Post*, I think we all need to congratulate Annie on her newest purchase," Myra said.

The women hugged Annie, high-fived her, and punched her lightly on the arm as they laughed and giggled about her latest acquisition.

Annie dropped her voice to a low whisper. "What will we do with it, girls? We need to start thinking about how we can make ownership work for us. Think about this: if we manage to get a pardon, we can just march into my paper and take it over." Then she said fretfully, "I don't know anything about running a newspaper."

"So, we'll learn," Kathryn said. "Is a pardon really a possibility? If we pull this off, assuming we take it on to begin with, won't they have to keep their promise?"

Nikki laughed, a strange sound in the quiet night. "Name me one time, just one time, when a politician kept his promise. When it comes to us, no one is going to help us but ourselves. Now, think about this. If we take it on, we need to do a little compiling of our own. It's called blackmail, ladies. Compared to our other . . . endeavors, blackmail is a drop in the bucket. And, don't forget for one minute that we have copies of all those files that were in Mitch Riley's safe. To me that's a hell of a bargaining chip."

"And we own the *Post.* All I have to do is sign off on it," Annie said.

"Oh, ladies, we are so golden we positively

shine!" Kathryn said.

"I guess that means we're going back to Washington," Isabelle said.

"Yes, that's what it means, dear. But this time we're going armed with our own brand of weapons — paper weapons," Myra said. "And I'm thinking we shouldn't be shy about mentioning them. The written word is all-powerful."

"Hear! Hear!" the others shouted, their voices ringing in the clear night.

Murphy and Grady both sat up on their haunches and howled at the waning moon.

Inside the dining hall, Charles stopped what he was doing and listened to the dogs' howling. He thought it was the most ominous sound he'd ever heard. His hand shook slightly when he poured the tequila into the mixer.

Chapter 5

Erin Powell barreled into her new offices at five twenty A.M., certain she'd beat Bert Navarro by a good ten minutes. She was chagrined to see that he was in one of the portable kitchens, the coffee already made and a box of donuts opened on the folding table. "Morning, boss," he drawled.

So much for hurrying and busting my butt, she thought sourly.

"Do you ever sleep?" she asked as she poured herself a cup of coffee.

"In this job I've learned how to power nap. For some reason I don't require a lot of sleep. I like getting here early so I don't have to fight morning traffic."

Erin eyed the sugary donuts and decided to pass.

At the same time, Bert was eyeing his new chief over his coffee mug. To his mind's eye she looked stressed, uncertain. Definitely not a good thing from where he was stand-

ing. "Guess we're the early birds. Tell
what you want me to do, Erin."

Erin's eyes narrowed as she tried to fig
out if Bert was one of the boys or a te
player.

When Erin didn't respond as quickly
he thought she should, he said — for go
or ill — "You need to get that chip off yo
shoulder, or the rest of the team will che
you up and spit you out. That's free, uns
licited advice, so take it for what it's wort
Just tell me what you want me to do, an
I'll do it. The Bureau taught me how to fo
low orders."

"Is it that obvious, Bert?"

Bert continued to drink from the mug in
his hand. "To me it is. I can't speak for the
others."

Erin turned around and walked out of the
kitchen, Bert on her heels. Inside the office
that was now hers to command, she turned
on the lights and looked over in the corner
to the supplies she'd requisitioned via e-mai
when she got home last night. "Talk to me
for starters. Tell me everything you kno
about the vigilantes. You were in on the la
three or four showdowns. I want everythin
No matter how insignificant you mig
think the detail is."

"What makes you think I know details?

was just another agent on duty." He watched as Erin slapped magnetic boards to the walls until all four surfaces were covered with the stark whiteboards. Colored magnetic markers hit the boards with loud plopping sounds.

Erin dusted her hands, dramatically, then removed her jacket and tossed it on one of the metal chairs. "You're not talking, Bert. Why is that?"

"I'm thinking you probably know more than I do. Like I said, I was just one of many agents sent into the field when things went down, and really don't have any firsthand knowledge of the women. Maybe you should share with me what you know, and we can compare." He thought about the catechism classes he took as a boy and how the nuns had drummed into his head that he would go straight to hell if he lied. He consoled himself with the thought that if he went to hell, he'd have a lot of friends there waiting for him. Everyone lied about everything these days. The end would justify the means one way or the other.

"You're friends with Deputy District Attorney Jack Emery and that guy Wong. How did that happen? Emery was engaged to marry Nikki Quinn. I heard all those stories way back when about how they squared off

in court. I don't know how much of it was rumor and how much was fact. Talk to me about those guys. Did you ever personally talk to any members of the vigilantes?"

It was on the tip of Bert's tongue to ask if going to bed with one of the vigilantes counted as talking, but he kept his mouth shut. It was so weird how the lies didn't bother him. One of these days he'd have to track down Sister Angela and confess. Then again, maybe he wouldn't. "Jack's a friend. A good friend. I go to the mandatory classes Wong conducts, and that's where we met and hit it off. He's first-rate. I earned my belt the hard way, have the bumps and bruises to prove it. No," he said with a straight face, "I have never personally talked to any of the vigilantes. I'm a little surprised, Erin, that you would ask me that question. Those women are not novices at what they do. The hard truth is they are so damn good at what they do, this whole damn Bureau can't catch them."

"That's because someone is helping them inside the Bureau. If not directly inside, then maybe close by. Like maybe Jack Emery or Wong. Even you, Bert. And before you can say it, yes, even me — except I haven't seen or talked to Nikki Quinn or Myra Rutledge in years and years."

Oh, shit! "So you say," he said airily. "Out of the six of us, you're the only one, as the director pointed out, who personally knew them. I guess what you're saying is that none of us are going to trust each other. I'm thinking that right now I should make an appointment to speak with the director to tell him to reassign me. If I bolt, so will the others, you know that, right, Erin?"

She did know that, and she didn't like it one little bit. She swallowed the bitter retort she was about to utter, and said, "This is day one, a clean slate. I will not allow personalities to get in the way. As of this minute, I trust and respect you. If you can say the same, let's give this our best shot."

"That'll work," Bert responded.

Erin looked at the magnetic boards, and said, "In a few hours, each one of these boards will be almost full. I want to start at the beginning. Those that are blank I can more or less fill in with my own personal thoughts and observations. To me the beginning is when Myra Rutledge's daughter was killed. Prior to that, Mrs. Rutledge was a sterling citizen. And so was Nikki Quinn."

Bert watched in amazement as Erin proceeded to write on the first board. He marveled at how she could multitask, scribble on the board, talk to him, and actually make sense while her gaze swept the clock and the doorway every few seconds.

"Bert, I want you to go through all the boxes in here. I understand that everything the Bureau has on the vigilantes is in them. You're going to have to go through the garbage to sort out their real accomplishments versus those that were and are attributed to them. They're given way too much credit, and that's part of what is making them so infamous. If they'd done half the things they're accused of, they would have burned out years ago. There just isn't that much time in the day, even if there are seven of them, to go to all corners of the world. The sightings will probably give you the most trouble."

Erin looked around at the magnetic boards as she decided which one she wanted to post the women's profiles on. She finally chose the board that would be directly in her line of vision as she sat at her desk.

Bert raised his eyes as he saw her move at the speed of light. Within a few minutes she had chosen pictures of the seven vigilantes and arranged them on the board. Underneath the collage, she placed the newspaper picture in living color of the infamous seven standing in front of the *Post* as they challenged the establishment. In spite of herself,

Erin grinned at their attire. *You're looking good, Nikki.* For a moment she envied her old friend.

Underneath both pictures she penciled in the words PERSONS OF INTEREST.

Bert's eyebrows shot upward when he saw the names she listed below: Jack Emery, Harry Wong, Judge Cornelia Easter, Lizzie Fox, Maggie Spritzer, Ted Robinson. Damn, she had the whole ball of wax. That was the precise moment at which he made a mental note not to underestimate the woman standing in front of him.

Sometime later, a shadow crossed the room as four figures, each with coffee cup in hand, blocked the light from the doorway. "You're late!" Erin barked. "As of this morning, your new hours are five thirty to whenever I say quitting time is." Without missing a beat, she added, "Joe, take these two pictures to the lab, have them blown up and laminated. Get three copies of each. Doug, I want you to ask Harry Wong to come in for an interview. Ask nicely. I don't want any blowback for anything we do from here on in.

"Pete, I want you to go to McLean and talk to Judge Cornelia Easter. I don't know why I say this, but I think the judge will relate better to you than any of the others.

Call it a hunch on my part. Charlie, request an audience with Deputy District Attorney Jack Emery. Again, be nice — *very* nice. Joe, after you drop off the pictures to be processed, I want you to find Lizzie Fox, Maggie Spritzer, and Ted Robinson. Bring them in for a little talk. You're still standing here, gentlemen, why is that? If you have questions, save them for later. My orders were clear. GO!"

Bert suppressed a grin. Gopher work. He decided to initiate a conversation. "So are we going on the theory that Myra Rutledge started up this . . . this group of women after her daughter died at the hands of a Chinese national with diplomatic immunity?"

"That's what I think happened. Something else happened shortly after Barbara Rutledge died. A woman named Marie Lewellen shot and killed a man right on the courthouse steps, the man who killed her own daughter. Of course she was arrested, and Myra put up her bail, a million dollars. Nikki Quinn was going to represent Lewellen. Not long after that, Lewellen disappeared. To this day she's never been found. Myra lost the whole million. The conjecture at that point was that if Lewellen could get away with it, why couldn't Myra? Who better to help her than her adopted daughter, Nikki, who owned a large law firm? All twelve members of that firm were women. Today the firm is still operating. We need to look into that, too. What that means is *you* need to look into that, Bert."

"So are you saying you think Nikki Quinn is the brains behind the vigilantes?"

"Actually, I am saying that. Nikki would be the perfect person to find the other recruits. Myra is incredibly rich, so she funded the operation. Then there's Charles Martin. Not much is known about him before he started working for Myra. He's almost a blank slate. He's Myra's live-in. He was head of security at her candy company before he retired. Someone with incredible knowledge, legal and covert as well, is pulling the strings."

"And you know this . . . how?"

Erin looked up from what she was doing. "I'm a listener. It's how you learn."

And that was all he was going to get, and Bert knew it. He continued with what he was doing, his thoughts going in all directions.

"I think if we gather an extensive dossier on the women, all the way back to the day when each was born, we can come up with an actual, true account of the things they've done. I don't know what to call their attacks. Acts of vengeance? Do you have a term, Bert?"

"Not really. For want of a better word, go with 'mission.' Either they've been doing paybacks for some wrong done to them, or they have some secret agenda no one is privy to. I agree with you, their profiles should give you the answers you're looking for."

"Okay. When we get up and running here tell me how you feel about this. You take Myra, Nikki, and Kathryn. I'll take Isabelle, Alexis, and Yoko. Countess de Silva is a no-brainer. We'll leave her till last."

Big mistake. "Okay, that should work. She's really rich, you know."

Erin nodded. "If you knew Myra the way I knew her . . . You'd never know she wasn't like every other mother in the world. She never flaunted her wealth, and neither did Barbara or Nikki. They were just ordinary people in my eyes."

Bert stopped what he was doing. "I was talking about Countess de Silva. Myra Rutledge is a pauper compared to the countess. I read in *Forbes* that she's one of the richest women in the world. She married some rich count from Spain. She had a fortune of her own. Cotton, tobacco, land." He cocked his head to the side and stared at his new boss.

"Wealth of that kind means *power.*"

"What are you telling me, Bert?"

"Just that that kind of money attracts power. The lady has it blowing out her ears. Power and wealth combined are a pretty unbeatable force."

"So, if I am to read between the lines, what you're actually saying is the FBI is no match for the vigilantes. You're saying her power and her wealth guarantee a walk for all seven women and that guy with the British accent. And we're just spinning our wheels."

Bert grinned as he nodded. "I say this with all honesty, I don't think we're any match for those women. Look what they did to Mitch Riley. He was the acting director of the FBI, for God's sake. They took him down even with all his security in place. They invaded his home. His *home,* Erin. They marched right in and took over. That doesn't say much for the FBI, now, does it? Right now, as we speak, Riley is probably making license plates in the federal pen for ten cents an hour. I read in the *Post* that organizations all over the world are vying for the vigilantes' help. I also read that the vigilantes can name their own price." This last was said with such awe that Erin glared at him.

Erin squared her shoulders. "What good is all the money in the world if you're a fugitive and can't spend it? No one is infallible. Everyone has an Achilles' heel. We just have to find theirs and act on it."

"That's not going to happen, Erin. Call it gut instinct on my part."

Erin stamped her foot. "Right now you aren't sounding very much like a team player, Bert. You're supposed to be doing a rah rah rah for the Bureau. Do you know something you aren't sharing?"

"Not at all. The vigilantes are well funded, the public is on their side, and they're smart. Every . . . uh . . . mission they've been on, they righted a wrong, and the public approves of what they've done. That means they're successful in the public's eyes. *They're women!*" he snapped, as though that summed up everything, and there was no need for further discussion.

"Someone is helping them. I don't care what you say, Bert. I repeat, either there's a mole here in the Bureau, or it's Emery or Wong or both. Nothing else computes."

Bert managed to look properly horrified at what Erin was saying. He shook his head. "It's not me. I'd stake my life and reputation that it isn't Jack or Wong. Both of them, myself included, swore to uphold the law. If you go after them and me, you're wasting time and manpower. But, it's your call and your career."

Erin felt frustrated. She liked and respected Bert. He hadn't gotten to be the director's number one by being a naysayer. She'd heard the scuttlebutt, and the smart money was betting that when Cummings retired, Bert was at the top of the short list for the director's job. She knew she needed to respond to his comment, so she simply said, "Yes, it is my call and my career, and I still say we have a mole who is playing both sides of the fence somewhere close to us. Let's just chalk it up to I'm a *woman* and I have instincts, and my instincts tell me that there is a mole among us."

Bert set aside the box that he was working on and picked up Erin's and his cups for coffee refills.

He was back in five minutes. He towered over her and her desk when he said, "I'd be remiss if I didn't offer this advice to you: Keep your suspicions and thoughts to yourself. If you insist on flaunting that I'm-a-woman thing, your task force is going to go after you, and since you're the only one who knows any of the vigilantes, your goose will be cooked. That's four against you and me. Who do you think the director is going to look at and believe?"

Erin felt her stomach muscles start to cramp up. "That almost sounds like a threat, Bert."

"No, it's not a threat. I know those guys. I know you think Charlie and Pete are the stable ones, and they are, but all those guys are brothers under the skin. All of them are good agents, and all have good records. Just so you know, Erin, I am not going to be your stool pigeon. I don't play those games. I'm here to do a job, and I'll do it to the best of my ability."

Erin knew Bert Navarro had just drawn his line in the sand. If she chose to cross it, it would be at her own peril. She made a mental note to pull Bert's jacket before she left at the end of the day. Bathtub reading for the evening.

"Thanks for the coffee," was all she said.

"No problem."

Chapter 6

The winds this Halloween evening were brisk on top of Big Pine Mountain, carrying the scent of the pungent pine that swept over the women walking the compound. It was their nightly routine: eat one of Charles's scrumptious dinners, then walk off the calories.

It was late, the waning moon was still high in the sky. Bright, shiny stars twinkled downward, bathing the compound in a beaming golden light. The candles in the cutout pumpkins flickered on the steps, lighting the way to the wide-planked porch. It was eerie, yet at the same time evoked memories of the carefree times of childhood.

At once the women all started to babble, sharing memories of trick-or-treating, wearing goblin and fairy-tale costumes as children as they tried to bamboozle neighborhood adults into giving them more candy rather than having tricks played on them.

"It's a different time today," Myra said sadly. "The papers are full of monsters who try to entice children into their webs, put razors in apples, and poison them with drugs in candies. This world is not one that I approve of."

"And that's why we do what we do," Nikki said gently as she remembered one particular Halloween when she and Barbara dressed up as clowns in costumes that Myra had sewn herself. They'd had so much fun that night. Somewhere, in an old trunk back in McLean, she had the costume packed away in tissue paper. She was saving it in case the day ever came when she had a little boy or girl to dress up for Halloween. Tears burned her eyes at the memory. Myra was right, this was a totally different time.

They reminisced then because somehow it made the loneliness that much easier to bear. Finally, when they ran out of memories to share, Annie stood up, and said, "Enough already, it's time to get down to work."

Together they circled the five-acre compound one last time, then walked back to the Big House to join Charles for what he fondly called a late-night meeting of the minds.

"You decided to take on the mission?" It

was more a statement than a question. The women nodded as one.

However, Nikki voiced a question, and the others waited expectantly for a response from Charles. "Where is the proof we asked for in regard to the pardon?"

"My contacts assure me that at the completion of the mission, it will be yours. Do I believe them? Not really. I see that you all have serious doubts, too, and that's a good thing. So, this would be my thinking . . . Build in a resolution if it doesn't come to pass. Put those seven fine, not to mention devious, minds to work, and figure out what you can do to even the score if the pardon doesn't come through."

"That's pretty iffy, Charles," Kathryn said. "We'll not only be walking a tightrope, we'll be ticking time bombs when it's time to split. We never have minutes to spare. We're always right down to the wire. Are you telling us we should go into this mission assuming the pardon is not going to come through? That doesn't make sense. Why should we help them at all if we know full well we're going to get stiffed in the end?" she objected.

"Think it all the way through, ladies," Charles said.

"We did think it through, Charles," Isabelle said. "That's all we talked about all day long. Obviously, we're missing something, so enlighten us."

"Well, for starters," Kathryn said, not allowing Charles time to respond, "there are way too many players in this gig to suit me. While there are seven of us, we work as a team. There are, as far as you've enlightened us, as many as six or seven . . . Possible clients. That cuts down our productivity, so to speak. Even with Jack, Harry, and Bert watching our backs, it's too uncertain."

The others nodded.

"There is that," Charles said blandly.

"How can we even it up, girls?" Alexis asked.

"Until we know *exactly* who and what we're up against, all we can do is study the profiles Charles gathered for us," Myra said as she opened her folder.

Charles clicked the remote control in his hand, and the plasma screen that took up one entire wall of the room came to life. A picture of an attractive woman appeared on the screen. "Meet Pamela Lock. Ms. Lock is her candidate's secret weapon as far as fund-raising goes. Since men are the primary donors, Ms. Lock, and no pun intended, has a lock on donations. It's said she can get money out of a turnip. Not only is she heading up the front-runner's fund-raising operation, she is a personal friend of Martine Connor, the woman who is almost a shoo-in to be running as the Democratic nominee for president against the incumbent. They went to Sarah Lawrence together and have remained friends.

"I'm sure her fellow alumna promised Ms. Lock a prestigious job in the new administration if she wins. This is my own personal thought, but it wouldn't surprise me one bit to hear she would be the new president's chief of staff if Martine Connor wins the election. And once Connor becomes the nominee of her party, Ms. Lock will undoubtedly become the head of the DNC's fund-raising operation.

"Ms. Lock comes from a well-to-do family that is heavily involved in politics. She's never married, has had many lovers. Her trust fund is robust. She likes to entertain. Lavishly. She knows just about everyone — politicians, movie stars, tradesmen, the little people. Her public persona is that she's friendly, warm, outgoing, always willing to do a favor as long as she gets something in return.

"In private, according to people who were once close to her — and that includes those of her former lovers who were willing to talk

— she's nothing like the person the public sees. She's a skinflint, a tightwad, counts the paper napkins, nickel-and-dimes the help. She makes everyone she's involved with sign a confidentiality agreement. She's a very litigious person. She also makes her lovers sign the same sort of agreement. One rather adventuresome young man, seven years her junior, decided to write a book about her. The iron hand came down, the guy disappeared, and Washington has not seen or heard from him since. That was two years ago."

"Does she have a weakness?" Annie asked.

"If she does, I haven't found it."

"Did Mitch Riley," Myra asked, "have a file on her? He had one on just about everyone in town. I can't see someone like Ms. Lock being the exception."

"Oh, he had a file on her all right. A sexual file. He had a seven-month affair with her a few years ago. She bought him a Rolex and other sundry gifts. Once a week she'd send him bottles of Cristal Champagne. He listed the hideaways they used to visit. But that's about it. There were a few . . . uh . . . compromising pictures. Polaroids. I think it's safe to say all of the lady's . . . assets . . . are her own."

"If the compromising pictures were blown

up to, say, poster size, how would they look?" Yoko asked.

Charles looked flustered.

"That good, eh?" Kathryn asked, tongue-in-cheek.

"I'm writing this down, Kathryn," Annie said. "That's item one. We blow up the pictures. Multiple copies. Just in case we decide to go that route."

"Anything else, Charles?"

"One other thing. Ms. Lock owns many properties. She has a getaway in South Carolina. She usually arrives at night after dark and leaves the same way. It seems to be her favorite getaway place. She owns an impressive piece of property in Tahoe, and an ocean villa in Maui, but she rarely if ever goes to either. She doesn't like flying, and the time in the air dries out her skin, or so says *People* magazine. When she goes to South Carolina, she drives.

"I found this next tidbit a little strange. It seems that Ms. Lock owns a rustic cabin in North Carolina. Around the bend from her cabin is another cabin that is owned by the RNC guy in charge of their fund-raising. His name is Baron Russell. He's forty-seven. We'll get to him in a bit."

Myra clucked her tongue like a mother hen. "Obviously, Ms. Lock has been a naughty girl."

Annie gasped. "Myra! Myra! Myra! I think it means she was shacked up with the RNC guy, which means they were screwing their tails off in one of those rustic cabins. That takes it beyond naughty, doncha think?"

Myra's face turned pink. "Thank you for pointing that out, Annie."

"By the way, Ms. Lock is forty-four. And before you can ask, yes, she has an impressive Rolodex that she guards with her life."

"If she guards the Rolodex with her life, how did someone get her list of donors?" Nikki asked.

"I can't answer that, Nikki. There's every possibility she's part of the scam. Right now, according to my sources, she's extremely upset, as she values her reputation above all else. You also have to consider that the RNC was also hit. Which then raises the question of whether Russell and Lock are in it together. It is also possible that the third party, whoever that might be, is trying to pit one against the other. In Washington, as you know, a scandal of any kind has major repercussions. You will have to sort it out and figure out how best to handle things," Charles said.

"Do we know who had access to their donor lists?" Myra asked.

"Supposedly, no one. Which in itself is suspicious," Charles replied.

Nikki's tone was sour when she spoke. "If that's true, where does that leave us? Who are we supposed to go after? Are there suspects? Where were these lists kept? In their homes? In a safe at the office? Are they only on paper or are there computer records, too? Which donors are making the most noise, and why are they agreeing to keep quiet? Having your identity stolen would have most people screaming at the top of their lungs. Give us something to go on, Charles. I'm not keen on going into the District blind and trying to wing it. We need some meat here; otherwise, I want no part of this."

The others agreed with Nikki.

"Let's not forget that your old childhood friend is heading up a task force to take us down," Kathryn said. "A dedicated FBI agent with her own agenda gives me a lot of concern. If it were a man heading up the task force, I would be a lot less worried. Ms. Powell is trying to prove something to her peers. She's going to be on this 24/7. I don't relish getting caught in the cross fire. Has Bert checked in yet?"

Charles smiled. "Yes, I agree, Kathryn, Ms. Powell is going to test your mettle. Bert will check in before retiring. Can we move along now?"

"Absolutely, dear," Myra said.

Charles clicked the remote. A picture of a tall, distinguished-looking man appeared on the screen. He was dressed casually and held a pipe in his hand. There were leather patches on the elbows of his tweed jacket. He was smiling for the camera, his pearly whites lighting up the screen.

"He looks like a country squire. I assume that was the look he was going for, right?" Alexis asked.

Charles ignored her sarcasm. "Mr. Russell is a bit of a rogue. He was married in his youth but was unable to remain faithful — to his wife's dismay. There were no children when they divorced two years later. He was engaged three more times to various socialites, but never managed to get to the altar a second time. He's gun-shy, according to the tabloids. He's every socialite's dream dinner guest. And the man loves it.

"He's wealthy, thanks to an indulgent grandparent who left him a small fortune. He does not squander his money and has a blue chip portfolio. He's the perfect man to raise money. He has charisma billowing out his ears. It's said the president invites him to the White House just to chat about football.

"Mr. Russell played football for Notre Dame during his college years and is a huge football fan. At the time he was often called a stallion on the field. He maintains a condo in the District, but the place he really calls home is North Carolina. Actually, it isn't far from where we sit at the moment. He goes there every chance he gets."

Charles pressed the remote, and the picture on the plasma TV changed. The women looked at a palatial home nestled in a grove of evergreens.

Annie jerked her finger toward the picture. "That takes log cabins to a whole new level."

"The house sits on five acres, is seven thousand square feet. It has all the amenities one could want. Indoor pool, not included in the square footage, outdoor pool, tennis court, stable that houses two horses. Russell loves to ride. The house boasts an indoor sauna and steam room, a gourmet kitchen. Russell likes to cook and is an accomplished chef — if you believe his PR.

"Strangely, he never takes women to his second home. He entertains friends, who drive to North Carolina for the weekend. Usually married couples. Once he was overheard saying he goes there to wash the stink of Washington off him. He calls his little getaway Stallion Springs."

The women guffawed at Charles's words.

"Is Russell involved with anyone right now?" Isabelle asked.

"There's nothing in his dossier to indicate any kind of a relationship."

"How about Ms. Lock? Is she involved with anyone at the moment?" Isabelle pursued.

"Likewise, there's nothing to indicate any sort of relationship. Both Russell and Lock are putting in some serious man-hours, if you'll pardon the expression. It's rare for them to leave their respective offices before ten at night. All indications are that they order take-out, go home to bed. They get up and do the same thing all over again the next day. That's the sum total of what I've been able to gather on both of them."

"Okay. We need a list of the office staff and any information you have on them. We'll want copies of their phone records and cell phone records, and let's get someone to hack into their office computers and their home computers. And I don't want to hear about privacy laws, Charles," Nikki said.

"It's being done as we speak, Nikki," Charles said.

"Just out of curiosity, dear," Myra asked, "what are the pundits in D.C. saying about Martine Connor's chance of making the White House her new home, assuming she gets the nomination? I'm afraid I haven't been keeping up with politics of late."

"Ms. Connor's chances are very good. With the sitting president's approval ratings hovering in the low twenties, any Democrat is an odds-on favorite to unseat him, and he knows it. Several members of his staff have been overheard making comments. Worried comments. They want four more years. More and more it looks like it would take a miracle for the Republicans to hold on to the White House."

Annie leaned forward. "If that miracle happens, Charles, what does it mean for us?"

"Big trouble, Annie. Very big trouble."

"Not if I own the *Post,*" Annie said.

Charles allowed himself a wide smile. "Yes, Annie, if you own the *Post,* you can call the political shots. You can sweep Ms. Connor right into 1600 Pennsylvania Avenue after you help to make her the Democrats' nominee."

It was Nikki's turn to lean across the table. "I think we might like to see everything there is to see on one Martine Connor.

Everything, Charles."

This time Charles laughed out loud as he slid a bright purple folder across the table. A very, very thick purple folder. "I thought you'd never ask."

Chapter 7

Harry Wong snapped his cell phone shut and resumed tying his sneakers. His mind raced as he tried to come to terms with what Bert had just told him on the phone; the bottom line being: don't fight it, go with the flow.

He knew someone was in the building, not because the intruder made a sound, he didn't. He smelled the man's scent, sensed his wariness, which Harry decided was a good thing. The shadows outside the work-out room afforded him all the cover he needed.

The intruder was well versed in stealth, something at which Harry also excelled. He waited until he saw the man's shadow crossing the narrow space near the kitchen. Harry counted silently, one, two, three, and the intruder was flat on his back, Harry's foot on his neck choking off his air supply. The man's arms flailed as his feet tried to go in all directions, to no avail.

Harry looked over his shoulder to make sure the hidden camera was working. The tiny light that was shining brightly between the fronds of a hanging plant reassured him. As Bert said, when dealing with the fibbies, the name of the game was CYA. Covering his ass was always paramount to what went on in his *dojo,* but he had thanked the agent for that bit of insight.

Harry eased the pressure on the intruder's neck for a second, just enough for the man to take a strangled breath. Then he clamped down his foot again. "Breaking and entering is against the law unless you have a warrant. Do you have a warrant? Blink once for yes, two for no." The man blinked furiously. "If you try to talk, you'll crush your larynx. Do you understand? Blink once for yes, two for no." The intruder blinked again. Harry eased up the pressure on the man's neck. "Don't move. I'm going to search you. If you move, my foot will be the last thing you ever see in this lifetime. Do you understand me? Blink once for yes, two for no." The intruder's eyelids blinked. "I like it when a guest follows instructions."

Harry knew what was going to happen next. He had trained federal agents and cops, and the first rule they learned at their various academies was that you never gave up your weapon. Harry slowly eased the pressure on the man's neck and slid his foot to the floor. True to form, the intruder rolled over, gasped for breath as his hands pummeled the floor. Then, like a jack-in-the-box, he was on his feet and swinging.

In the blink of an eye the intruder was airborne. Harry winced when he heard the loud thump as the flying body hit the wall. It sprawled like a broken doll. "If my calculations are right, you now have a broken collarbone and a fractured hip. You are one sorry sack of shit, mister. But to show you my heart is in the right place, I'm going to call 911 because I don't want you dying in my *dojo.*" His fingers pressed the keys on his cell phone.

Strange sounds came from the man's mouth. Harry rather thought he was being called a son of a bitch and that the man was a federal agent. "No shit! You're a federal agent? Why didn't you say so instead of breaking and entering? A man's home and his work space are his castles. You're supposed to announce yourself, show me your creds. I read that in the FBI manual. What do you do? You sneak in here, no warrant in hand, and you think I'm going to serve you tea and cakes? Not in this lifetime. By the way, I got it all on film. For posterity. Ah, I think I hear a siren. Your new ride . . . Mr. FBI Agent. To the hospital."

Harry walked over to the door that led to the street. He stopped long enough next to the sprawled man and looked down at him. "You really do look like a sorry sack of shit." The agent, in obvious pain, cursed. Harry thought he said, *"Fuck you."* "I refuse to tolerate profanity in my place of business," he said virtuously. To prove his point, his clenched fist shot out and a couple of the man's capped teeth popped out of his mouth like speeding bullets. Harry blinked, raced back to the camera, and erased the last ten seconds of activity from the tape. He offered up a jaunty salute, then sauntered to the front door.

Both EMS workers were women. Large women. No-nonsense women. Harry knew them well. He'd trained them free of charge in return for emergency services when one or more of his clients managed to get injured. It kept his liability insurance at affordable rates. "No need to be gentle, Irma. Just dump him in the wagon and take the scenic route to the hospital. He *says* he's a federal agent. I didn't check his creds, so maybe he is and maybe he isn't. He broke in here intent on harming me."

The big woman grinned as she pushed the gurney closer to the agent. Her partner, a woman named Heidi, who looked as big as an oak tree, glared down at the man, who seemed to be insisting they look at his credentials.

"What's he saying, Irma?" Heidi asked.

"Beats me. Do you know what he's saying, Harry?"

Harry shrugged.

Harry waved as the ambulance peeled away, siren wailing, lights flashing. He smiled when he thought of the route Irma would be driving. It wouldn't surprise him one little bit to find out she'd have either engine trouble or a flat tire along the way.

Harry removed the tape, walked into his office, and made three additional copies. He shoved the original tape in an envelope, stuck on sufficient postage, and addressed it to Charles's mail drop. He'd find a mailbox on the way home. He addressed the second one to Elias Cummings at the FBI. The last two went into his pocket.

Harry took one last look around, locked all the doors, and left by the back entrance. He fired up the Ducati, sat a moment as he thought about the past thirty minutes. Then he laughed as he pulled out his cell phone, powered up, and was speaking to Jack

Emery within seconds. "Listen up, big guy, I have a story to tell you."

Jack cursed long and loud the moment he broke the connection with Harry. Intending to call Bert, he turned on the phone again, but then the doorbell rang. "Shit!" Well, where was it written that he had to answer the door? Nowhere, that's where. The bell shrilled again. Confident that his evening caller couldn't see through the door, Jack meandered back to the kitchen, where he popped a longneck Bud and sat down. He powered up his cell phone and punched in Bert's number. The agent answered on the first ring.

"Yeah, yeah, it's supposed to be a roundup, strike all of you at one time. How long you planning on holding out?" Bert demanded.

"Till hell freezes over. Give me the low-down on Charlie Akers."

"Nice guy. Thorough agent, dots all his I's and crosses all the T's. Goes by the book. Retirement is right around the corner for him. He's a good family man, sweet home-maker wife, two kids in college. He's not going to get violent. He'll try to reason with you, talk nicely to get you to go to headquarters for a chat. He's like a dog with a bone.

He'll sit outside all night. What I'd do if I was you would be go out the back door and walk around to the front, whenever you're ready, and pretend you just got home.

"Word just came down a few minutes ago that Harry put Doug Parks in the hospital. Well, let's put it this way, he's on his way to the hospital. Seems the ambulance had a flat tire. Those two Amazons didn't want to get their hands dirty and called AAA. Parks's condition isn't life-threatening. Then they got caught up in a couple of traffic bottlenecks. Life's a bitch sometimes. Any news, Jack?"

"At the moment, no. How's it looking on your end?"

"Busy. Powell is like a dog chasing her tail. She doesn't know which way to go, so she's going in all directions. It's amusing to a degree. We have a six A.M. meeting to report our progress. It will be zip. She's going to go nuclear when she hears about Doug Parks. One guy out of commission. If we could just figure out a way to take out Joe Landos, I'd feel a lot better. Any ideas?"

Jack swigged from the longneck. "Not at the moment. I'll call."

Jack finished his beer and opened a second. The front doorbell continued to ring. For one wild moment he thought about turning the power off but nixed the idea. This might be a good time to change the sheets on his bed and take a shower. He could pretend he'd just gotten out of the shower after a nap. Shit!

Contemplating his dilemma, Jack continued to drink. If he kept up with his drinking, he wouldn't have a problem. Yeah, yeah, there was nothing worse than interrogating a drunk.

At the end of the day, he knew the fibs would haul his ass into their offices, even dragging him out of the courtroom, if necessary, which wouldn't do his reputation one bit of good. He slammed the empty into the recycle bin and stomped his way to the front door. He yanked it open, and barked, "Yeah?"

The man looked like someone's father, which he was. His hair was almost gray, neatly parted and combed. Brown eyes, strong jaw. A compact kind of guy, but gravity was winning out. He was dressed neatly in a dark suit, a spit shine on his shoes. He held out his credentials as he verbally identified himself. "Take your time, Mr. Emery, make sure you're comfortable with my credentials." He sounded, Jack thought, like he was giving directions to a football stadium.

"So you're Special Agent Charles Akers. I bet your colleagues call you Charlie. What can I do for you, Special Agent Akers? I hesitate to point this out, but it is seven o'clock at night. My workday ends at five. What that means to you is you're invading my personal space and my private time."

"And you think I give a good rat's ass about that, Mr. Emery?"

Whoa. So there was still some fire in the belly. Now Special Agent Akers's tone sounded like he was giving parking directions at the local jail.

"Guess not. Gotta make sure that pension stays intact. What do you want, Akers?"

"I'd be more than pleased if you'd accompany me down to the Hoover Building."

Jack's mind raced. "Do I have a choice?"

"Not really," Special Agent Akers said jovially.

"Okay, let me get my jacket. Just so you know, I had a poker game scheduled for nine o'clock. I need to call someone to cancel. That won't be a problem, will it, Special Agent Akers?"

"Five minutes. If you aren't standing next to me, I'll be breaking down your door."

"Understood." Jack slammed the door shut. Ten seconds later he had Maddy, the office manager at Nikki's firm, on the phone. "Listen up, Maddy, this is Jack. The FBI is here at the house to haul my ass downtown. I'm going to need a lawyer, ASAP. The best of the best. Fifteen minutes and I'll be at the Hoover Building. Unless this guy takes the long way. And I'd like the press there when they walk me in. A picture of me being hauled in will make for a Kodak moment. Can you do it?"

The voice on the other end of the phone made a very unladylike sound. "Consider it done."

Jack heaved a mighty sigh of relief as he reached for his jacket and slipped into it.

He dropped the cell phone into the bottom of the umbrella stand and fished out a second one from his jacket. He speed dialed Harry's number and waited for the martial arts expert to speak. "They're here to take me downtown. If anyone asks, I called you to cancel our poker game. Be alert, Harry, the shit is starting to fly."

"Gotcha."

Jack went out the front door and locked it behind him.

"What took you so long, Mr. Emery?"

"I had to go to the bathroom, Special Agent Akers. I know for a fact you guardians of the law aren't big on bathroom breaks when you drag someone in for questioning. I think that's against my civil rights."

"Shut up, Mr. Emery. Get in the car."

Jack knew he needed to stall for time. He wasn't sure Maddy could get her people to the Hoover Building before he arrived. "Look, Special Agent Akers, I don't mind your coming here and asking me to accompany you downtown, but I do object to your not telling me why. Let's cut the bullshit and tell me why you're dragging me out of my home at this hour of the night."

"All in good time. Think of this as a come-to-Jesus meeting. We'd like some input from you. We're a generous bunch, so we'll share what we have, and perhaps we can all learn something."

Jack did a quick little dance. "You see, you see! That's just it. Learn what? Share what? I'm all for both, but I need a clue. You want me to cooperate, you need to give a little, Special Agent Akers. Being the Deputy District Attorney for the District of Columbia, I'm hardly a novice at interrogations. In fact, Special Agent Akers, you might want to remember that when you work in the District you are subject to its laws, and I represent those laws. 'Nuff said?"

"It's not my place to enlighten you, Mr. Emery. My boss will be doing that. I'm following her orders. Think of me as a foot soldier. A messenger."

Jack worked up some more outrage, hoping his eyes were bulging. "Her! Did you say *her?* A woman? Well, no woman is going to tell me what to do. What are you, some pussy? A wuss? You take orders from *a woman!* Well, damn. Now I really do feel sorry for you. Nah, I don't think I'm interested in going with you."

He turned around to walk back up the steps to the house. He heard the click of the agent's gun but didn't stop. No one was going to shoot a deputy district attorney on the steps of his house right here in Georgetown. No way, no how. He fit the key in the lock. He risked a glance down at his wrist. He'd wasted almost ten minutes. That was good. Another ten, and things should be in place.

"Stop right there, Mr. Emery."

"Or what?" Jack asked, opening the door. He turned around. "So shoot me! Make the eleven o'clock news. There goes your pension, big guy! You'll be up to your ass in political bullshit till those retirement papers are moldy. That means no monthly income. So, asshole, take your best shot!"

"You think this is a joke, don't you? It's not. I asked you nicely. I'm going to ask you nicely one more time. If you refuse to accompany me, I'm going to have to call for backup."

"Dead or alive, is that it? Someone to lie for you when you shoot me. You guys suck, you know that? I didn't do anything. I didn't break any laws. I'm an officer of the court. You now, you're a different story. You might think you're the eight-hundred-pound gorilla, but you're not. What are you waiting for? I thought you were going to shoot me."

"Shut the hell up," Akers said as he reviewed his options, which weren't looking too good at the moment. All he could think about were the words Emery said about his pension and the eleven o'clock news. Hell could freeze over before they'd turn over his pension money to him. He knew all about bureaucracy.

Did he really want to call for backup? Emery was right, the Bureau would look at him as a wuss. His colleagues would whisper and snicker behind their hands that he was playing it safe till retirement. Talk about being between a rock and a hard place.

Emery was looking at him like a cat who'd just licked up a whole bowl of cream. A shudder rippled up and down Akers's spine. The son of a bitch was up to something. He saw that Emery was about to close the door when he shouted, "Okay, okay, get back here. I'll tell you what I know, which isn't that much. My boss, my *temporary* boss, Erin Powell, has been appointed to head up a special task force created by the director himself to bring the vigilantes to justice once and for all. She asked me to bring you in for a chat. A chat, Mr. Emery. You are not under arrest. But in about five minutes if you do not accompany me quietly into this car, you *will be* under arrest. Obstructing a federal agent is not going to look good on your record, just as not bringing you in won't look good on mine. We're both reasonable people, so let's cooperate with one another. And, no, working for a woman who is PMSing isn't a fun thing for me, either. I take orders just like you do."

Jack pointedly looked at his watch. Fifteen minutes had elapsed. With travel time to the Bureau, Maddy should have her people in place. He turned around and locked the door for a second time. "Okay," he said agreeably.

Akers blinked. Just like that, the jerk was agreeing to go with him. It hit him then like a lightning bolt. Emery had been stalling. "Fuck!"

Powell was going to crucify him.

■ ■ ■ ■

Akers drove like the Hounds of Hell were on his tail. Jack bellowed and snarled for him to slow down, but Akers ignored him. "You're going eighty miles an hour. That's against the law. This is the goddamn District. We have laws here! And as an officer of the court I may just have to file an official report on this," Jack bellowed as he grasped the handgrip above the door.

"Shut the fuck up. I'm wise to you. You've been stalling me. Well, that's going to get you exactly nowhere."

Eight minutes later, the dark sedan pulled to the curb in front of the Hoover Building. The crowd of people jostling one another looked to be in the hundreds. It was all Jack could do not to laugh out loud.

"Wow! Thanks, Akers, this is a hell of a welcome! You guys go all-out, don't you?" Jack asked as he climbed out of the car.

"Get back in this damn car, do you hear me?" Akers sputtered.

There were print reporters, Ted Robinson and his partner Joe Espinosa at the head of the pack. There were anchors from all the news channels. And then there were the lawyers lined up three deep. Jack looked around as though he was a movie star. "I am Deputy District Attorney Jack Emery. E-m-e-r-y. This guy who brought me here is Special Agent Charles Akers. A-k-e-r-s. Get my good side, boys. I wish I could comment, but I have no idea why I'm here. All I know is there's someone in there," Jack said, pointing to the building, "who is in charge of yet another task force to bring down the vigilantes. Her name is Erin Powell. You spell that with two L's, I think. P-o-w-e-l-l."

The crowd literally seemed to swell. Agents appeared with drawn guns. Jack managed to look stunned and horrified at the same time. Lights brighter than stadium floods sprang up everywhere. Microphones were being thrust into his face. He tried to back away, the lights all around him nearly blinding him.

A slender woman appeared out of nowhere. Even with all the lights glaring in his face, Jack could make out the look of panic on the woman's face. It had to be Akers's temporary boss, Special Agent Powell with two L's. A squadron of other agents behind her, she shouted for the crowd to disperse. No one moved. The media was on it like white on rice, and they smelled news.

"Back off, you are on government property!" Powell shouted.

Cameras clicked, and more microphones appeared. She angrily batted them out of the way.

"Arrest anyone who doesn't move!" Powell screamed to be heard over the uproar.

Jack leaned over to the nearest reporter, and said, "You didn't get this from me, but Powell used to know a couple of the vigilantes. Like in best friends. Nikki Quinn and Myra Rutledge. And she's in charge of this task force. What's wrong with this picture?"

"You shitting me, Emery?"

"Gospel, buddy. I swear on my mother."

Jack moved slightly to get away from the reporter as he watched what was going on around him. He spotted Harry Wong. He reached out a long arm and yanked the reporter closer. He hissed again. "See that guy over there, the skinny one with the yellow Windbreaker? Talk to him. He's a wealth of information. I think he has a video you might want to see." The young reporter looked at Jack suspiciously but moved off to do his bidding. He managed a wink in Harry's direction. Harry nodded.

It took twenty minutes before the agents had the doorway clear except for thirteen women.

Erin Powell looked at her agents and demanded they move the women, who looked like they were rooted to the concrete, away from the doorway. A tight huddle formed as the male and female agents snapped and snarled at one another. Jack watched as Erin Powell exploded in a verbal tirade. "I don't care who they are, move them out of here."

A tall, beautiful woman stepped forward. More than once Jack had heard her referred to as the sexiest woman alive. Jack almost blacked out when she approached Erin Powell and slapped a wad of paper into the agent's hand. "Lizzie Fox, representing Jack Emery. These ladies behind me are my co-counsel, all twelve of them!"

Lizzie turned to the media and announced in a loud, crystal-clear voice, "Ladies and gentlemen, I'm Lizzie Fox, Mr. Emery's attorney. Call me for any and all interviews, and I or my staff will cooperate. Fully." She looked directly into the camera and offered up a sizzling wink. The cameraman filming her looked like his pants were on fire. It was all Jack could do not to laugh out loud.

The late news started off with a film clip of that sizzling wink as the anchor announced, "The Silver Fox is back in town, and woe to those who are hiding out in the Hoover Building."

CHAPTER 8

The women were getting ready for bed when three sharp bonging sounds from the bell in the compound reverberated over the mountain. They stopped what they were doing, looked at one another, their expressions a mixture of excitement and dread. Three bongs of the bell meant drop what you're doing and report in. Robes flapping in the evening breeze, slippers slapping at the ground, the women ran toward the Big House, each wondering what crisis warranted the call.

Charles greeted the women at the door, Myra standing behind him. Both wore robes and were smiling from ear to ear. As one, the women relaxed.

"What? What?" Kathryn demanded.

"Something rather amusing, ladies. Or let's say the vigilantes are one-up. I am referring to a breaking news cable special that ended a few minutes ago. I taped the episode, and later I'll catch the D.C. eleven o'clock local news for fuller coverage."

Nikki gasped when Jack Emery appeared on the screen. One hand flew to her heart, the other to her lips as she watched the scene being played out on the large plasma screen.

The women hooted and hollered, their fists shooting in the air as the unruly crowd shouted and bellowed.

Nikki moved closer to the screen. "Oh, my God! Those are my lawyers! The whole firm is there! How'd that happen? What's going on, Charles? Sweet mother, that's Lizzie. Did she just say she's representing Jack? Charles, say something and say it right now. *Now!*" she shrieked.

The plasma screen went dark. Charles held up his hand to silence the women, who were, naturally, all talking at once. "Believe it or not, I just got a call from Nellie a few minutes before I rang the bell. As you could see, Jack was rather busy, as was Harry. Bert couldn't get to a phone. He said he's being watched like a hawk by Erin Powell. He did manage to alert Nellie, who, like I said, just phoned me."

"All well and good but what happened to cause that kind of meltdown?" Nikki asked, pointing to the blank screen in front of them.

"It seems Ms. Powell sent the members of her task force out to bring in our friends. When it came to Harry, Agent Parks entered his *dojo* unannounced and without a warrant. Harry was closing up and thought it was an intruder and managed to . . . uh . . . take him out. Agent Parks is in the hospital as we speak. I seriously doubt if he will be returning to Ms. Powell's task force. Harry's security camera caught it all on tape. A copy is on the way to my mail drop.

"As for Jack, Agent Akers showed up and asked him to accompany him to the Hoover Building. Jack agreed, then changed his mind and things went downhill after that. He managed to call Maddy, and she rounded up all the attorneys at your firm, along with Lizzie. They were waiting at the Hoover Building when Agent Akers arrived with Jack. Oh, yes, Maddy and Lizzie alerted the media, and that's what the circus atmosphere was all about. I like it when my people are proactive."

"Where's Jack now?" Nikki asked.

"Inside the Hoover Building, I assume. Ms. Powell can hold him for seventy-two hours and deny him a lawyer, but I don't think that will happen. Lizzie was front and center, it's all over the news. Elias Cummings won't allow anything to go awry. The Bureau does not need any more bad publicity. That's all I know."

"I thought Lizzie had gone to ground with Justice Barnes. What's she doing back in the District?" Annie asked.

Charles removed his glasses and looked over at Annie. "Actually, I called her in. She's here to oversee the final details of your purchase of the *Post,* Annie. Of course, no one knows that. Her cover story is she's been on a sabbatical, but she's back in the game again. Of course, we're the only ones who know that."

"That makes me feel a lot better," Annie said. "Lizzie you can trust."

"Does that mean Maggie Spritzer is back in town, too?" Isabelle asked.

"That's what it means, Isabelle," Charles said. "As a matter of fact, Ms. Spritzer will be in a position of power when the sale becomes final."

"Very clever, Charles. How did you manage all of that?" Nikki asked.

"With a great deal of help. That's another way of saying, we have it covered."

"What's going to happen now, dear?" Myra asked.

"Well, for one thing, Lizzie has more than a nodding acquaintance with Martine Connor, the presumptive Democratic candidate for the presidency. She handled some of Ms. Connor's legal business in the past. Both women belonged to many of the same organizations. She also knows Pamela Lock quite well. When the three of them were together, it always made the news. Speculation ran rampant about three high-powered women getting together. Invariably something political happened that got laid at their respective doorsteps. Fortunately for all of them, and us as well, no hint of scandal was ever attached to any of them. I don't think I'd be out of line or off the mark if I said that if Martine Connor goes to the White House, Lizzie Fox will end up being the new White House counsel, if not the attorney general. I'm not certain where Ms. Lock will end up, although, as I indicated earlier, my personal guess is that she would be the new president's chief of staff. But even if I'm wrong, she'll be someplace high in the new administration."

Nikki's eyes narrowed. "This is getting complicated, Charles. Too many agendas, is my thinking. The only person who hasn't reared his ugly head is Ted Robinson."

"Wait five minutes," Charles quipped. "When I replay the tape for you, you'll see that he is right in front of the pack, along with his pal Joseph Espinosa."

Just as Charles was about to press the remote to rerun the tape, his cell phone rang. The women waited, whispering among themselves.

Myra's whisper was the loudest and held the most concern. "I do hope Nellie is okay with all this. She tends to get jittery when her little world is rocked."

"Yes, but when it comes to crunch time, Nellie comes through," Annie said. "Don't forget, she is personal friends with Elias Cummings. The truth is, I think each one of them is afraid of the other. For them it works."

Myra chewed on her lower lip, wishing she knew what was going on with her old friend.

Retired Judge Cornelia Easter, Nellie to close friends, settled herself in her favorite chair hoping for some welcome sleep. It had been a busy, stressful evening. She stared down at the encrypted phone in her hand that had started the ball rolling earlier. She closed her eyes in the hopes she could forget what had just transpired. She shuddered as she thought about the message she'd just gotten from Special Agent Bert Navarro. She stroked the cat on her lap, a yellow tabby named Jasper, and calmed almost immediately. A second cat, Miss Patty, wiggled and squirmed and clawed her way to the headrest on the recliner. She nuzzled into Nellie's neck and immediately started to purr. Nellie smiled. She loved her cats, all ten of them, and a new litter was on the way out in the barn. New life. She rejoiced in it even if it was an animal life.

Just three hours ago — or was it four hours? — her phone had chirped to life . . .

She hated to disturb the two cats, but she had to get up and go out to the kitchen so she could see the security monitors. According to Agent Navarro, Special Agent Pete Mangello was about due to appear on her monitor. "Play hardball, Judge," had been Bert's parting comment before the connection was broken.

Nellie started to twitch again as she sat down at the kitchen table. She got up almost immediately to fix herself a stiff drink. She carried it back to the table and sat back down, her eyes on the monitor above the kitchen door, all compliments of the federal government when she had retired. As her security detail said, she was buttoned up tight. No one could get onto her property unless she opened the monster security gates. On top of that she had a secret weapon, well, two secret weapons. Two magnificent German shepherd guard dogs that were trained to guard her with their lives, again, compliments of the government.

Nellie turned her head to look in the laundry room, where the two shepherds were lying, nose to nose. Sisters, trained from puppyhood. Jam and Jelly. Her saviors. The best, though, was that they adored all ten cats and romped through the big old house until the rafters shook. It was not uncommon for one or two of the old cats to snuggle up next to both dogs for long winter naps.

At first she'd been leery about having two dogs, but once she became involved with the vigilantes, she knew it was a good idea, and she had no regrets. She whistled softly, and both shepherds padded out to her side, waiting for her to scratch them behind the ears. They licked at her old gnarled hands and looked at her with bright eyes as though to say, *"I know you're in pain."* For a few brief moments Nellie felt like she was in a cocoon of safety, her guardians all at her feet.

The moment was shattered a few seconds later when the hair on the back of both dogs' necks stood on end. Nellie looked up at the monitor and saw the dark sedan sitting at the entrance to the gate. She waited for the audio to kick in and heard the man announce himself as Special Agent Peter Mangello. "I would like a few words with you, Your Honor."

Nellie got up and walked over to the intercom. "About what?" she asked curtly.

"I'd like to discuss the matter inside, ma'am, if you don't mind."

"But you see, Special Agent Mangello, I do mind. I've retired for the evening, and, had you called ahead, I could have saved you the trip all the way out here. I *never* see unauthorized visitors. That's why I make appointments."

Both dogs pawed the floor, growling softly deep in their throats. The cats, all ten of them, were like a little herd as they scurried to and fro, not liking their mistress's tone of voice.

"Your Honor, I'm here with Director Cummings's approval. Call him if you have any doubts. I really need to speak with you, and I don't want to have to come back with a warrant. I can simply plow down these gates, and see where that gets us. I'm an FBI agent, the *F* stands for federal . . ."

Nellie's hackles rose. Like she needed to be apprised of the law. "And I am a retired *federal* judge. Did you just threaten me,

Special Agent Mangello?" Nellie heard the aggrieved sigh at the other end of the intercom.

"No, ma'am. Please, call Director Cummings. If you don't have the number, I can give it to you."

"Call him yourself. I told you, I have retired for the evening. Good night, Special Agent Mangello." Nellie clicked off the intercom, then shut down the security panel. She looked down at the dogs, who looked like they were ready to feast on someone's legs or buttocks. She spoke soothingly and led them back to the living room, where they took up their positions on either end of the sofa. They remained alert, their eyes bright and shiny. The cats were still scurrying and leaping from couch to chair, to the floor and up to the tables. Finally, they lined up on the sofa between the two dogs as though they were waiting to get their pictures taken. In spite of herself, Nellie laughed.

She then checked the time at the bottom of her TV screen. She'd been watching The Shopping Channel. She would never admit it to anyone that she was addicted to it. She corrected the thought almost immediately. In a weak moment she'd confided to Myra about her shopping mania. She couldn't remember if she'd told her to keep it a secret or not.

While her thoughts raced, Nellie's eyes were glued to the screen, where a pretty young thing was trying to convince the viewing audience that their lives wouldn't be complete if they didn't immediately order the stainless steel slow cooker with nine different bells and whistles even people in outer space would be clamoring for before the hour ran out. She decided to pass on the extraordinary offer.

Nellie figured it would take Elias Cummings at least eight minutes to call her. Why had Mangello neglected to mention that he was a member of a special task force? Why had he said Elias was his boss? Technically, Cummings was Mangello's boss, but according to Bert Navarro, a young woman named Erin Powell was heading a designer task force. Mangello, Navarro, and three other agents were currently reporting directly to her.

Nellie continued to watch the digital numbers tick over at the bottom of the screen. She almost whooped with pleasure when the house's landline rang. Nellie reached down into the work bag attached to her chair and pulled out the phone. "Good evening, Elias," she said, before the director could identify himself. "Why are you and your people bothering me at this time of night? I've retired for the evening. You need to call and make an appointment if you want to talk to me. Isn't that what you do, Elias? Now you can say something, Elias."

"You never sleep, Nellie," the director said. "You told me that yourself." The director's voice was calm, and he sounded amused.

"You weren't listening, Elias. I didn't say I was sleeping. I said I had retired for the evening. That means I am dressed in my sleeping attire, I am buttoned up, so to speak, security-wise. I am sitting here with my animals drinking my one allotted drink of the day. Make an appointment."

"Stop being such a curmudgeon, Nellie, or I'll haul your butt in here and do it the hard way."

"That sounds suspiciously like a threat, Elias. I will not tolerate that. Your man threatened me before, too. And if you try to, as you put it, haul my butt to your offices, what do you think I'll be doing?"

"God only knows," Director Cummings grumbled. "C'mon, Nellie, my guy just wants to ask you a few questions. If you don't cooperate, I mean it, I *will* haul you in here."

"Oh, all right," Nellie agreed. "I'll give him exactly fifteen minutes. I'm going to make a few calls to ensure that your person leaves on schedule. Are we clear on that, Elias? Guess you got your balls in the wringer again, eh?" Nellie added, just as she broke the connection. Sometimes you just had to say what was on your mind.

To the animals' dismay, Nellie hauled herself to her feet again, trundled out to the kitchen, clicked on the intercom, spoke briefly, then pressed the button that would open the iron gates. Next she called Charles, who promised to call Bert and anyone else he could think of.

"That's bullshit, Charles. I want you to call Lizzie Fox. I like the way she kicks ass and gets right in everybody's faces. If he isn't off my property after the allotted time, I'll shoot him. Just so you know. Do you hear me, Charles?"

"I do, Nellie. Relax and go back to The Shopping Channel. I'll take care of things."

Nellie was miffed. "How do you know about The Shopping Channel?"

"You told Myra who told Annie who then told me. They said you're addicted. Are you saying it was supposed to be a secret?"

Nellie broke the connection. Obviously no one could keep a secret, herself included.

Chapter 9

Erin Powell was more than a little frazzled and hoped it didn't show. Her people were looking at her strangely. Then again, maybe that was just her imagination. She looked at the huge clock hanging on the wall, a reminder that she'd had no dinner. A Power-Bar hardly qualified as one of the major food groups.

Nine o'clock. And her people were standing around staring at her with pity in their eyes. She licked at her dry lips. "Someone better tell me right now how that circus in front of the building happened. The director called and chewed out my ass, so now I'm going to chew you out. Charlie, what happened?"

"Emery pulled a fast one. You said to be polite. I was polite. The guy is slick. He is, after all, the deputy district attorney for D.C.," Akers said, as if that was explanation enough. "It's not like he's simply some private citizen who's intimidated by agents of the federal government."

"Where is he?"

Akers shuffled his feet. "Room 3."

"And Doug is in the hospital. That never should have happened. Is there an update on his condition?" she asked.

Joe Landos smirked. "He's okay. That means he'll live, but he'll be on disability for about six weeks. Let's be honest here, Doug did it all wrong. Wong has a sterling rep, and the locals are on his side. Cummings likes him a lot. There's a video bearing out everything Wong said. We took a big black eye on that one."

"Are you telling me Doug acted like a rookie? What the hell was he thinking?"

"I guess you'll have to ask Doug that yourself. I just got an update from the hospital. I didn't personally talk to him," Landos said.

Erin hated the self-satisfied look on the agent's face. They were all getting off on the fiasco that had gone down. And she didn't see one iota of respect for her in any of their faces. Her back stiffened. "Why isn't Lizzie Fox in Room 4, Joe?"

"Are you kidding? You can't be serious if you think I should have hauled her in in front of that mob out there. It was a judgment call. Come morning, I'll serve her up with your breakfast."

Erin knew Landos was right, but that didn't mean she had to like it. She turned around and homed in on Pete Mangello. "Well?"

Mangello glared at the woman standing in front of him. "I had to fucking threaten a federal judge. Then I had to have Director Cummings call her. She refused to co-operate," he explained, defensively.

It was Erin's turn to glare. "You did *WHAT?* You went over my head? How dare you do that! How dare you! You know the chain of command, Mangello. Do you expect me to overlook this?"

Mangello's eyes narrowed. "Look, Erin, Judge Easter is one sharp lady. She doesn't go the bullshit route. She's also got some powerful friends. Friends attached to the media. If I had suggested she call you, she would have laughed in my face. She only deals with people of her own caliber. I made a judgment call, just like Joe did. I talked to her and got exactly nowhere. And, that was *after* she talked to Director Cummings. Just in case you don't know this, let me be the first to tell you that Lizzie Fox is also her attorney of record. As she kicked me out, Lizzie was just arriving, and *she* threatened *me.* Said if I ever tried talking to her client without her being present, she'd cut off my balls and shove them up my ass. That's a direct quote. Then she added that she'd call in the media so they could watch her do it. You know she's a media darling. She loves the limelight. Like I need shit like that on my record. And the Bureau, as Director Cummings has said, does not need any more bad press. You're pulling in negative points by the bushel, Erin."

"You're making that woman sound like some kind of avenger," Erin snarled. "I want her in here as soon as possible. Joe, do you hear me?"

"Yes, ma'am," Landos drawled.

Erin pointed to the one clean board hanging on the wall. The name Lizzie Fox was at the top in bright red marker. "Fill it in, gentlemen, and don't leave anything out. I don't care how inconsequential you might think it is. We do not need to be blindsided by some media-hungry sexpot."

The men standing in front of Erin laughed. Bert laughed the loudest. Erin wished the floor would open up and swallow her whole.

Whoa! Bert blinked as he envisioned the catfight that was more than likely going to ensue the moment Lizzie Fox walked into the building for her Q&A. He almost pitied Powell.

Erin was halfway out the door when the phone on the desk rang. Being the nearest, Bert answered. He schooled his face to blankness and flattened his voice when he said, "Director Cummings for you, Erin." He handed her the phone.

Erin's heart fluttered in her chest. This was a call she wished she could take in private, but she knew that wasn't going to happen.

"Powell," she said curtly. She listened but was unable to hide the dismay she was experiencing. "Yes, sir. With all due respect, *sir,* I thought I was running this task force, meaning I'd make the decisions. Yes, sir, they were my orders. No sir, federal agents do not threaten . . . Again, sir, with all due respect, my people react to the situation they're dealing with at the time. No, sir, Deputy District Attorney Emery has not been questioned as yet. I was on my way to speak with him when you called. Let him go! Did you just say let him go? I understand about the unfortunate circus atmosphere. That was beyond my control, sir. Surely you aren't holding me accountable for what happened outside. I didn't even know it was going on until after it had gotten out of hand. Yes, I am very quickly coming to understand just who Ms. Fox is. Yes, sir. I understand, sir. Yes, sir."

Bert swiveled around. This was the part where he almost felt sorry for Erin Powell. He thought she was going to cry any moment. He understood her humiliation. "You might want to rethink your strategy, Erin. You're dealing with some very powerful people, who know even more powerful people. They know how to play the game. You're the new kid on the block. Their rules are not your rules. Do you want me to show Emery out of the building?"

Erin squared her shoulders. "I think I can handle it, Bert."

The agents watched Erin leave the office, her back ramrod straight.

"She looks like she's going to her own execution. I give her one more week," Landos said.

"She's in over her head," Mangello said. "Two weeks, maybe three, but three is a stretch. She's going to cave."

"I can't believe the director appointed her to head this task force. Some women's group must have gotten to him," Akers said.

"Jesus, it's only her second day on the job," Bert said. "Give her a break. You know what, Pete, you were out of line when you had Cummings call the judge. In case you don't know this, women hold grudges, and they are sneaky. You know that old saying, 'Don't get mad, get even.' Some woman coined that phrase. Everyone knows that. You got, what, nine more months till you retire, right? I'd start worrying if I were you."

Mangello looked sick at Bert's words. He looked down at his watch, and said, "I'm outta here, it's almost ten o'clock."

Joe and Charlie followed him. Bert was left standing alone in front of the blank board. Nothing like driving a wedge between all the team players, he thought smugly. His next big decision was, should he leave or wait for Erin to get back in the office? He looked at the blank board and — grinning — wrote, "femme fatale." He reached for his jacket. If he was lucky, he'd meet up with Jack outside. As he packed up his briefcase, he wondered how old Jack was doing going up against Erin Powell. Jack knew how to dance his way around interrogations. Bert knew Jack could reduce Erin to a basket case without batting an eye.

Just as the thought entered Bert's head, Jack Emery was doing exactly that.

As a show of courtesy, Jack stood when Erin Powell entered the room. He knew why she was here. She'd gotten orders to release him, but she wasn't going to let him know that. He knew from past experience how the fibs worked. Astute at reading people, Jack knew she had her marching orders, and those orders were to send one Deputy District Attorney Emery on his way.

Jack shrugged his arms to settle the sleeves of his jacket more comfortably. He made his way to the door before Powell stiff-armed him. "You going somewhere, Emery?"

"As a matter of fact, yes, I'm going home. It's late, and I'm tired. Please, I'm asking you nicely, drop the arm."

Erin narrowed her eyes. "And if I don't?" The challenge was there, but Jack just laughed.

"You want to go a few rounds with Cummings, be my guest. I'm outta here, and before I leave I want to go on the record as saying I do not appreciate the strong-arm tactics you and yours used this evening."

"No one strong-armed you, Emery. You think you're above the law, don't you?"

"No. Actually, *I am the law in this jurisdiction,* and I take it very seriously. If you want to talk to me, call my office in the morning and make an appointment. I'll be glad to comply, but only with my lawyer in attendance."

"You do know what the penalty is for lying to a federal agent, don't you?"

"You betcha. By the way, I am assuming you're Special Agent Erin Powell. Aren't you guys supposed to identify yourselves? We're a lot more professional where I work. Good night, Agent Powell."

The arm went back up. Jack gently slipped it aside and stepped through the doorway.

"Were you responsible for that circus out front? Remember what I said about lying to a federal officer."

"Well, yeah," Jack drawled. "I put in a call to my lawyer. That was it. You guys aren't very good at crowd containment, now are you?"

"Get the hell out of here, Emery," Erin snarled.

Jack grinned. "See, now you're getting it. That's what I've been trying to do for the last ten minutes. Give my regards to Director Cummings."

Five minutes later Jack was breathing in the last minutes of the fresh October air. He was about to head for the curb, where he could smoke a cigarette until he could hail a cab. He heard the voice but couldn't tell where it came from. Bert.

"Wait five minutes, walk around the corner, and I'll pick you up."

Jack nonchalantly fired up a cigarette, made a pretense of looking for a cab. He took a couple of deep drags until he was sure five minutes had gone by before he turned and walked to the corner.

Just as he turned his back to the front door of the Hoover Building, Erin Powell walked outside. Her gaze immediately went to the figure walking toward the corner. Where was Emery going? It took her only a second to make the decision to follow the man who'd just made a fool out of her. At the corner she stopped and watched as Jack got into a black Mustang. The split second the door opened, and the dome light came on, she recognized Bert Navarro. Everyone on the floor knew Bert Navarro drove a restored 1965 Mustang. Her stomach crunched itself into a tight knot. "Crap."

"My boss just saw you getting into my car, Jack," Bert said as he put the car in gear and peeled out onto the road.

"So what? It's late, you're giving me a ride home. Let them make a federal case out of it. No pun intended. What the hell is going on?"

Bert laughed. "Harry took out Parks earlier, but you already know that. Seems it took almost an hour for him to be transported to the hospital. Snafus along the way. He's out of the loop now. Harry's people following orders. The director called Erin and told her to let you go. She bristled at that order and gave him an argument, for all the good it did her. She lost face in front of the guys, and she's going to take that to heart. Nellie made short work of Mangello. Seems he threatened her. Erin read us all the riot act and was bellowing about chain of command. She's in over her head. Right now she's got a hate on for Lizzie Fox. We all know how that's going to turn out."

Jack grinned in the darkness of the car. "Someone should tell Ms. Powell she's out of her league."

"I'm not really sure about that, Jack. You don't know Erin Powell. She might be temporarily, and I stress the word 'temporarily,' out of her league, but she'll fall back and regroup. She's a good agent. She's got what it takes, but, unfortunately, this task force is a thankless job. If it can get off the ground, she's the one to do it. Having said that, my money is on the Silver Fox."

Jack started to laugh and couldn't stop.

"I'd buy a ticket to see that little meeting when it takes place."

"No problem. I'll record it for you."

"Oh, if they only knew," Jack said.

Both men laughed uproariously.

Sixteen minutes later, Bert pulled the Mustang to the curb outside of Jack's house. "You want to come in for a beer? It's late, and if you want to stay over, it's no problem. Actually, it might be a good idea. I have to call Charles, and if we hustle our butts, we'll make the eleven o'clock news."

"You got anything to eat in there? I'm not talking about those weeds you call vegetables. Man food."

"Got tons of frozen dinners and some leftover Chinese. Fridge full of beer."

"Then I'm your man. Let me get my go-bag out of the trunk."

The go-bag was a bag of supplies most agents kept in their cars in case they were directed to hop a plane or train on the spur of the moment. The bag contained shaving gear, clean underwear, and several shirts, along with a warm-up suit. The trick was to remember to repack the bag once it was used.

"Nice night, doncha think, Jack?" Bert asked, slamming the trunk.

"Winter's coming. I hate winter," Jack

said, opening the door.

Down the block a car stopped, the headlights off. Erin Powell watched as Bert opened his trunk and took out a bag. "Well, well, what have we here?"

Bert turned around in the open doorway, then lifted his arm and waved in Erin's direction. "You knew she was back there, right?"

"Oh, yeah. This will give her something else to spin her wheels about."

When Erin saw Bert wave at her before the door closed, she wanted to spit. Instead, she banged her head on the steering wheel. *I must be a piss-poor excuse for a federal agent.*

There was no one around to dispute her assessment.

CHAPTER 10

It was four minutes past eight on November 1 when Lizzie Fox climbed out of a sleek black town car in front of the Hoover Building and told the driver to wait. She shrugged her elegant shoulders, gave a slight tug to a clingy skirt that could have been fitted into her ear if she was short of closet space.

Ted Robinson, with Joe Espinosa at his side, gawked at the ravishing woman walking toward them. Long legs that went all the way to her throat, Betty Grable legs if you were from a certain lascivious era, deep cleavage, a tan that was so perfect it had to have come from a tanning bed. Ted just knew the tan was a *full*-body tan. The luxurious mane of silvery hair was piled high on her head, making her five-eleven height even more impressive. The makeup she wore was so flawless as to be indistinguishable. She wore enough bling to light up a dark night.

"Now that's one fine, Goddamn good-lookin' woman," Espinosa muttered under his breath. "What the hell is she doing here at this hour of the morning, do you suppose?"

Ted laughed, an unholy sound.

Ted and Joe weren't the only ones admiring the long-legged beauty. People stopped, moved out of the way, then turned to watch the lithe figure cross the open area to the front door of the Hoover Building.

Ted jumped in front of her, and said, "Hey, Lizzie, remember me? Can I have a few words with you?"

Lizzie slowly and deliberately looked Ted over like he was a worm on a stick, one she was going to shake to the ground and stomp on. Instead, she smiled, stepped to the side, and offered up a dazzling smile that had made more than one sitting judge rule in her favor. "Anything for the press. Make sure you get me full face. I don't like side shots."

"Absolutely," Espinosa leered, as he focused the camera.

"So whatcha doing here, Lizzie?"

Lizzie offered up another dazzling smile. "Actually, Mr. Robinson, I was invited here this morning." She looked around, then up at the sky. "Do you think it's going to rain today? And here I am without an umbrella."

"Who invited you?" Ted asked as he flicked the small recorder into the ON position.

"Some . . . person . . . I can't seem to remember her name. Emily, Emma, something like that."

"Erin Powell?" Ted volunteered.

"Something like that. Whatever . . ."

"Why?" Ted asked bluntly.

Lizzie wagged a playful finger under Ted's nose. "Now you know I can't be telling you things like that," she drawled.

"Does this command invitation have anything to do with the fracas that went down here last night?"

Lizzie winked and smiled. "You're the reporter, Mr. Robinson."

"By the way, where've you been, Lizzie? I've been trying to find you for months."

Lizzie winked again, and Ted got weak in the knees. He wondered what it would be like to take this bombshell to bed.

"If I told you that, then I'd have to kill you. Now, if there isn't anything else, I'm running late. I don't want Ms. Whatever-her-name-is to get her panties in a wad. If I'm not out in an hour, send in the troops, okay?"

"Gotcha. Can I quote you on that, Lizzie?"

"Of course. Will you gentlemen be staying on when the sale of the *Post* goes through?"

Ted looked like he was sucking on a sour lemon. "I hope so."

Lizzie leaned closer to the reporter, and whispered, "I can make it happen, Ted. I'm overseeing the final legalities. I have an idea. Let's do lunch before you write this up. I like the Squire's Pub. Oneish or thereabouts."

"You shitting me, Lizzie? How'd that happen?" Excitement rang in Ted's voice as he hopped from one foot to the other. "I'll be there."

Lizzie shrugged her elegant shoulders. Never modest, she said, "Because I'm the best of the best, that's why. What other reason could there possibly be?"

Ted was in such shock he was speechless for the first time in his life. So speechless he didn't make a move when he saw Jack Emery and Judge Easter walk through the doors behind Lizzie.

When he finally found his tongue, he looked at Espinosa, and said, "Holy shit! Did you just hear what I heard? I think we should buy some hip waders because there's going to be a bloodbath around here sooner rather than later."

"Yep."

■ ■ ■ ■

Erin Powell saw *her* coming, and so did the others. She cringed inwardly while outwardly hoping the others weren't picking up on it. That was wishful thinking on her part. She hated, absolutely hated, the smirks on her fellow agents' faces. Except for Bert Navarro, who looked like he was studying the *Mona Lisa* with a critical eye. She had yet to deal with Bert concerning last night's activities.

"Good morning, people," Lizzie said in her best low, sultry, come-hither voice. "I understand you wish to have a dialogue with me. I'm here. Time is money in my business. So, I'd appreciate it if we could get right to it. Oh, yes, one other thing. Do not ever, ever, ever, ever pull crap like this on me again, or you'll be in the Mojave stapling papers." The voice was now so sensual and earthy-sounding that all the agents, Bert included, wore sappy expressions as they rushed to escort her to the conference room, to get her a comfortable chair, and make offers of coffee.

"Can I run out and get you a latte?" Landos asked.

Lizzie batted her inch-long eyelashes, and

replied, "Agent . . ."

"Landos, Joe Landos," the agent said, falling all over himself.

"That would be just lovely, Agent Landos. Thank you for being so considerate."

Landos was out of the building faster than greased lightning.

Lizzie looked around and made a face. The room was spartan, folding chairs, long metal table that was scratched and scarred. In the middle was a huge coffee stain that no one had bothered to clean. The walls were blinding white, the floor battleship gray. She eyed the chair and made a pretense of checking for dirt so that her five-thousand-dollar Armani suit wouldn't get dirty. She finally sat down but ever so gingerly on the edge of the chair. The minuscule skirt hiked up so far the agents looked away discreetly.

"How's it going, Lizzie?" Bert asked with a show of familiarity.

Lizzie offered up her dazzling smile, and said, "Ask me when I leave here, sweetie. Now, tell me, what can I do for you fine gentlemen and . . . uh, lady?"

Bert knew immediately what Lizzie was doing. She'd drawn her line in the sand and would not deal with Erin. Lizzie never dealt with women. As in never. She'd decided she would deal with Bert, and that was that.

Erin sensed where it was all going and stepped in front of Bert. "I'm Special Agent Erin Powell. I'm heading up this elite task force on Director Cummings's orders."

Lizzie ignored Erin's outstretched hand, her expression clearly showing what she thought of that order. Erin flushed and withdrew her hand as though she'd been stung by a bee.

"As I was saying, Ms. Fox, we'd like to ask you a few questions, and you can be on your way."

"Questions about what?"

Lizzie crossed her legs. Erin heard the indrawn breath of her fellow agents. Why did everything have to be about sex?

"About the vigilantes. You were the attorney of record."

"And it's all privileged. I'm afraid I can't help you."

Erin wondered if she looked as desperate as she felt. Probably. "Oh, but you will. I'm in control here. I can hold you for seventy-two hours if I so choose."

Lizzie stood up. "You can try, but before you do that, I suggest you call Director Cummings to see if that's really the route you want to take. Since you probably know two of the vigilantes better than I do, why don't you just make up something and run with it? I was simply their attorney for a few hours. And then, poof, they absconded. End of story. Now, Bert, please show me where my two clients are so I can advise them of their rights. By the way, there are some reporters out front. If you want to pursue push coming to shove, let's do it, Special Agent Powell. I told them if I wasn't out in an hour to contact Director Cummings, who has an open-door policy, and inquire as to my whereabouts."

Erin's stomach rumbled. She was glad she hadn't eaten any breakfast. She'd not only just lost the battle, she'd lost the war as well. Still, she needed to go down fighting. She was just about to order her agents to arrest Lizzie Fox, and she'd take the heat, when Director Cummings poked his head in the door. Seeing Lizzie, his face lit up like a hundred-watt bulb.

"Nice to see you, Lizzie."

Oh, shit, Erin thought. *They're on a first-name basis.*

"Nice to see you, too, Director."

"I understand you've been away, out of town. Nice to see that you're back. Where were you?" he asked in his most folksy manner.

Lizzie laughed, the sound tinkling all over

the office. She wagged a playful finger, then held out her left hand where a ring with a diamond as big as a headlight gleamed. "Here and there, Director. A lady never kisses and tells, you know that. Ah, here is my latte. Thank you so much, Agent Landos. Wasn't that sweet of him? Your agents are such nice, understanding people. I was just explaining to Ms. Emily . . . Emma . . . sorry, whatever her name is, that she couldn't arrest me and hold me for seventy-two hours because then all sorts of problems would come up. Isn't that right, Director? It goes without saying that I shared everything I could — which is really nothing, since it is all privileged. We both know you can't hold me. Unless, of course, you're trying to make a statement of some kind, which will go against you in a court of law.

"I have an idea, Director. Why don't you walk me down to where my clients are waiting for me." Without waiting for a response, Lizzie untangled her long legs, stood up, and smoothed down her skimpy skirt. All eyes, even Erin's, were on her beautiful, long, toned legs.

When the director and Lizzie were out of earshot, Landos leaned forward, and asked Erin, "Guess she showed you, huh?"

Erin walked over to her desk. She sat

down, looked at her agents, and said, "Yes, I guess she did," so softly the men had to strain to hear her words. All but Bert wore baffled expressions as they stared at their boss.

"Charlie and Pete, don't you have someplace to be? I believe Judge Easter and Deputy District Attorney Emery are waiting for you. Joe, pick up Ted Robinson and haul him in here. From what I'm told, he knows more than anyone else about the vigilantes."

"He's a nut job, Erin. No one pays attention to him. He sees vigilantes in his dreams. He's a joke," Landos said.

"So bring him in so I can get a good laugh. I need one right now. I thought I told you to bring in Maggie Spritzer."

Landos looked for a moment like he was going to give Erin an argument but decided against it. "I would if I could find her. No one knows where she is."

"Just like no one knew where that sexpot was?"

"Meow!" Landos said as he left the office.

Erin spun her chair around so that she was facing Bert. "You want to tell me about last night?"

"No, actually I don't. When I'm off duty, my time is my own. More to the point, do you want to tell me why you were following me?"

"Actually, I don't, Bert."

"Then I guess we should get to the business at hand. What do you want me to do?"

What she really wanted was to cry on his shoulder. Anyone's shoulder. She schooled her face to impassiveness when she spoke. "It's getting to the point that no one is going to talk to us even if we sweat them. And you were right, Bert. Powerful people are behind those vigilantes. When they bring in Robinson, I'm going to do the interrogation. I'll decide if he's a crackpot or not. Give me your professional opinion of Lizzie Fox, Bert. Aside from the obvious."

"She's not shy. She's flamboyant and has the goods to pull it off. She doesn't lie when she says she is the best of the best. Bottom line, she is. As the young people say today, the lady has it going on. She's got enough favors due her in this town to keep her going till hell freezes over. All she has to do is call them in, and you're out in the cold, Erin. Right now she's going to play with you. She's going to bait you, then she'll strike with that dazzling killer smile of hers. You won't know what hit you. I've seen her in action."

Erin shivered inside her suit jacket. She

was stung to the quick by Bert's assessment. "You must think I'm a total dud. Why is that?"

"You let her get to you. You played right into her hands. I don't think you're a dud. I think you're out of your league here, is what I think. For starters, you had no clue who or what Lizzie Fox is. Always know your adversary, Interrogation 101. Instead of wasting your time following me around, use your time more constructively. This is a thankless job, and you aren't going to get those women. Accept it."

Erin digested the information, not liking it. "There's a mole here somewhere."

"Maybe so. Find him or her and sweat them. Now, what do you want me to do?"

"Finish going through the boxes. Finish up the boards so that everything reads chronologically. Somewhere there's a clue that everyone's missed. Find it. I mean it, Bert, find it, or my thinking where you're concerned is not going to be pretty. I'm going to be all over you if you zero out again. I'm going out. Call me on my cell if you need me."

"Okay, boss."

Bert looked around. He knew the room was bugged, so he didn't bother to check it out. He felt a small shiver of apprehension knowing Erin Powell thought he was the mole. Like all women, she was going to be like a dog with a bone where he was concerned.

As he got down to his thankless job, he wondered how Jack and Nellie were faring. Who the hell was doing the questioning? The director? If it was Charlie and Pete, it would be a disaster. Both men had the finesse of a bull in a china shop. And where was Erin going so early in the morning? Talk about a cluster fuck. This was right up there with the best of them.

Three doors down on the right, Director Cummings was thinking along the same lines. Obviously, this little meeting was a mistake, and he had to save face some way. He waved off Agents Akers and Mangello, who were about to storm the room.

"I'm sorry about this. Please, allow me to apologize. This task force is just starting up, and some of my agents got a little overzealous. You're all free to go, but I'd like it if you'd agree to come in and talk when we get a little more organized. An informal Q&A."

"Elias, this is nonsense," Nellie said. "I have nothing to say that I haven't told you several times already. You need to move to higher ground, get some fresh ideas. We're the old guard, been there, done that. Speaking strictly for myself, I have had no contact with the women you call the vigilantes. I heard the case in court. That's the sum total of my involvement. Aside from what I told your predecessor, who tried to do me in with that dossier he compiled, there is nothing I can tell you. Can't we please leave it at that so I can get on with my retirement?"

"Of course, Nellie," the director said agreeably. "To show there are no hard feelings, allow me to take you to breakfast. I insist, Nellie."

"Well, since you put it that way, I guess I am hungry."

"Wonderful."

The director looked at Jack and Lizzie and extended the invitation. Both declined.

"You taking this all down, Lizzie?" he asked, his folksy voice ringing in the large empty room.

Lizzie pointed to her head to indicate she had it all stored in her brain. She made a production of standing up then and almost blew the director's socks off when she leaned over and kissed his cheek. Jack, cell phone in hand, clicked once, then twice, and the picture was stored. Nellie, seeing the little byplay, almost laughed out loud.

"Shall we?" the director asked, standing aside so his guests could exit the door.

"I'll just be a minute, Nellie. I want to get my jacket."

"Take your time, Elias. I'm retired and have all the time in the world."

"Nice seeing you again, Your Honor," Jack said as he cupped Lizzie's elbow in his hand to usher her out the door.

Neither spoke until they were outside in the brisk air. "What the hell is going on, Jack? What was that dog-and-pony show all about?" Lizzie demanded as she waved to Ted Robinson. He waved back.

"When I find out, I'll let you know. See ya," Jack said, heading to the curb to hail a cab.

He looked back once to see Ted Robinson glaring at him. He shivered in the crisp air as he climbed into the cab. He barked out the address of the courthouse, then leaned back to think about what had just happened inside 935 Pennsylvania Avenue.

CHAPTER 11

After leaving her office just before noon, Lizzie Fox had the driver of the town car take her back to her home in the pricey neighborhood above Dupont Circle. She signed the credit card form, added a generous tip, and slid out of the car, thanking the driver.

Key in hand, she opened the solid oak door, then closed it behind her as she kicked off her spiked heels. They sailed across the room, landing with a plop next to a luxurious white sofa. Her antenna went up almost immediately. Someone was in the house, even though it was deathly silent. She tiptoed over to the sofa and picked up one of the stilettos. Carrying it like a weapon, she moved cautiously through the house. She stopped long enough in the dining room to slide open one of the drawers, where she kept a fully loaded gun. Shoe in one hand, gun in the other, she slowly inched open the swinging door that led into the kitchen. Her jaw dropped and her eyes bulged when she saw Judge Cornelia Easter sitting at her kitchen table.

"Damn, Nellie, I could have shot you and asked questions later. How'd you get in here?"

Nellie offered up a tight little smile. "While I was sitting on the bench, over the years many people stood before me on trial. One gentleman enlightened us in great detail about how to break and enter without getting caught. Believe it or not, I took notes in case anyone else came before me and tried to snow me."

"I guess he wasn't such an expert if he got caught," Lizzie said, snapping the safety on the gun in her hand and stuffing it into a kitchen drawer.

"Oh, he didn't get caught breaking and entering. He wanted to convince me he retired from such nefarious doings by explaining his résumé to me. He was charged with highjacking an eighteen-wheeler full of designer shoes that he had family members selling at a flea market in Alexandria. His smart-ass lawyer got him off by convincing the jury his client was at the wrong place at the right time. I could use a good cup of coffee right now. Tell me, dear, what's going on and what do we have to do?"

Lizzie removed her suit jacket and hung it over the back of one of the kitchen chairs before she set about grinding beans and filling the coffeemaker with water. She set out cups and saucers, cream and sugar. "I'm not sure, Nellie. We lucked out this morning, with Elias showing up the way he did. Coincidence? I don't believe in coincidences, Nellie. Never have. Was it all a setup to make us nervous? Possibly a warning of things to come."

"Did something happen out of the norm? Myra told me the girls are getting ready to take on something, but she was vague on details. Do you think it's just the bad press the FBI is getting from the media? They have become a laughingstock on the 24-hour cable news channels."

"I think that's part of it. I've interacted with the agents assigned to this special task force on occasion. However, today was the first time I met Erin Powell. How she got up to bat on this gig is beyond me. All female fibs want to make a name for themselves. I have no reason to think Powell is any different. The best thing we have going for us right now is that Bert is on the inside, but there's a problem there, too. Powell followed Bert last night when he gave Jack a ride home, then spent the night, since he had to be in the office by five thirty. He managed to text message me about it as I was riding down in the elevator. So he's on Powell's radar screen. He said she believes there's a mole in the FBI who helps the vigilantes. Don't worry about Bert, he knows how to cover his ass."

Nellie wondered what exactly *interacting with the agents on occasion* really meant, but she'd bite off her tongue before she asked. So she just nodded and waited for whatever Lizzie was going to say next. With Lizzie it was always a bombshell a minute.

"Well, it's my opinion that something somewhere is going down for Elias to form this special task force. It's got to be more than the bad press. Every organization gets bad press and lives to fight another day. I'm thinking, and again, this is just my opinion, but I think it's all a setup to trap the vigilantes somehow," Nellie said.

Lizzie got up to pour the coffee. She patted Nellie's bony shoulder on the way. "It's funny, Nellie, that you should say that because I've been thinking exactly the same thing. At least we're on the same page. All we have to do is wait to see how it all shakes out. With Bert on the inside, I'm thinking we won't have long to wait.

"Listen, Nellie, I want to change my clothes. I made a lunch date with Ted Robinson. He's going to meet me at the Squire's Pub. I'm going to try to turn him." At the judge's startled look, Lizzie laughed. "I admit it's a daunting task but not impossible. Enjoy the coffee. I won't be long."

Nellie blinked. And it only took her not quite five minutes to dump the bombshell. In spite of herself, Nellie burst out laughing. She didn't have a doubt in the world that Lizzie could turn Robinson but at what cost?

Nellie finished her coffee and was calling her driver to pick her up when Lizzie appeared in the doorway. Nellie's eyebrows shot up to her hairline. The statuesque lawyer sported skintight black leather pants, scarlet knee-high leather boots with spike heels, and a short, candy-apple red bomber jacket. To Nellie's practiced eye it didn't look like she was wearing *anything* under the jacket. She was still sporting the headlight diamond on her left hand. The wild mane of silvery hair shimmered in the kitchen's fluorescent light. "Oh, my," was all Nellie could muster in the way of words.

Lizzie did a perfect pirouette. "Sex makes the world go round. I have a meeting at two with Annie's lawyers and the ones representing the owners of the *Post*."

"Oh, my," Nellie said again.

"You know that old saying, Nellie, 'First you bullshit them, then you dazzle them, and when they're gasping for breath, you either hand them a pen or call an ambulance.' Works every time."

"No, I can't say I ever heard that before. I just know about catching more flies with honey than vinegar. I guess that makes me sound old."

Lizzie laughed as she rinsed the coffeemaker and pulled the plug. "I'm not trying to catch flies, Nellie. I'm trying to outswim the sharks. Not to worry, I have a lock on it."

"Well, in that case I won't worry. You look . . . You look . . . spectacular."

Lizzie laughed again because she knew Nellie meant every word. "I'm outta here. The door will lock behind you. Stay as long as you like. I'll call you later this afternoon. Check in with me if you hear from Jack or Bert, okay?"

"Is it okay if I smoke while I wait for my driver?"

"No problem. There are some cigarettes in the kitchen drawer. There's an ashtray in there, too. I puff on one now and then when my stress level hits a high note."

Nellie couldn't imagine Lizzie Fox ever getting stressed out. She was the cockiest, the most confident, arrogant female she'd ever met. Of course, it could all be a façade for all Nellie knew. She waved to Lizzie's retreating back. She didn't light her cigarette until she heard the front door close behind the lawyer.

Nellie blew a perfect smoke ring before she closed her eyes. Where was all of this headed and what was the outcome going to be? She wished she was psychic.

The Squire's Pub was a watering hole for government lawyers, White House personnel, and assorted white-collar bureaucrats with designer briefcases. It was a place to be *seen.* The pub was huge, and always, no matter the hour of the day or night, filled to overflowing. The bar was long, solid mahogany, with matching walls and stained glass windows. Politicians vied and cajoled to have their pictures mounted on those walls. It was a known fact that some of the more aggressive Washingtonians went so far as to try bribing the owner, a Brit named Graham Abernathy.

Abernathy loved women. Adored women. Lusted after women. One in particular:

Lizzie Fox. And she traded on that love, adoration, and lust. Translation . . . Abernathy was Lizzie's informant, her source, her snitch, her stool pigeon, and she'd go to jail before she ever revealed his name.

When the plate glass door with the ornate grillwork on the inside opened, the whole room stopped what they were doing to stare at the ravishing creature about to grace the room with her presence. Abernathy saw her first and leaped over the bar with the agility of a ballet dancer. The crowd parted as he swung the lawyer high in the air until she was breathless. "I've missed you, luv!"

"Wow!" Lizzie laughed as she brushed at her hair. "I need to come here more often."

"How about helping me out for the next hour or so?" the big, burly man with the twinkling eyes asked.

"Love to," Lizzie said. It wouldn't be the first time she stepped behind the bar to mix and hand out drinks for Abernathy. One time she'd worked an hour and made three hundred dollars in tips, which she donated to the local SPCA. Her feet left the floor, and in the blink of an eye, she was behind the bar and taking her first order.

"That rock on your hand is new. Talk to me, luv," Abernathy said over the clinking of glassware and the chatter at the bar.

Lizzie laughed. “Keeps the wolves at bay. It’s one of those fancy new synthetics,” she hissed in his ear.

“So I still have a chance, eh?”

“You darling man, you’ve always had a chance. To be my best friend. I love your wife and kids. Besides, what would that lovely wife of yours say if we took off and canoodled behind the bar? She’d damn well kill you, that’s what she would do.”

“That she would, luv. She says it’s okay to look, but I mustn’t touch.”

“Katy is a wise woman, and I’d be first in line to help her kill you if you ever stray. Tell me,” she said out of the corner of her mouth as she shook up a martini, “what’s going on? I’ve been on a sabbatical, so I’m not up on the latest. I’m meeting a reporter from the *Post* in a bit, so I can’t stay here long. You got anything worth hanging around for?”

“I do, luv. It’s meaty. I thought about you when I heard it, but you weren’t answering your cell phone.”

“No cell phone usage where I was. Listen, Graham, I have a meeting after I ditch the reporter. If things go off on schedule, I can be back here at four. That will give us an hour before the cocktail crowd shows up. Will that work for you?”

"It will, luv, it will." He grinned when he watched Lizzie stick a five-dollar bill into her cleavage.

Lizzie worked quickly, uncapping long-necks, pouring white wine, and shaking up cocktails, all the while keeping up a chirpy banter with the men three deep at the bar.

On more than one occasion Graham had called her at the courthouse to tell her that her opposing counsel was drowning his sorrows at the bar. More times than she cared to admit, her adversaries returned to court after the lunch break in a sluggish mood, their eyes glazed, thanks to Graham's heavy hand with the bottle. Sure it was dirty pool, sure it was a shade unethical, but Lizzie Fox played to win. There was no place in the courtroom for losers except maybe as the defendant or the plaintiff.

It was 12:50 when Lizzie looked up to see Ted Robinson at the bar. "Find a green table, and I'll join you."

Green tables were always reserved for Graham's special guests. Lizzie had no problem trading on the *special guest* part. She slapped down a cocktail napkin and a Corona with a wedge of lime stuck in the opening in front of a bald-headed judge in a Savile Row suit. She winked at the judge, who winked back. She slid the ten-dollar bill to Graham, wiped her hands on the bar towel before she walked out from behind the bar. Carrying a Diet Coke and a Bud longneck, she fought her way through the crowd of admiring men and envious women without spilling a drop.

"On the house, Robinson, but you get to leave the tip."

Ted nodded as he upended the bottle. "What's up, Lizzie? You okay with me recording our conversation?"

"No, I'm not comfortable with that. We're off the record here, okay?"

"I'm easy. Okay by me."

"The fibs are looking for you. They want to sweat you on the vigilantes. You seem to be the only one in this town with knowledge of them. I am well aware of your . . . ah . . . passion, to bring the ladies to justice. How am I doing so far?"

Ted shrugged. "Go on."

"So what are you going to say when they haul you in and hold you for seventy-two hours?"

"And you need to know this . . . why? You soliciting business, Lizzie?"

Lizzie managed to look outraged. "Sweetie, I have prospective clients lined up from here to Baltimore. I can pick and choose. You don't look like you could pay my retainer, much less my hourly rate — which, by the way, is seven hundred dollars."

"You're right about that, I can't afford it. Are you telling me in a roundabout way that I need a lawyer? The *Post* has lawyers that are at my disposal."

"Not anymore they don't. All those buttoned-up guys got their walking papers. Didn't you hear? There are new owners in town who are bringing in their own people."

Ted's stomach started to rumble. He stared at the woman sitting across from him and decided she was telling him the truth. "Okay, I'm going to need a lawyer. You take time payments?"

Lizzie winced. "What would you say to a trade-off?"

Ted thumped his bottle down on the table. "What kind of trade-off?"

"Keep your lip zipped when you're hauled in. All you say is you're obsessed with the vigilantes. Deniability will take you a long way. You did hear about that new task force Cummings started up, right? Call me and I'll represent you. For free."

"Why are you being so damn generous all of a sudden, Lizzie? You're one of them, aren't you?"

"No," Lizzie lied with a straight face. "I'm

still pissed that they jumped their bond and left me holding the bag. Don't try to spin it any other way, Ted."

"Wait just a damn fucking minute. You just threatened me. Either I play ball with you, for whatever your reasons are, or . . . What's the *or,* Lizzie?"

Lizzie leaned back in the green-upholstered chair and folded her hands on the table in front of her. "I never threaten. I make promises."

Ted looked into his empty bottle and grimaced. Lizzie reached for it and held it up high for a waiter to see it. A fresh bottle appeared like magic.

"And if I play ball, I get . . . what?"

"A twofer. You get me to represent you, and you get to keep your job. Win-win," she said happily.

Ted thought Lizzie looked like a barracuda, with him caught between its jaws. "God's a guy. You're full of yourself, Lizzie. No one is that influential."

"I'm handling the transfer of the *Post.* In fact, when I leave here, I'm heading to the *Post* to wrap up some final details. We can share a cab if you like. Bet you don't know who the new EIC is. Sullivan is being put out to pasture. New broom sweeps clean. You want to keep your job, do what I say. I

can guarantee Espinosa his job as well."
"A contract?"
"Do you want a contract?"
"Well, yeah. I'd hate for some new EIC to hold my job over my head. Five years. Guarantee my package if the new deal doesn't go through. Upgrade my health benefits and my expense account."
"Deal," Lizzie said. "And I get what?"
"My silence. Isn't that what this is all about? Who's coming on board as the new EIC? I've heard rumors. The guy from the *Times?*"
"Not even close. Maggie Spritzer."
Ted's eyes rolled back in his head. He clutched at the edge of the green table till he could focus on Lizzie. "That was beyond cruel, even for you, Lizzie."
Lizzie laughed. "Why is the truth cruel? Ms. Spritzer will be at the meeting. So do we have a deal or not?"
"Yeah," Ted said. "But all bets are off if I catch you breaking the law. If that happens, you'll be standing in the tall grass, and I'll personally stuff the contract up your . . . whatever. I do have some ethics left, you know. We still on the same page now?" Ted asked coldly.
"Oh, yeah. We're on the same page. Now, I want you to call the FBI and ask for Erin

Powell. Say you heard they want you to come in. Make an appointment, then call me, and I'll meet you there.

"So are we sharing that cab or not?"

Ted slugged down the rest of the beer in his bottle, slapped a ten-dollar bill on the table, and stood up. "Why the hell not?"

"Yeah, why the hell not," Lizzie said.

Chapter 12

The women were armed with rakes and paper bags as they moved about the compound. Raking and bagging leaves and debris was the same as doing a ten-mile run, Charles said as they pelted him with pinecones to show what they thought of his order.

They worked in teams of two each, while the seventh Sister, Yoko, trimmed back the autumn chrysanthemums that graced the perimeter of the compound. They talked among themselves as they worked, their voices excited at first, then sobering at the possibilities that might confront them once they arrived back in Washington.

Annie scooped up a load of leaves to dump into the bag Alexis was holding open. "We're going to be staying in a house down the street from the ex-national security advisor. You remember Mr. Woodley, right? It was before my time with the Sisters, but

Myra told me everything. I'm sorry I missed that little caper."

"Do I ever? I'm sorry you missed it, too, Annie. It was a mind bender from the git-go." Alexis grinned.

"Well, Charles said Paula, the ex-NSA's wife, told him a house was for sale, so we bought it. We're going to be flight attendants. Myra and I will be the den mothers or cook and housekeeper. Mrs. Woodley invited us for tea after we move in. Myra thinks Mrs. Woodley just wants to torment her husband with the sight of us, which Myra said is okay with all of us. I said I thought that would be fine. I'm really looking forward to meeting both of them." Annie laughed, then Alexis doubled over as she formed a mental picture of the man they'd turned into a virtual vegetable.

"According to Charles, you girls will have the proper airline uniforms and the requisite luggage. And you will be coming and going, so no one will be suspicious. As Mrs. Woodley said, it's pretty much a mind-your-own-business kind of neighborhood, so we shouldn't draw too much attention. For the past few days some women from an acting studio have been going in and out, dressed as flight attendants, so the neighbors could see them. Their gig is up tomorrow, when we show up one by one. You know what they say about the best-laid plans of mice and men, right?"

Alexis laughed as she snapped a plastic tie around the neck of the bag that they would later haul to the side of the mountain, open, and dump the leaves. The mountain was their personal landfill.

"What's so funny?" Nikki asked as she dragged a huge bag of leaves over to where the others were piled up. "This is a thankless task. By tonight there will be just as many leaves as we've raked up on the ground. I don't want to do this again. It would be different if we could burn them, but we can't. I have blisters that have blisters of their own, even wearing these gloves." To prove her point, she peeled off the work gloves to reveal huge blisters on the palms of her hands. "Better yet, I quit!" she said dramatically.

That was all the others had to hear. They threw down their rakes and their work gloves, marched over to the steps of the Big House, and sat down.

Yoko closed her pruning shears and joined the others. "I can't believe we're going to Washington tomorrow." Her eyes sparkled as she sat down on the bottom step. "This trip, I want to take a drive past my old shop just to see what's going on. We always had mountains of pumpkins for the children. I worked so hard to make it festive for the little ones. On Saturdays we did a hayride. I don't care what Charles says, I'm going. Do you all hear me? I'm going to do that."

"We're all going to do it, Yoko. If the gods are in the right position, maybe we can all take the hayride. Wouldn't that be great?" Nikki asked.

The others clapped enthusiastically.

Charles appeared in the open doorway. "What is it I'm going to say that you won't like?" Before anyone could reply, he looked at the wild disarray in the middle of the compound and knew instantly his chicks had quit on him. He backed inside and closed the door.

"Coward!" Kathryn shouted.

"So, where were we," Myra asked, "before Sir Charles made his presence known?"

"We were saying how excited we all are to be going back to Washington. Imagine having tea with the Woodleys. I can hardly wait," Alexis said.

"So our game plan hinges in part on Lizzie. Let's make sure we have this down right. She's going to get one of us into Pamela Lock's inner circle by trading on an old friendship, not to mention that Lizzie has acted as legal counsel to both Lock and the woman who will be her party's presidential nominee. One of us will be a high-powered, well-connected volunteer with her own Rolodex along with the proper credentials Charles will set up. Said volunteer will have her own assistant. It will be the same for the RNC operation. One high-powered, well-connected volunteer plus assistant. Do I have that right?" Kathryn asked.

"That's my understanding, which means there are three of us left doing . . . what?" Alexis asked.

"Don't even go there if you're planning on planting Myra and me in that Kalorama house being den mothers. We want in, don't we, Myra?" Annie demanded.

Myra fingered the pearls at her neck. "Yes. Absolutely, we want in. We are not going to sit on our . . . our duffs, this time around. We are definitely in." *God, did she just say that?* Obviously she did because the others were looking at her with a great deal of interest. Or maybe it was respect. She did love getting respect.

"I wouldn't mind sitting this one out," Isabelle said. "I can run errands, chauffeur anyone who needs to go somewhere. Just tell me what to do, and I'll do it."

"Trust me, no one is going to be sitting

around. We just have to refine the plan a little more and get it up and running," Nikki said.

"Nikki, what's your gut feeling? Do you think a pardon is even a remote possibility?" Myra asked, her tone so wistful, Nikki felt herself choke up.

"No, Myra, I don't. I'm sorry. For the president's chief of staff to promise something like that is just too unbelievable, but in doing so, I think the man tipped his hand. I think he's involved somehow. I can almost guarantee the president knows nothing about that particular wild promise."

"Think about this, Nikki," Annie said. "What if we can get Lizzie to . . . uh . . . drop a few little hints that we might be willing to help if Martine Connor offers us the same deal should she make it to the White House? All is fair in love and war, and this is war. To the victor go the spoils, that kind of thing. This is our survival we're talking about. I for one have no trouble working to make Ms. Connor her party's nominee. We help to get her the nomination, then do everything we can to get Connor into office, using the *Post* to support her against the incumbent."

The others thought about it, looked at Annie, and, as one, nodded.

"That'll work for me," Kathryn said.

The others nodded.

"I don't know about helping the Democrats," Myra fretted.

"Get over it, Myra. You're going to love helping *this* Democrat," Annie said. "More to the point, you can't vote, anyway. Think of it as just a word you have trouble saying. End of story. Well, no, that's not really the end of the story, you're going to have to plan a huge party, a big, glorious fundraiser. We can blackmail all those Hollywood people that were on the fringe of Michael Lyons's smarmy life. We also have the file Mitchell Riley kept on all those people with money. We can blackmail every single one of them to donate generously to the fundraiser."

Myra didn't know if she could bring herself to help a Democrat or not. She shrugged. She'd worry about her political affiliations later. She did know how to plan and throw a party, though.

The Sisters looked at Annie in awe, their jaws slack at her suggestion.

"Why are you looking at me like that? Blackmail is a pimple compared to what we've been doing," Annie said airily.

"Annie does have a point, girls. Personally, I love the idea," Kathryn said. "Let's make our fabulous fund-raiser in New York, so we can shop. I need some new clothes."

The girls hooted with laughter because, as they all knew, Kathryn used to live in jeans and flannel shirts — but since hooking up with Bert Navarro, she was into clothes, perfume, and enticing animal-print undies. She flushed but held her ground.

"Okay, New York it is. Anything outside of Washington will give us more cover. I think we should call it a soirée for Ms. Connor. A hundred thousand a plate. Ten to a table. How many on our guest list? How much do we want to raise to get her the nomination?" Annie asked, excitement ringing in her voice.

"Ten million sounds like a nice, healthy number. Connor can buy a lot of airtime in the big primary states for that kind of money," Nikki observed.

Annie clapped her hands together. "Myra and I will head it up. I think the Waldorf-Astoria will do nicely. Don't you think so, Myra?"

Myra was speechless as she fingered her pearls. All she could do was nod. What would Charles say when he found out they might be helping a Democrat become her party's nominee and then take the White House from the Republican incumbent?

Annie clapped her hands again. "Okay, it's done. We can promise Ms. Connor the ten million without blinking. Think, girls, what else can we promise her to sweeten the deal?"

"We have a lot of time for that. We can arrange a whole host of things to bring in money as long as we're in blackmail mode. For now, we're just making promises to see if she's receptive. While she might be leading in the polls against the guys trying to get the nomination, she's still strapped for funds. Hey, we're women, we can make it happen. We dangle the carrot, see if she takes the bait, then get to work," Nikki said. "No sense spinning our wheels until we see if it will fly."

The women's fists shot in the air to a chorus of, "I like it . . . I think it will work, too . . . She's a woman, and women stick together."

"We need to go over that file on Martine Connor that Charles gave us," Kathryn said. "We need to know everything about her from the day she was born so we don't get sandbagged along the way. Lizzie can help us with that. We need to make Martine Connor a household name. Maybe Charles can help us with that."

The front door of the Big House opened.

Charles stood in the doorway with a silver tray in his hand and a manila folder under his arm. "Peanut butter and jelly sandwiches, pumpkin tarts, and hot tea for lunch, ladies. In the envelope is the updated, guaranteed-to-be complete file on Martine Connor, and will be of more help to you than the first one I gave you." He turned around and closed the door.

"How *does* he do that?" Alexis grumbled.

"By listening at the door," Annie snapped as she bit into her sandwich. She chewed furiously, and when she finished her sandwich, she looked down at her watch and then at the Sisters. "Lizzie should be at the *Post* about now. I wish I was a fly on the wall to see how that's all going to work out. Not that I'm worried, it's a done deal. I just never owned a newspaper before. What if I screw up? What if things don't work out? Then what? It's such a massive undertaking," she babbled.

"I can't believe that's you talking, Annie," Myra said. "Aren't you always the eternal optimist? Where is this worry coming from all of a sudden? The glass is always half-full as opposed to half-empty with you. Why are you so worried now when it's too late to back out? It's not like you're going to be running the paper; other people will be doing that," she finished, with a bite to her tone.

Isabelle started to laugh and couldn't stop. "The part I like best is that Maggie is going to be Ted Robinson's boss. Close your eyes and visualize how that's going to play out. I think I might pay to see that if it was on pay-per-view."

While Annie and Myra cleaned up the luncheon debris, which was almost nil, the others went back to raking leaves.

"I thought they quit," Annie said, looking over her shoulder.

"No one quits on Charles and lives to talk about it. You know that, Annie." Myra smiled. "Not even us, so get ready to rake as soon as we take all these things back to the kitchen. He's watching us, you know."

"I know, I know," Annie said cheerfully, her good mood restored.

At the same time as the Sisters were raking the leaves, Lizzie Fox and Ted Robinson were taking the elevator up to the fifth floor of the *Post,* where the two parted company, Ted to his newly assigned cubicle and Lizzie to the conference room. She knew her way, having been there four times, but always late at night after the paper had been put to bed.

They were waiting for her, and to a man they stood when she entered the room. The bright-red leg-hugging boots with the four-inch heels did not go unnoticed. Nor did the clinging leather pants miss inspection.

Maggie Spritzer, dressed in a conservative charcoal-gray suit befitting her new position at the paper, was the one who walked around the long table and hugged Lizzie, to everyone but Lizzie's amazement. They watched bug-eyed as Lizzie hugged Maggie with a bone-crushing embrace.

"Gentlemen," Lizzie said by way of greeting. "Please sit down and let's get to work." Before she opened her one-of-a-kind briefcase, she looked around at the faces of the men she was dealing with. They looked like sharks but were so in the box she discounted them entirely. All they wanted to do was nitpick. Lizzie Fox did not nitpick. She slammed and rammed, and if you were still standing, she'd sucker punch you right out of the room.

Lizzie slapped stack after stack of papers, all earmarked with red sticky note arrows, on the table in front of her. She looked around again, and said, "I have exactly seventy minutes to wrap this up. The new owner has informed me that if we don't get it done in that time period, I am to walk out of this room and the deal is off. I do not play games, gentlemen. From this minute on until the clock runs out, it's my way or it's the highway. It's up to you. Now, let's go to page 16 in the yellow folder. Shame on you for trying to slip that past me. It's gone. Let's move on to page 74 in the red folder . . ."

Sixty-eight minutes later the digital kitchen timer in Lizzie's briefcase pinged.

"That's it, gentlemen. Thank you for your cooperation, your willingness to try to screw me — and you see where that got you. We have ourselves a deal. I hope your client is as happy as my client. I won't say it's been nice doing business with you because it has not been a pleasant experience."

Lizzie stood, the scarlet bomber jacket gaping at the neckline. She exhaled, and the jacket settled itself nicely over her chest. She focused on Maggie, and said, "It's officially yours, dear. Make it work." She offered up a jaunty salute and was gone a minute later. She left in her wake a dozen sweating, frustrated, angry, belligerent lawyers who did everything but paw the floor and howl.

It was all Maggie could do not to burst out laughing.

"Coffee, anyone?" she asked in her new

editor-in-chief voice. She had no takers, so she poured herself a cup from a fancy silver urn and liberally laced it with real cream and four sugars. She sat back down and sipped at her coffee, her eyes on the skedaddling posse of high-powered lawyers. And all it had taken was one very sexy, brainy woman to put them in their place. She did laugh then, but there was no one to hear her because the last man out the door slammed it shut.

"And this, Maggie Spritzer, is the first day of your new life here at the *Post.* Yah, Maggie," she mumbled as she congratulated herself. "This is better than any Pulitzer I could have ever dreamed about."

Chapter 13

It was an inky-black night, and while not clandestine, the evening had all the makings of a spook meeting. Part of it might have been the black rental cars, the black clothing worn by the women. As Lizzie Fox put it, you can never be too careful in Alphabet City. She was, of course, referring to the nation's capital, where it was harder to keep a secret than it was to catch a greased pig.

In the wild hope she could thwart any unwelcome scrutiny, Lizzie had donned a chestnut-brown wig to cover her trademark hair. A baseball cap and a black Nike running suit along with black running shoes completed her attire. Her two companions were similarly attired. Just three women meeting for coffee after a workout at the local gym. Ironically, not one of the trio had seen the inside of a gym in years.

The meeting was in a shabby coffeehouse in a shabby part of town, where people stared into their coffee cups wondering where they could panhandle next or how to get their next fix. It was the ideal location for a late-evening rendezvous.

It took all of ten minutes for the women to play catch-up. Lizzie brought the social talk to a close by saying, "And here you are, Marty, the prohibitive favorite to be the Democratic nominee. Damn if I'm not impressed. And you, Pam, I can't believe you're still trailing in the money polls."

Martine Connor pulled the bill of her baseball cap even lower and allowed a small grin. "I tried for months to get hold of you, Lizzie. I wanted to see if you'd come aboard. I could use someone like you in my corner. They're shredding me out there. And on top of that, some scum . . . Well, that's why we're all here. Tell me, what if anything can you do for us?"

With Martine it was never *I*, but always *we* or *us*. Lizzie looked at the striking woman sitting across from her and thought she looked tired and worried.

"Pam and I both know you're the go-to woman, so here we are."

Lizzie looked across the table, liking what she was seeing, two dedicated women hell-bent on putting the first woman ever in the White House.

Martine Connor was not a beautiful woman. But she wasn't ugly, either. Her features were blunt and could be softened with the right makeup and hairstyle, something she rarely took the time to bother with. Now, this minute, she looked like someone's aunt from next door. She'd never worried about designer clothes or fancy cars. There were those who called her a Plain Jane, while others called her a misfit. She'd worked hard all her life, fighting to survive. An orphan, she'd made her own way early and stayed on the path she'd chosen — education. Working two jobs and going to school for her doctorate left no time for fooling around. Life was too serious. Squeaky clean to the core, she was the perfect presidential candidate. She wasn't politically tested. Yet. But she had almost a whole year to get there. There was little doubt that she would win the nomination. The big question in everyone's mind was, could she, the first woman presidential nominee, unseat the incumbent, a man — even a man whose approval numbers were heading toward single-digit territory? The voting public was divided on whether the president should be a man whose competence and policies were, to say the least, seriously suspect, or a competent woman with a reputation for hard work and absolute integrity. And though it would never be put that way in their diatribes, so were the media and the pundits.

"I needed to take a break and get away. To say I was burned out would be putting it mildly. But, I'm back. I guess this little meeting is because you need my help. I'm more than willing, but let's put our cards on the table. Tell me everything. And I do mean everything. By the way, I left the firm, gave them back their partnership. I'm on my own these days. I have no backup. But I do have sources and friends. I have a lot of outstanding IOUs I can call in. My new offices are in Georgetown. I haven't officially moved in yet, maybe later this week if the paint smell goes away."

She was about to say she was around the corner from Nikki's old offices, but changed her mind at the last second. All in good time. "I'd be more than happy to work with both of you. We can worry about the bill later. Let's just make a plan and see if it's doable."

Pamela Lock grimaced. "We've been screwed, Lizzie. Somehow, someone got hold of my donor list, and is threatening to sell it off to the highest bidder. We have some heavy hitters on that list. In this marvelous age of computers, all it takes is a few keystrokes, and people's lives can be forever ruined. If that happens, it's goodbye White House for Martine. Hell, she might not even get the nomination. I have guarded that list with my life, so I have no idea how it got into other hands. But there's something fishy about the whole deal. Something about it all isn't sitting right with me. I know this sounds crazy, but I have this feeling it's all a setup."

Lizzie clucked her tongue. There was disgust in her voice when she said, "Always pay attention to your gut feelings. Instinct never lets you down. Did you ever hear the term 'hacker'?"

"Of course I've heard it, and I even know how it's done. I had the best of the best installing firewalls to make my computer system impregnable, and still they got through. If that's what happened. The GOP will have a field day with this. Bastards! I'm sure they're behind this in some way. To be honest, Lizzie, I don't know where the hell to turn or what to do."

Lizzie looked at the two of them, knowing the answer to the question before she even asked it. "And aside from being your legal counsel, what is it you want from me?"

Martine and Pamela looked at one another, but it was Martine who spoke. "We want to know if you can . . . I don't know how to say this . . . We want to know if you can somehow, some way, reach out to . . . to the vigilantes. There, I said it," she gasped, her face a rosy pink with the effort it cost her.

Lizzie sipped at the bitter coffee in her cup. She was more than pleased with herself. She was never wrong. She could read people a mile away. "What makes you think I can somehow, some way, contact the vigilantes?"

"Oh, come on, Lizzie, this is me and Martine you're talking to. You were their attorney when they got busted. That means you know them."

"Well, yeah, and they hung me out to dry when they absconded. Did you forget about that?" Lizzie responded, hoping that her feigned outrage came across as genuine.

"Well, yeah," Pamela drawled, mimicking Lizzie's words. "They had help. Who do you turn to in your blackest hours? You! That's who. I know you helped them. I think that Judge Easter and that DDA, I forget his name, were in on it, too. It's the only way it could have gone down. Don't worry, your secret is safe with us. Now, how about it? Can we engage their services or not? We don't have time to screw around here, Lizzie. And before you can ask what's in it for you, our response is whatever you want."

Martine Connor nodded in agreement. "Whatever you want, Lizzie, name it, and it's yours. Just so you know, Pam and I will both go to our deaths before we'd utter a word about *them*."

A waitress as tired-looking as the café she worked in approached and refilled their coffee cups. Lizzie could hardly believe she'd consumed a whole cup of the vile brew. She gulped at her fresh cup, looked at the two women sitting across from her, and said, "They'll be here tomorrow. It was a preemptive strike on my part. Now I'm going to tell you something you don't know. The Republicans have also contacted them. The RNC was hit just like you were. Or so they say. Pure and simple, it's an identity theft ring. Or so they claim. They held out a really large carrot to the vigilantes. I don't know if you can match it. That's the gopher in the woodpile, ladies."

Pamela snorted. "Are you telling me Baron Russell was hit, too? I don't believe it! He can't keep a secret to save his life. What's the carrot he dangled?" she asked suspiciously.

Lizzie looked at the coffee in her cup as

she sucked on her lower lip. When she released it, she said, "A presidential pardon." She watched to see what the women's reactions were and saw outrage, anger, and disbelief.

"Son of a bitch!" Pam seethed.

"Unbelievable," Martine whispered. "That would mean someone in the White House okayed it. Is that possible, Lizzie?"

"Think about it. It got the vigilantes' attention, now, didn't it? Being as smart and as astute as I am, I pretty much figured out you guys got hit, too. Or are in on it in some way. That's why I went preemptive. Which one of you hit the message board?"

Pam pointed to herself. "I didn't know what else to do, so I put out some discreet feelers and tried a message board. I figured since it was anonymous, I didn't have anything to lose. But do you think the White House is in on it?"

"I find it highly unlikely. It's my understanding the . . . uh . . . ladies asked for written confirmation on paper that contains the presidential seal. I don't see that happening, and neither do they."

"They're actually arriving tomorrow?" Pam asked, her voice full of awe.

"Yes. You will have a new fund-raising volunteer showing up for work the following day. Don't get friendly. Give her free rein and sit back and watch."

Lizzie addressed her next comments to Martine. "You're going to have to promise me something. In writing. Nothing less is acceptable. And for this help, you are going to get the biggest, the most glamorous, the most anticipated event in political history. A soirée in New York at the Waldorf-Astoria. If everyone's calculations are right, it should bring in $10 million. That's a lot of airtime in a lot of primary states and enough to fund your campaign staff for quite a while, Martine."

"And they can do this . . . how?" Martine asked.

"Did you forget who one of their members is? Only one of the richest women in the world. I'm also now going to tell you a secret. You both have to swear to me on all our lives that you will never divulge what I'm going to tell you. Agreed?" Martine and Pam nodded. Martine slapped her hand down first on the table. Pam put hers on top, and Lizzie put both her hands on top of theirs. It was as binding a promise as there was.

"Guess who the new owner of the *Post* is?"

Both women stared at Lizzie, totally

speechless. Lizzie nodded. "You know what that means for you, Martine, right?"

Lizzie could see her old friend swallow hard. She knew, just knew, Martine was seeing herself walking into the Oval Office and taking her seat behind the desk. Suddenly she burst out laughing.

"I hope you'll keep a picture of me behind your desk," Lizzie said.

Martine finally found her voice. "Dear God, tell me my luck is finally turning."

"Only if you can keep that promise. That's our bottom line here, Martine."

"I'll find a way, Lizzie. Trust me."

Lizzie believed her, but lawyer and cynic that she was, she said, "If you don't, Martine, I will go after you, and so will the vigilantes. So be forewarned."

"Well, damn," was all Pam Lock could think of to say.

"Okay, ladies, let's make it work for us. No more meetings like this from here on in. Tomorrow, or no later than the day after, I'll have special phones for you. No one, not even the Secret Service, can access them. You keep them on your person at all times. Are we good to go?"

Both women nodded.

Lizzie paid the check and left a fifty-dollar tip for the waitress. She was almost to her car when she wondered if her good deed was a mistake. She took a moment to remember how tired the older woman looked and the place where she worked, and decided she was an I-didn't-see-anyone-like-that, I-mind-my-own-business kind of woman. And, the coffee shop was that kind of place. Lizzie felt better with her assessment.

Fat little bomblets of rain started to fall as Lizzie unlocked the rental car. She tried to remember if the weatherman had predicted rain for tonight or tomorrow. In the end, did it really matter? She decided that with everything she had on her plate, she didn't care one way or the other.

Lizzie was an excellent driver. She liked to drive fast, had a heavy foot, but at the same time she did her best to obey all driving laws and had a sparkling-clean record.

It was too early to go home to her empty house. Her nerves were twanging all over the place with all that had been discussed during the past hour. She looked at the clock on the dashboard. It wasn't that late. Maybe a visit to old Jack would be in order. She seemed to recall that he said he never went to bed before midnight.

Before she knew it, she was on 13th Street and on her way to Jack's house in Georgetown. Now, wasn't he going to be surprised to see her at this hour of the night?

Eight minutes later, Lizzie was ringing Jack's doorbell. She took a step backward and waited while Jack peered at her through the peephole. She waved like an idiot.

"Kind of late for a social call, isn't it, Counselor?" Jack asked, stepping back to allow her to enter.

"One should never assume or presume, Jack. Ask yourself why I would be paying you a social call at this hour of the night. This is strictly business. Bet you didn't even know it was raining outside."

She wondered why she had said that. Was it because she was always uncomfortable in Jack Emery's presence? Did she harbor secret feelings for the deputy district attorney? She laughed inwardly at the absurd thought. Maybe it was because, intellectually, he was her match. And he was just as clever and devious as she was. In a courtroom they were like snapping, snarling wildcats. Even the judges couldn't believe the two of them, and constantly reprimanded them. Once, several years ago, a judge had slapped them both in jail for twenty-four hours and fined them each five thousand dollars. Jack had bought her a drink when they got out of jail. She respected Jack Emery more than she did any other person in the world. Maybe she felt inferior to Jack in some cockamamie way. Yeah, yeah, that had to be it.

"So, you want a beer, some mac and cheese? What?"

"No to the food, yes to the beer." She couldn't resist the urge to let loose with, "Georgetown, we have a problem."

"Well, shit, it took you long enough to spit it out. C'mon out to the kitchen and make the rest of my night miserable. What'd you do to your hair? You look . . ."

"Like shit?" Lizzie reached up and yanked off the chestnut-brown wig. Her crop of silvery hair fell in tight ringlets to her shoulders. She shook it loose, then scratched at her head. "I was in disguise tonight."

"You're gonna tell me why, right? And, no, I didn't know it was raining outside. Not that I really care."

"I had a meeting at a coffee joint in southwest Washington with Martine Connor and Pamela Lock. You want to hear the details?"

Jack popped two bottles of Budweiser and handed one to Lizzie. When she looked at him questioningly, he said, "Dishwasher's on the fritz. I hate doing dishes, so drink it out of the bottle. If it's good enough for me it's good enough for you. Spit it out, Counselor."

"Neither one knew that the RNC's donor list was heisted. They thought the RNC had lifted theirs. I clued them in. By the way, they called the meeting. All three of us agreed it looks like some kind of setup. As you know, I did legal work for both Martine and Pam for years. I think it's safe to say we're friends. I trust them, and they trust me. The reason for the meet was to ask me to get in touch with the vigilantes because they want to hire them to get to the bottom of this mess. Before you chew my head off, both of them put two and two together and know we're all in this up to our eyebrows. They're women, they never said a word nor will they say anything in the future. I let them both know, friends or not, I'd go after both of them if word ever leaks out. We made a deal, Jack."

Jack cringed. "What kind of deal, Lizzie?"

"What kind do you think, Jack? The only kind of deal I make is to benefit my client or, in this case, clients. The vigilantes are my clients. Martine gave me her word that she'd grant them a full pardon if she gets in the White House. Here," she said, tossing a cassette tape across the table, "I got it on record. Not that I don't trust her, because I do, but I always cover my ass, you know that. Take it to your office and keep it secure. Make some copies just to be on the safe side. Alarm system or not, my office can always be broken into, as we well know. The courthouse, now, ain't no one gonna break in there. And, no, neither Martine nor Pam knew I was taping them. I left plenty of room at the beginning of the tape to add a few sentences. I'm not a novice at this, Jack. Hey, do you have any munchies, chips or something?"

Jack looked disgusted. "I don't eat that crap. You want an apple or a banana?"

Lizzie sighed. "No. I'll hit up a fast-food place on the way home and get some French fries. Tell Charles I need two of those special phones for Martine and Pam so they can communicate with me. I won't take no for an answer."

Jack slugged back the rest of his beer and then plunked the bottle down on the table. Lizzie did the same thing and nodded that she'd take a second beer. Jack uncapped two fresh bottles and handed one over to her. "What did you have to promise, Lizzie?"

"The vigilantes' help. And I told them about Annie and Myra organizing a fund-raising event in New York at the Waldorf-

Astoria. Ten million bucks, if Myra and Annie can pull it off, will buy a lot of television spots in key primary states. A few more events like that will almost guarantee her getting the nomination and walking into the Oval Office."

Jack's head was swimming with the possibilities he was hearing. A full presidential pardon meant Nikki and the others could come back, and they could all lead normal lives. He and Nikki could get married and maybe have some kids. They'd get a couple of dogs and live happily ever after. The naked desire in his eyes was almost more than Lizzie could bear when he said, "Tell me the truth, what are the chances of that really happening?"

"As good as it's going to get. I'll make it happen, Jack. Trust me, okay? I have friends."

Jack leaned back in his chair as he contemplated Lizzie's promise. For some ungodly reason, he believed her. He felt so mellow, so relaxed he almost fell off his chair. "How come you aren't tied down with some guy? You should be married by now. What the hell are you waiting for, Lizzie? You want to be an old maid?"

Jesus, did I just say that? At the stricken look on Lizzie's face he knew the four beers he'd had prior to her arrival and the two since then were loosening his tongue.

"Hey, forget I said that, okay? Your personal life is none of my business. I'm sorry, Lizzie. I had too many beers this evening."

Lizzie shrugged as she got up to leave. Then she sat back down and leaned across the table to hold Jack's gaze with her own. She started to talk and didn't blink once, to Jack's amazement.

"Sometimes, Jack, a person is only capable of loving once. I'm one of those people. I had a relationship during my first year of law school. His name was Eric. He was the reason I got up in the morning. I loved him more than anything in the world. I couldn't see straight. He was all I thought about from morning till night. I almost flunked out that first year.

"Eric was the kindest, the most gentle man that ever walked the earth. He was graduating that year first in his class. He had almost every law firm in the country vying for his services. All he had to do was pick one, and he was literally guaranteed seven figures a year. That was just to start. The signing bonuses they promised were out of this world.

"What I didn't know at the time was Eric's family background. He always kind of brushed it all away and never went into any detail. Mother died when he was in high school. Two sisters who lived in upstate New York. Three nieces, two nephews. Father retired. That was all I knew. He never went home. Never got phone calls or mail from them — that I knew of, anyway. I thought maybe there was friction, but it wasn't my business. I was so wrapped up in *us,* I didn't care about *them.* Oh, Eric and I had such plans. Such wonderful plans. We were going to have the perfect life. All I wanted was to have his kids. That's all he wanted, too.

"Graduation night we went to a party at a restaurant. By the way, no one from his family showed up for his graduation. Even then I didn't think it all that strange. There were eight of us, four couples who palled around that first year. We were drinking cheap champagne and eating glorious Italian food. I got up to go to the ladies' room when suddenly I heard gunfire. Tipsy as I was, I knew that sound when I heard it. I went into one of the stalls and stood on the seat so no one would see me. It was a slaughter, pure and simple. All the people in the restaurant, the owners, the help. It was in the papers for weeks and months. The police found me a long time later.

"They stuck me in a hospital, and I had a

breakdown. It took almost two years before I could function normally. I finished school, first in my class, thank you very much. And, as they say, the rest is history."

Jack watched as Lizzie swiped at the tears dripping down her cheeks.

Jack bolted upright. He was stone-cold sober now. "That's not the end of it, is it, Lizzie? I remember now. You took the family on, one by one. The name was Savarone, right? That's how you made your name. You took them on, and you fucking well won. That whole posse is still behind bars without the possibility of parole."

"It's all over, Jack, but, yeah, I took them on, and I won. His own father had Eric killed. Do you believe that? I couldn't wrap my mind around that. Eric wouldn't work for the family. He divorced himself from them. The father lost face, or whatever it is that happens to people like that. They took Eric's life because he didn't want to be a gangster's mouthpiece. I gotta go home now, Jack."

"Lizzie, stay the night. It's really raining out there, I can hear it on the windows. Georgetown floods when it rains. There's a guest room. Clean sheets and all, your own bathroom. You're too emotional to drive in weather like this."

"Gee, Jack, I didn't know you cared."

Hearing the sarcasm, Jack grinned. "Now that's the Lizzie I know and love. I'll bet you ten bucks I know why you're never in town on weekends."

"Why's that?"

"You go to the cemetery, right? You take flowers, you sit there and tell Eric about all your cases. You cry, then you come home and wait for the next weekend to do it all over again. I know because I did the same thing when my mother died. You gotta let it go, Lizzie."

"I don't know how, Jack. Don't you think I've tried? This is my life. I'm not unhappy with it. We never had this talk, right?"

"What talk?"

"Where'd you say that guest room was?"

"Second floor, second room on the left. There's even a toothbrush and stuff in the linen closet. Nikki knew how to keep up a house."

"I'm gonna make it happen for you, Jack. One of us deserves the brass ring, and I'm glad it's you." She leaned over and kissed him on the cheek, and a few seconds later he heard her walking up the steps.

Jack jabbed at his eyes, which were burning so badly he thought they were going to pop right out of his head.

CHAPTER 14

A blustery wind was rocketing the cable car as the Sisters climbed in to share it with assorted cardboard cartons already inside. As the car slid down its well-oiled tracks and descended the mountain, Charles looked at Murphy and Grady, and said, "They'll be back, you know that. Now, who wants some dinner and a nice walk around the compound? I think my arm is in good shape this evening for throwing sticks, boys."

Both dogs looked at him, and Charles knew they related to two of those words, "dinner" and "sticks." "Okay, then let's do it!" Charles waited, though, the dogs nipping at his pants leg until the cable car was back in its nest.

The stiff wind at his back pushed him ahead in his trek to the Big House.

Charles felt lost, but the feeling was nothing new to him. He always felt this way when his chicks left the nest to do what they did best, righting a wrong only they could make right.

Leaves fell like snow. By tomorrow all the leaves from the trees would be gone and just the rich resin scent of the pines would permeate the mountain. Winter was coming. Charles couldn't decide if he liked that idea or not, but there was nothing he could do about it.

In the kitchen, he prepared the dogs' dinner, crumbling bits of bacon and adding a cup of diced vegetables into the kibble mix before adding a spoonful of gravy to each bowl. When the dogs finished eating, they both sat back on their haunches to wait for their dessert, half a Pop-Tart each. Both dogs were partial to strawberry. They barked their thanks and walked away to the front porch, where they would wait for the stick-throwing part of their nightly routine.

Charles looked around at the cluttered kitchen as he prepared to clean it all up. He might have sent his chicks into a lion's den, but he'd sent them with full stomachs. He smiled when they had all oohed and ahhed over his pot roast and potato pancakes. At the last minute, using the last of the cabbage from the garden, he'd made a cabbage casserole that all the women ignored until Kathryn, who would eat anything, sampled it and pronounced it spectacular. He looked at the empty dish and smiled. If only life's problems could be reduced to planning, cooking, and serving meals.

An hour later, his evening ritual with the dogs complete, Charles settled himself in the command center and waited for all his operatives to check in. His eyes stayed glued to the monitor in front of him as he waited for reports to come through. While he waited, he checked off the timing sequence of his operation the way he did every evening, even when a mission wasn't in progress. He sighed. Such was his life. But he wouldn't change his life and what he was doing for all the money in the world.

As Charles was settling into his think mode, and his chicks were tooling along I-95, just inside the District of Columbia, in Kalorama, to be precise, Paula Woodley, a previous beneficiary of the vigilantes' help, stared across the dining room table at her husband, or, more accurately, a caricature of her husband, the former national security advisor to the current Republican president.

Paula Woodley was an excellent cook, and the food piled on the table reflected her expertise in the kitchen. Tonight she'd prepared all of her husband's favorite foods, knowing he wouldn't be able to eat a bite of them. It was a real southern dinner: true southern-fried chicken, the crust golden and crunchy; She-Crab Soup; macaroni and cheese with six different cheeses; and a medley of okra, tomatoes, zucchini, and little pearl onions. She devoured everything on her plate. The little jar of baby food in front of her husband remained untouched. His eyes spewed hatred at the woman sitting across from him.

"Either you stuff that glop down your throat, or I will force-feed you, Mr. Woodley. We both know how much you like that." Since the day the vigilantes had rescued her and reduced her husband to his current state, Paula never called the man sitting across from her anything but Mr. Woodley.

Confined to a wheelchair, Woodley was totally dependent on Paula, as dependent as a newborn baby.

As always, Paula kept up a running dialogue as she ate. Now, though, she was licking her fingers and staring at her husband. "I'm having apple pie for dessert. You used to love my apple pie. Do you remember the time you pushed my hands down on top of the hot stove because I made a peach pie instead of an apple pie?" She waved her hands to show the scars on the palms of her hands. "I made five apple pies today, Mr. Woodley — three as a housewarming present for our new neighbors. I'll be taking them over shortly. Goodness, maybe I didn't tell you about our new neighbors. Well, guess who is moving in almost on top of us! I see, you give up. The vigilantes, that's who. I'm sure I can convince them to stop in for a . . . little visit. I hope you won't be inhospitable and embarrass me. I've worked very hard to join in the neighborhood. I just love playing bridge and going to lunches while you sit here and vegetate. The neighbors never ask about you anymore. You're a nonentity, Mr. Woodley."

Paula carved herself a large slice of pie and slid it onto her plate. She got up, went to the kitchen, and came back with a carton of ice cream and a small silver pot of coffee. She ate slowly, savoring each bite while sipping at her coffee. "Do you remember the time you threw the scalding coffee between my breasts? You'd like to do that again, wouldn't you? I can see it in your eyes. Oh, well, Mr. Woodley, that is not going to happen, ever again. I thought I told you to eat. If I have to count to three, Mr. Woodley, you won't like it."

The ugly, hateful man sitting in the wheelchair struggled to pick up the spoon next to the little jar of baby food. Paula watched the effort it cost her husband to struggle to eat. She enjoyed every moment of his discomfort. She wondered when he was going to give up the fight and die. She knew she could help things along, and no one would ever be the wiser, but seeing him suffer day after day, week after week, month after month for all the beatings he'd inflicted on her, all her broken bones, the loss of vision in her left eye, was much more appealing.

Paula kept her husband confined to one room no bigger than a compact kitchen. The room contained a hospital bed, a metal chest of sorts that held a twelve-inch black and white television set with rabbit ears, and one chair for visitors. Except no one came to visit. A home health aide came every evening at seven o'clock to bathe her husband and get him into bed at night. A different home health aide came by in the morning at eight o'clock to get him ready for the day. He was shaved, diapered, and dressed in outfits that resembled hospital scrubs to begin his day of watching the weather channel on the small set. It was the only channel that would come through with the rabbit ears.

Three times a day, Paula made a production of wheeling him out to the dining room so he could watch her eat.

Paula sighed as though it was all too much for her. She finished her dessert and coffee and set about clearing the table. She returned to the dining room with a mint she popped into Woodley's mouth. "Your dessert, Mr. Woodley. Time to go back to your room. I'm sick of looking at you. Do you remember the time you dragged me over to the fireplace and burned my feet? I couldn't walk for months. I had to crawl, and even then you kicked me and broke my ribs. Your 'keeper' will be here shortly. Good night, Mr. Woodley. I hope your sleep is filled with nightmares detailing every atrocity known to man." This last was said so cheerfully, the man in the wheelchair tried to lash out at his tormentor, but she cuffed him upside the head, then gave him a second whack for good measure. She closed the door with a loud bang.

Back in her newly decorated kitchen, which was now so cheerful that she couldn't wait to go into it in the morning, Paula sat down and poured herself a second cup of coffee. She looked over at the pies sitting on the counter. She hadn't baked them yet. It was her intention to carry them down the street and bake them there so that when her saviors arrived — and that's how she thought of the vigilantes — they would have the aroma of the baking pies to greet them. It was a small thing for having her life saved, but it was the only thing she was really good at — cooking and baking. She knew her old friends would understand. She could hardly wait to see them.

She'd almost turned herself inside out the day Nikki Quinn called and asked for her help. She remembered how she'd squealed, "Anything, I'll do anything. Just tell me what you want me to do." And Nikki had told her.

Paula Woodley let her mind wander as she waited for the evening home health aide to arrive. She had been on the brink of death, actually waiting to die, due to severe internal bleeding from one of her husband's beatings, when the vigilantes swooped in to save her. Her recovery had been long, painful, and tortuous. Mr. Woodley had been returned to her by the government several months after she'd gotten out of the hospital. She remembered so clearly how she'd stared at him, wondering who the man in the wheelchair was. She'd already been told that virtually every bone in his body had been broken, but unable to comprehend such a thing, she'd merely chalked it up to media hype.

And then when she'd seen him with her own eyes, she'd acted like a lunatic as she danced around his wheelchair, laughing hysterically. "You're mine now, Mr. Woodley. All mine, and I will remind you hourly that I am the only one you have, you son of a bitch!" She remembered how he'd cried, how he'd tried to speak but couldn't.

The first thing she'd done was brew a pot of coffee. When it finished brewing and was scalding hot, she'd poured it into a cup with a huge red #1 on it that someone had given him at Christmastime. She'd filled it to the brim and carried it into the den, where he waited for her. She took up a position right in front of her husband and stuck her finger in the cup. It hadn't cooled one bit on the short walk from the kitchen to the den. With slow deliberation she'd inched her way forward. Reading the intent in her eyes, Woodley tried to move the wheelchair, but she reached out with her foot and set the brake. With a steady hand she poured the coffee down into his crotch. She knew he was screaming because his mouth moved. A few seconds into the silent scream, he blacked out. When he came to, Paula tossed him a jar of Vaseline and walked away.

The next day and every day that followed, she would taunt him with what she was going to do to him. Though she would rarely follow through on her threats, and even when she did there was no real damage done and very little pain, just knowing he lived in perpetual fear — the way she had during their married life — was enough for her.

Paula turned when she heard a soft knock on the pane of glass in the kitchen door. She got up to unlock it. "Good evening, Joseph," she said cheerfully. "Your patient is waiting for you. He had a wonderful day and ate a robust dinner. I baked a pie for you. Be sure to take it when you leave. I have to go down the street now. New people moved in today, and I'm in charge of the welcoming committee. Just be sure the door locks behind you when you leave. I might even be back before you leave, but just in case I'm not, I will be at 11063. If there's a problem, you can always reach me on my cell."

Joseph Nesbitt was a man of few words. He'd heard the stories, the rumors concerning his patient and the beating he'd taken at the hands of the vigilantes. He wasn't sure if a woman or a group of women would have the stomach to do to the man what had been done to him. When he voiced his opinions to his wife, she'd laughed in his face and added a few more things that *could* have been done that the vigilantes had skipped. Every evening when he got home after settling his patient for the night, his wife would quiz him. Ethel was a big vigilante fan, as were all her friends. Sometimes he made up stories just to entertain her. She'd always clap her hands and say that the man should die already, and that his wife was a saint. He wasn't so sure about the saint part. Sometimes he thought Mrs. Woodley hated her husband. She was good to Joseph, though, always making him pies and cakes or sending him home with a complete dinner. She paid for his gas and travel time and was more than generous during the holidays. He hoped Woodley lasted a long time so he could reap even more benefits. His wife loved Mrs. Woodley's apple pies. He hoped he would remember to pick up some ice cream on his way home.

"Don't worry about a thing, Mrs. Woodley. Take your time. I'll stay an extra hour and read the paper to Mr. Woodley. He likes to be kept up on the goings-on in government."

Nesbitt waited until Paula settled the unbaked pies on a baking sheet and left the house before he cut himself a slice of pie and ate it. It wasn't until he was done that he realized he forgot to put ice cream on it. He slid his dish and knife and fork into the dishwasher and turned it on before he ambled down the hall to his patient, the day's paper folded and stuck in his hip pocket.

Just when Joseph was getting his patient ready for the night, Paula Woodley was sliding her pies in the preheated oven and set about seeing to the house. She fluffed up the cushions on the chairs and sofas, checked the sheets on the beds, and made sure there were plenty of towels available, along with an assortment of bath salts, powders, combs, brushes, toothbrushes, and everything else for the comfort and convenience of seven wonderful women.

Back in the kitchen, she savored the aroma of the baking pies as she checked the contents of the pantry and refrigerator. Earlier in the afternoon, when she was frying her own chicken, she'd cooked up a huge platter and had had to make two trips to carry it and a tray of her macaroni and cheese for the women to eat on their arrival.

She'd shopped in the morning, filling the

refrigerator with vegetables, fruit, juice, eggs, bacon, and milk. Yesterday she'd laid in a supply of coffee beans and even bought a new coffeemaker. Six of the vigilantes were big coffee drinkers, as she recalled. She'd also purchased all kinds of teas, not knowing which blends the little vigilante liked best.

She looked around. The kitchen was a pretty one, with light oak cabinets, and red-checkered curtains and place mats. She'd added a bright bowl of autumn flowers to the middle of the table. The vigilantes' home away from home. She did take a moment to wonder where the women actually lived these days. Then again, it was none of her business. What she did know was she would go to her death before she ever admitted she'd helped them. Their secrets, whatever they were, were safe with her.

By nine o'clock the pies were done and cooling on the counter. She'd turned down the beds and turned on the outside lights. Satisfied that she had done all Nikki had asked of her, she left the house by the kitchen door and walked down the street to her own home.

It would rain before morning, she thought. When it was damp and rainy, Mr. Woodley was in a great deal of pain. When she said her prayers at night, Paula Woodley always prayed for rain.

She was about to walk up her driveway when she noticed her neighbor walking his dog, a delightful little furball named Maxine. She passed a few pleasantries with her neighbor, then went into the house. She was glad that Joseph was gone. She wasn't much in the mood for small talk this evening.

Paula checked to make sure the aide had taken his pie. He had. She poured herself a glass of milk and cut a slice of pie for herself. She did love apple pie. When she was finished, she washed and dried her dishes and made her way to her bathroom, where she ran a hot bath. While the water was running, she walked back to the little room where her husband now lived. She opened the door, poked her head in, and said, "I think it's going to rain before morning. Good night, Mr. Woodley."

Paula pulled the door shut and locked it. There was no need to lock the door, but she did it anyway because she slept better knowing her husband was behind a locked door. She also locked her own bedroom door.

Paula looked at her naked body with all its scars, her eyes narrowing in momentary anger. Still, this was the part of the day she loved best, settling down into the warm tub with the rich cypress-lavender blend of salts she favored. This was when she turned her mind off and truly relaxed.

An hour later, as she was turning down her own bed, she saw a pair of headlights sweeping down the street. She sighed with happiness as she peered out the window to see a white van pull into the driveway at 11063 and into the garage.

The vigilantes had arrived.

Paula Woodley slept like a baby that night.

Chapter 15

Erin Powell knew she looked like she'd been ridden hard and hung up wet. Right now she'd give her right arm for just a few minutes of sleep, but she knew that wasn't going to happen. Humiliated and chastised by the director himself for her running of the task force and the mistakes he'd said she made rankled big-time. There was nothing worse than being made to look like a failure in front of your colleagues, but she'd bitten the bullet and sucked it up, more determined than ever to make it all work for her. Although it wasn't like she had anything worthwhile to work with. Sightings, mostly bogus, were virtually impossible to sort out. The vigilantes covered their tracks. It had taken her hours to come to terms with the fact that there simply were no clues worth focusing on. But, according to the director, the clock was ticking.

It was close to midnight when she realized

that she wasn't getting anywhere, but then she opened a thin folder of newspaper clippings. She knew immediately that she was onto something when she tried to match the vigilantes' profiles against the articles in the folder. But then again, she'd thought she was on the right track when she'd ordered her agents to bring in the key players for interrogation. She couldn't quite shake the feeling that she was right, but the director had chopped her off at the knees. Everyone had lawyered up with the same damn woman, Lizzie Fox. That alone told her more than she needed to know. She had a wild and crazy thought that maybe the director himself was setting her up for . . . for what? She had no clue, and the idea that he might have a hidden agenda was preposterous — wasn't it?

Erin looked down at her watch.

She had second-guessed herself last night and decided to stay and work late rather than lug all the heavy file boxes home. "Late" had turned into an all-nighter, and she was paying for it now.

She should go to the lavatory to freshen up a bit before her colleagues arrived. She thought about the long trek down the hall to the bathroom and nixed the idea. She ran her fingers through her hair and added some lipstick. She didn't feel one bit better.

The empty coffeepot glared at her. She'd sent her secretary/assistant, Althea, home at three o'clock and told her to be back at six. It was almost six now. She wasn't sure if she could drink another cup of coffee, but maybe the aroma would help to keep her awake.

It was Althea who had compiled the short list and explained why she thought it was the most credible. Althea was analytical to the nth degree. She was one of those rare people who could look at a maze and figure it out within minutes.

Erin remembered exactly when Althea had come to stand over her desk, and said, "Seven women, right? So, seven happenings or episodes or whatever you want to call them. Acts of vengeance would be my words of choice. All we have to do is find mention of seven acts of vengeance, and we'll be able to nail it down.

"Remember now, when we first heard about the vigilantes, there were supposedly seven women. We know this because they were apprehended in California when they zeroed in on that movie star. But — and this is the big *but* — there was someone new to the seven, that countess whatever her name is.

"I remember reading about her a year or so ago. She lived on some mountain in Spain and was a wealthy recluse. Her entire family was wiped out in a storm in the ocean. And, get this, she grew up with Myra Rutledge, as did Judge Easter. That's all background."

"And this means what? Seven women, seven acts of vengeance. So what?" Erin asked.

"What it means is the countess wasn't in on it in the beginning. She stepped in at the end. Why? Did they lose a member of the group? In one of those articles, I think it was the one that talked about the national security advisor, he said there were six women. All we have to do is pinpoint the dates, find out who died at that time, or something over the top that made the papers, and we can attribute it to the vigilantes."

"That's all well and good, Althea, but what is that going to get us? Is it going to help us find them? Will the people involved even talk to us? They're not going to want the notoriety, and they'll all lawyer up in a heartbeat. We need to know where the vigilantes are so we can catch them and put them in prison where they belong."

"I hate to be the one to tell you this, Erin,

but you are not going to catch those women. They are so well connected it's unbelievable. Just think about the circuses that took place when there was a sighting — like Elvis, only seven times bigger. The public is behind them. One hundred percent." Althea's voice was so flat and sounded so ominous that Erin flinched. "And you know what else, I think you're right, and this is all a setup. You're the Judas goat on this one."

To a certain extent, it all made sense, but the big question was, why? *Judas goat, my ass,* had been Erin's first thought.

But now she was so fuzzy-minded that she was inclined to go along with Althea's way of thinking. *Should I play this close to my vest, or should I share it with the members of the task force?* Her heart kicked up an extra beat at the thought.

She let her mind run wild. Why would the director set her up? Why would he put the FBI in such a position? Was he secretly on the side of the vigilantes? He was a personal friend of Judge Easter, he'd gotten Mitch Riley's job when the vigilantes tossed him to the feds. Did the vigilantes go after Riley so that Cummings could step into his job? Stranger things had happened. Was this task force just something the director started up to throw everyone off his trail or was it to appease . . . who? Certainly not the media.

Erin rubbed her red eyes, which were full of grit. When she opened them, she saw Althea already standing by the coffeepot. She could hear the slow, steady drip, which was almost mesmerizing.

"I see you didn't go home. You look awful, Erin. You don't owe this place your life, you know. Did you come up with anything?"

Erin tapped a file on her desk. "I read through the vigilantes' profiles at least ten times each. At this point I know just about everything there is to know about them. I cross-checked their files with the incident files that you pulled. And, yes, there are seven. In some instances it might be a stretch, but I think we can tie all seven together as long as we don't use glue.

"For instance, Myra Rutledge's daughter was killed by a Chinese guy with diplomatic immunity. He thumbed his nose at all of us, and nothing was done to him. Then suddenly he disappears, and everyone connected to him is recalled to China. Ted Robinson somehow came up with the theory, or be it fact, that Myra's Gulfstream plane made a trip to China. Not long after that, there were reports that John Chai, the man who killed Barbara Rutledge, was seen in the province where he lived. The rumor, according to Robinson, was that the man had been skinned alive and was insane. I think that was Myra's revenge.

"Moving right along here to Alexis Thorne. She went to prison for something she claims she didn't do. The two people who framed her, Arden Gillespie and Roland Sullivan, ended up in prison with tattoos all over their bodies but mostly on their faces. The name that was tattooed was Sara Whittier. That's Alexis Thorne's birth name. That's two down. She was cleared and her record expunged. She walked away with a tidy sum of money when guess who sued on her behalf? Lizzie Fox was her attorney. No one ever mentioned that. That proves to me that Lizzie Fox knew at least one member of the vigilantes before she represented them at the end when they were caught.

"I can't connect a particular vigilante to what happened to the national security advisor. It might have been a freebie, for all I know. He, by the way, is more or less a vegetable. His wife takes care of him. That makes three.

"Four is Senator Mitchell Webster. There was talk he was going to be Cartwright's running mate for the presidential election. He disappeared off the face of the earth. His wife was Dr. Julia Webster. She disappeared, too. Her car was seen at Myra Rutledge's estate more than once, along with the other vigilantes' cars. This is all according to Ted Robinson, who verified it with pictures in which Julia Webster's license plates are clearly visible. Their story was they played cards or dominos or some damn thing. For whatever reason, the countess is the one who replaced Dr. Webster. Robinson said there were rumors that the senator had HIV. Which would then lead you to believe he infected his wife. It's possible that she died. We have no solid proof on any of it. Mitch Webster was never seen or heard of again.

"Five is Kathryn Lucas. I searched for hours and couldn't find anything the vigilantes would or could do for her. Until I came across an article sent by one of the wire clipping services — about three guys in California who got their balls chopped off and mailed to them. In Ziploc bags, no less. Now, ask yourself who could or would do something like that? A doctor, and Julia Webster was a doctor. The article said the testicles were surgically removed. The deed doesn't seem to fit any of the other vigilantes, so I'm giving it to Lucas. I'm thinking she might have been raped, but that's just a guess on my part. Slicing off some guy's balls is making a pretty strong statement. *Three* guys getting their jewels hacked off is an even bigger statement. Those women are cold and heartless. They fit the bill."

"What are you going to do about it?" Althea asked. "Let's just say for the sake of argument that the ladies did those things. What can you do about it? What can the FBI do about it? First you have to catch them. So, give me the why of it all."

"See! See! That's what makes me think you were on the money when you agreed with me that just maybe the director is setting me up," Erin whispered, having heard conversation outside the door. Her crew reporting for work. "Not a word of this to anyone, Althea."

They were looking cocky, even Bert, which surprised Erin. She knew they liked it that the director had dressed her down and did everything but call her a fool. *Well, we'll see how it all ends and who's left standing,* she thought. It was a bitter thought, and she was stuck with it.

Erin stood up and walked over to the last whiteboard. At five in the morning she'd filled it in. "Take a look at this," was all she said.

The agents moved on her order and read

all her notations. Mangello even put on his reading glasses to make sure he didn't miss anything.

Bert took the initiative. "I see what you've done. By process of elimination in all the sightings and by cross-referencing, you've tied the vigilantes to these particular seven incidents. And what does that mean to us? For all we know there could be twenty-seven or fifty-seven incidents that we don't know about. I see you didn't include the incident with the G-String Girls, when it was said the vigilantes actually did their D.C. performance. What's your objective here?"

The other agents smirked. Erin's eyes narrowed. If they only knew what she was thinking. She knew in her gut that Navarro was the mole in the office, but she couldn't prove it. She'd become convinced he was her mole when she was sorting through all the reports at four in the morning. He was involved in just about all the incidents involving the vigilantes. He was the director's number one, and suddenly he was her number one. The word "spy" came to her mind. And he was a friend, a good pal, of Jack Emery. He also had easy access to Judge Easter. After her own surveillance of Bert the night before, it didn't come as a startling revelation. She played it cool, or what she hoped passed for cool, as she stared him in the eye. "If I have to explain it to you, then you need to go back to the Academy." She had to get him out of her hair, and she knew just how to do it.

Navarro's hackles rose, but he didn't say a word. He knew more was coming. He also knew he wasn't going to like it.

"Landos, you're going to the federal pen to talk to Arden Gillespie and Roland Sullivan. I want you to squeeze them for all they're worth. If you shake the tree hard enough, something might fall to the ground. Record the conversation. If it looks like they might know something not on the record, you can barter a little, and we can talk to the federal prosecutor. See what they have to say about Sara Whittier, aka Alexis Thorne, being one of the vigilantes.

"Agent Akers, you stay in the District and get me everything you can on Senator Mitchell Webster. Try to tie down the wife's current residence. She's a doctor, so you might want to try the AMA.

"Mangello, there's not much known on John Chai other than that he killed Myra Rutledge's daughter. I want you to go to the Chinese Embassy and ruffle their feathers. See what you can find out. By nature the Chinese are a closemouthed lot, but they have American employees. Concentrate on them. Then I want you to go after the woman who fouled up Isabelle Flanders's life. I think her name was Rosemary. She was in a mental hospital. She might be in better shape now, so see what you can get out of her.

"That leaves you, Bert. I want you on the next plane to Chicago. Then you go to California. Two of those three guys who are minus their balls now live in Chicago. The third is still in California. If you go over my head to the director on this, you will be eating shit for the rest of your life. Are we clear on that?"

"Yes, ma'am," Bert said smartly. "Do we dare ask what you'll be doing, Erin? Since you're so big on all of us trusting each other, I for one would like to know."

The others muttered something that sounded like, *"Yeah, we want to know."*

"I'm going out to Kalorama to talk to the former NSA and his wife. One of those woman-to-woman talks that might give us the pot of gold at the end of the rainbow." It happened so quickly she almost missed it — the flicker of alarm in Navarro's eyes. Whatever it was she thought she saw, it was gone in a nanosecond. Erin felt a thrill of excitement, making her wonder if it was what she had said or where she was going that sparked the alarm in Navarro's eyes.

"You're all still standing here. Move! Go! Bert, you only have ninety minutes to catch your flight. You have an e-ticket. Call in every two hours after you arrive. That goes for the rest of you, too. If I'm not here, Althea will patch the calls through to me. That's an order."

Mumbling among themselves, the agents closed the door behind them.

"She's got a hard-on for you, Navarro. What'd you do?" Landos asked. "Not that ending up in California is such a bad gig, but I sure as hell would hate to have to interrogate three guys who gave up their balls to a group of vicious women. I think she wants you out of the way. C'mon, Bert, what'd you do to piss her off?"

"I was too lazy to drive home the other night, and Georgetown was flooded, so I bunked at Jack Emery's. Powell followed me. End of story. I saw her, and she knew it. She's not the best at tailing someone. I spotted her from the git-go."

Landos whistled. "That would do it. She probably thinks you two have a thing going on. You know . . . She's a real priss, and you know what else, I think she's still a virgin. Have yourself a ball in the land of milk and honey and don't forget to call in every two hours, that's an order."

In spite of himself, Bert laughed at Landos's falsetto voice. "Screw you and the horse you rode in on, Landos." Bert could hear his fellow agents laughing all the way down the hall.

Bert's thoughts were all over the map as he rode down in the elevator. Powell was onto him. He read it in her eyes, in her body language. While she might suspect him, he'd left no footprints for her to home in on. The FBI dealt in facts. Hard proof. Maybe it was time for Erin Powell to disappear. And it was time to call Jack Emery. And, of course, Kathryn, to tell her where he was going and why.

The neat, tidy rooms Paula Woodley had prepared now looked like a cyclone had whipped through, leaving papers and boxes everywhere. The Sisters stopped what they were doing to take a break.

Alexis suggested breakfast and fresh coffee and offered to prepare it. "The sun will be up in a few minutes, we need to freshen up."

They'd been at it since their arrival, mapping out their strategy on how best to proceed with their new mission. The apple pie, the fried chicken, and the mac and cheese had been devoured within minutes. Now, according to Alexis, it was time to refuel.

It was a team effort in the kitchen. The women worked in harmony, all the while talking about their night's work. Alexis did the cooking, Isabelle cleaned up the mess they'd left on their arrival. Kathryn set the table, and Yoko made coffee and tea. Nikki bundled up their trash, while Myra and Annie did their best to tidy up the den and living room, where their "blackmail files" were stacked in the order of importance. Their telephone campaign would begin after breakfast.

More than anything, the group appeared to be a middle-aged collection of women with two den mothers enjoying a collaborative breakfast after a party night. Right now they were all staring in awe at the double-yolk eggs Alexis was cracking into the fry pan.

They were just starting to eat when Kathryn's cell phone rang. Startled, she looked down at the number, and said, "It's Bert!" She said hello, then listened. Several times her eyebrows rose before she clicked off without saying a word.

Forks poised, coffee cups at their lips, the

women waited.

"It's not good. Well, maybe not terrible, but still, not good. You know what? I'm not hungry." Kathryn pushed her plate away and looked at her Sisters. "It's Erin Powell! Bert said she's coming out here to talk to Mrs. Woodley and her husband."

Nikki jerked upright. "Mrs. Woodley would have called us. She knows the rules."

"I'm not saying she does know. Maybe Powell is going unannounced. Element of surprise, that kind of thing. You need to call and warn her. Like *now,* Nikki. Don't let her get blindsided."

Nikki got up and walked back into the den, where she picked up her cell to call Paula Woodley, who answered on the third ring, sounding sleepy. The woman came instantly awake when Nikki explained the situation.

"Don't worry, dear. I know what to do."

Nikki sighed with relief when she powered down and returned to her scrambled eggs. "Mrs. Woodley understands. Damn, I forgot to thank her for last night's feast and for everything she did for us."

"I'm sure you'll get the chance to speak with her again. Don't worry about it, dear," Myra said soothingly.

CHAPTER 16

Their breakfast over, the cleanup in progress, the mood was somber at 11063 Benton Street.

Myra broke the silence by saying, "Nikki, dear, I think you should call Lizzie Fox. Mrs. Woodley is going to need some legal representation."

"I think you're right, Myra. You're ahead of me this time. I should have called her the moment I hung up from speaking with Paula. It's just . . . Something is niggling at me. I can't quite put my finger on it, and I know it's important. I can't . . . I'm sure whatever it is, it will come to me." The frustration in Nikki's voice was evident to everyone in the room.

"It always works that way, dear. My advice to you is to clear your mind, go on to other things, and before you know it, whatever it is will be crystal clear to you," Myra said. Her worried gaze as she stared at her adopted daughter belied her cheerful voice.

Their break over, the women dispersed to get showered and dressed for the new day. Forty minutes later, Isabelle and Kathryn walked into the living room dressed in airline uniforms. Alexis immediately opened her Red Bag and got to work. It took only thirty minutes for both women's appearance to be altered. The Sisters stood back to appraise both women with a critical eye. Altered brow lines, colored contact lenses, a dab of latex here, a fragile, thin prosthesis in both mouths, and Kathryn Lucas and Isabelle Flanders no longer existed. In their place stood Amelia Whitehouse and Constance Carford.

Annie clapped her hands with enthusiasm as Kathryn and Isabelle whirled and twirled for their benefit.

"You're good to go, girls," Alexis said. "Don't forget your airline bags by the front door. We need the neighbors to believe the myth Charles created that this is a group house for airline attendants."

"I hope our new car arrived," Kathryn said. "I hate driving that van."

"Someone dropped it off in the middle of the night. You will be driving a two-year-old Mitsubishi. Enjoy your day, ladies," Nikki said.

The plan was for Kathryn and Isabelle to shed their airline uniforms at the first gas station they came to and dress in casual attire before they presented themselves at the Connor campaign's fund-raising headquarters.

While Myra and Annie returned to their fund-raising activities and Alexis inventoried her impressive Red Bag, Nikki felt at loose ends. She desperately needed to remember what it was that was making her so uneasy. And, she wanted to talk to Jack so badly she could taste it. She looked over at Yoko, who was talking on her cell phone. She had to be talking to Harry Wong, the love of her life.

Nikki walked over to the huge bay window and looked out. The street was quiet. If there were children on the block, they were in school at this hour of the morning. If elderly people lived nearby, it was unlikely any of them would venture out before noon. There were no dog walkers, no one raking leaves, no delivery trucks, and no sign of a mailman. Benton Street was just like every other street in Middle America at nine o'clock in the morning.

Nikki finally inched one of the club chairs closer to the window but still far enough away that anyone meandering out on the street wouldn't see her if they cast a glance in her direction. When she couldn't stand it another second, she keyed in Jack's number and waited for him to pick up. "It's me. Hey, you, what are you doing?" Nikki smiled at her own greeting. "We're here. Guess that's pretty obvious. I can't wait to see you." She then gave Jack a quick rundown on the Woodleys, Lizzie, and what they'd been doing all night long.

She finally wound down by saying, "Something is really bothering me, Jack. I can't wrap my mind around it yet. But, my gut is telling me whatever it is means success or failure for this mission. I've tried everything, but I just can't get a handle on it. Help me out here, Jack."

"Was it something I said? Something someone else said, one of the girls? Did Charles say something that you didn't react to? Or was it maybe something vague you saw on the message boards?"

Nikki groaned. "That's just it, I don't know. Myra says I have to shift into my neutral zone, and it will eventually come to me. But by the time I finally 'get it,' it might be too late. I don't want to start something we're not going to be able to handle. We were ambushed once, and I don't ever want that to happen again. Is there any way you can make it out here to see me?"

It was Jack's turn to groan. "If only. The short answer is no, for the moment. I know I'm being watched. Erin Powell has us all in her crosshairs. I wish you could have heard Bert when he found out she was shipping him to Chicago and then California. He was royally pissed.

"Bert has himself convinced, and in this case I tend to agree with him, that Powell believes he's her mole. She went preemptive by shipping him off, which only means she's about to do something she doesn't want him to know about. If she believes he is her mole, she won't want him tipping her hand."

"You mean like Erin's coming out here to Kalorama to talk to the Woodleys?"

"No, something else. He heard about that at their morning briefing. Bert thinks she has some trick up her sleeve. She's walking a fine line right now and the director came down on her and she didn't like it. If she fails with this task force, she might as well get out and go into the private sector. The fibs don't like failure when it comes to their agents."

Something tweaked Nikki, but it was gone before she could latch on to it. Damn, she'd almost had it. "Any other news we should know about?"

"I wish. Turn on your television. The big news is the sale of the *Post* going through. Everyone is weighing in with their opinions. The GOP isn't real happy. The Dems are gloating. Guess they have some inside info no one else has. The hunt is on for the owner. The people on the hill aren't buying the information that's being peddled. Maggie has been on every show going, and she just smiles and gives away nothing. She doesn't look like the Maggie we know. I'm telling you right now, and remember I'm the one who said it first, she's going to rule that paper with two iron fists. I'm actually meeting her for lunch today. Judge Easter is going to be in the same restaurant just by chance. Anything you want me to tell either one of them?"

"Actually, Jack, I do. I want you to tell Maggie to assign some reporters to keep tabs on the Connor campaign's fund-raising operation. Tell her to give a lot of space to Pam Lock and the great job she's doing for her candidate. Kathryn and Isabelle should be arriving at that office any second now. Have them tell the reporters about the soirée that's being planned at the Waldorf-Astoria. Tell her to pull out all the stops."

"I can do that. I miss you, Nik. As much as I want to see you, I won't put you and the others in any danger by trying to do so. Not to worry, we'll make it happen, but only when it's safe. Listen, I'm running late. I've got fourteen minutes to make it to the courthouse. I'll call you. I love you more than all the stars in the sky."

"And I love you more than all the sand on the beach."

There was a smile on Nikki's face when she closed her cell phone. She looked around to see if any of the others were watching. They weren't, so she closed her eyes and for a few seconds conjured up Jack holding her in his arms as he whispered in her ear. When her eyes started to burn, she forced herself to concentrate on the street in front of the house.

Nikki heard the high-powered twang of the engine before she saw the sleek silver Porsche slow to a crawl before it swept into the Woodleys's driveway. She fought the wild urge to run out into the street to hug Lizzie. Instead, she called over her shoulder, "Lizzie just arrived." Now all she had to do was wait for Erin Powell to show up. Her watch said it was exactly nine o'clock. Paula Woodley had phoned to inform her the moment Powell called her to set up the meeting for nine thirty.

Never good at waiting, Nikki paced, her

thoughts going in all directions. She walked back to the kitchen mumbling about making fresh coffee. She whispered to Yoko to take her place at the window. Yoko immediately bobbed up from her lotus position to stand by the window, the cell glued to her ear. Whatever Harry was saying to her made her smile. Nikki felt jealous and yet happy for Yoko. Sometimes life just wasn't fair.

At the same time she knew Paula Woodley was in good hands.

Moments before Lizzie Fox arrived, Paula paid the morning health aide, who had cleaned up her husband for the day, then locked the door behind him. She rushed back to the barren room and wheeled the chair out to the den, which had a magnificent seventy-six-inch plasma television set. She whirled around and dropped to her knees to stare into her husband's eyes.

"Listen to me very carefully, Mr. Woodley. If you so much as blink or give any indication that things aren't all warm and fuzzy here in our abode, you will regret it because I will walk away from here and call the vigilantes back to finish the job on you." Suddenly Paula went off into peals of laughter. "If you could kill me with your eyes, you would. I see it. It makes me happy, Mr. Woodley, because I know how you're suffering. Know this, you son of a bitch, I hate you ten times more than you hate me. No, that's a lie, I hate you a thousand times more than you hate me.

"Ooh, I hear a car. That must be our new lawyer. The vigilantes recommended her. I hear she's superb. Not that she's going to do *you* any good. When the FBI agent gets here, just drool and slobber all over yourself. You will keep those crooked fingers of yours under your blanket and remember what I said, no blinking. I'll be watching you. And when they leave, after you play at eating your lunch, the vigilantes are coming for dessert. That's what you have to look forward to. If you even think about making any of those gurgling, gargling sounds, I will personally choke you. Remember that time you did choke me and almost crushed my larynx? I couldn't talk for months and had to be fed through a tube in my stomach, and my tongue swelled up to twice its normal size. I'll go you one better and yank your damn tongue out by the roots and stuff it up your ass. Now, blink to show me we're together on all this."

Karl Woodley blinked right on cue.

"That's a good boy, Mr. Woodley. Ah, the

doorbell is ringing. I bet you can't wait to meet our new lawyer. Mind your manners, Mr. Woodley," Paula trilled as she danced her way to the front door.

The introductions made, Paula escorted her new attorney out to the kitchen, where she poured her a cup of fine Kona coffee. Paula noticed the tremor in Lizzie's hands when she picked up her coffee cup. She smiled. "It's always a shock when people first see Mr. Woodley. I, of course, am used to it. I like looking at him. Sometimes I just sit and stare at him and thank God for what the vigilantes did to him. I'd be dead now if it wasn't for them."

Lizzie didn't know what to say. She knew Paula Woodley's story and marveled at the woman's guts. "Can . . . can Mr. Woodley talk?"

"In a manner of speaking. He makes noises. I understand him. No one else can. The agent won't get a thing out of him. Me either, because I wasn't here when Mr. Woodley was attacked. I can't imagine what she hopes either of us can tell her. Do *you* know why she's coming here? Are you one of them, Ms. Fox?"

"In a manner of speaking I know. The director of the FBI appointed a new task force, and Ms. Powell is heading it up. All indications are that there's a serious push on to capture the ladies. Am I one of them? Yes, Mrs. Woodley, I am. This is very good coffee."

"That's funny you should say that. Mr. Woodley had a standing order with some company in Hawaii to send coffee to us once a week. It was expensive. I wasn't allowed to drink it. Maxwell House was good enough for me. I make a point of grinding the beans in front of him and drinking the whole pot myself. He gets water with his toast in the morning. Do you think I'm too sadistic?"

She sounded to Lizzie's ears like she was asking if she thought it would rain before noon.

Lizzie squared her shoulders. "After what you went through at his hands, no. I just don't understand why you haven't killed him. If you ever decide to do that, I'll represent you."

"Thank you, Lizzie. I'll be sure to remember your offer when it gets to the point where I'm tired of tormenting him. Oh, dear, there's the doorbell. Shall I bring Ms. Powell out to the kitchen, or shall we adjourn to the den?"

"I'll come with you. I will answer for you at times. If I hold up my hand, that means you don't answer whatever question she poses for you. Do you understand, Mrs. Woodley?"

"Perfectly, and call me Paula."

Lizzie Fox stayed in the den out of Karl Woodley's sight as she waited for Paula to return with Erin Powell. The attorney was dressed in a power suit of steel gray, with a scarlet blouse and gray suede shoes. Her silvery mane of hair was done into a fashionable chignon. She wore her headlight diamond earrings and no other jewelry. On the coffee table was her ostrich-skin briefcase that cost more than Powell's yearly salary. A gift from a grateful client. She did love fine things.

Lizzie Fox waited patiently. It was one of the many things she was extremely good at. Then, like a cobra in bright sunlight, she'd strike. She could hear the voices at the front door but couldn't make out the words. She continued to wait.

Paula opened the door and waited while Erin Powell fished out her credentials. Paula pulled a pair of reading glasses out of her pocket, put them on, and read all the fine print. She spent a few extra seconds studying the shield and even rubbed her fingers over it before she nodded and stepped aside for the agent to enter.

Erin Powell felt her heart plummet to her stomach when she got her first look at Karl Woodley. Nothing could have prepared her for what she was seeing. She tried in vain to cover her shock.

"It's all right. Most people react that way when they first meet Mr. Woodley. Both of us are used to it." She turned when she heard foot taps on the hardwood floor. "This is our attorney, Elizabeth Fox. Ms. Fox, this is Special Agent Erin Powell."

Erin's heart plummeted from its hiding place in her stomach all the way to her feet. She was trying to think of something to say when Lizzie Fox beat her to the punch.

"We really have to stop meeting like this, Ms. Powell."

Erin's eyes narrowed, and she offered up a tight little smile. "I just have a few questions for your clients." Of course, that was a lie, she had a whole list of questions, but seeing Woodley's condition and Lizzie Fox at the same time, the list immediately dwindled down to just a few.

Excellent hostess that she was, Paula motioned to the sofa and chairs. The three women took their seats, but not before Paula turned her husband's chair so he could face the trio. She sat back and waited for the agent to begin her questioning, the picture of complete cooperation.

Erin began by placing a small recorder on the coffee table. Lizzie held up her hand, then set a matching recorder next to Powell's.

"What can either of you tell me about the night the vigilantes invaded your home?" Erin asked, not caring who answered the question.

Paula shrugged. "I can't tell you anything. I wasn't here. Actually, I was in the hospital. Your people have all my hospital records, my doctor's affidavits. I see no reason to make me go through all that again."

"I understand." Erin turned and addressed Karl Woodley. "Is there anything you can tell me? I need to know how many women were here that night."

Woodley stared at her but didn't move or blink. His gaze immediately went back to the television screen.

"There were six women," Paula said.

Lizzie chirped up. "That's hearsay. Mrs. Woodley wasn't in the room that night. She's just telling you what someone told her."

Erin nodded. She went back to Woodley. "Were there any men here? The reports say there were five or six men. Can you verify that?"

Karl Woodley ignored the agent and the question. Erin turned to Paula, but she was looking at Lizzie when she asked, "What did your husband specifically say to you about the home invasion?"

Paula looked at Lizzie, who nodded that she could answer the question.

"Nothing."

Erin allowed her dismay to show. "How is that possible? When you recovered from your stay in the hospital, and Mr. Woodley came home, you must have discussed what happened."

Lizzie nodded again to show Paula she could answer the question.

"You would think that, wouldn't you? It didn't happen. Believe me, I tried. I think the memory was just too terrible, and he blocked it out. All you have to do is look at him to know how badly it all went that terrible night. I'm really sorry that I can't be of more help. If you recall, I did try explaining all that to you on the phone this morning. You could have saved yourself a trip out here."

Erin didn't think she looked sorry at all, and Lizzie Fox looked almost gleeful. Her stomach muscles bunched themselves in a knot. Her tone was surly, contrary-sounding when she asked, "Can't he blink, wave his fingers?"

Lizzie shrugged. "Ask him yourself, Agent Powell."

Erin knew when she was being taken down the garden path. Her shoulders stiffened. No smart-ass lawyer in a Chanel suit was going to get the best of her. She moved then, lightning quick, and asked, "Mr. Woodley, how would you like to come down to headquarters where we can ask you some questions? I can have your doctors standing by. I know you can communicate, we just have to figure out the best way to do it. Just blink if you want to do that."

Karl Woodley blinked defiantly. Erin turned to the lawyer and Mrs. Woodley. "I'll get the paperwork in order and have an ambulance to take Mr. Woodley down to headquarters."

"I don't think so, Agent Powell. I think we need to do another test before you put my client through any more misery. Paula, dear, I think you should be the one to ask your husband the question. Blinking is a natural occurrence, Agent Powell. We all do it a hundred times a minute or some absurd number like that," Lizzie said.

A smile on her face, her voice gentle, Paula leaned over and touched her husband's hand. "Darling, did you understand what Agent Powell just asked you? If you did, and if you want to go to the FBI Building, blink twice."

Karl Woodley stared at the television screen. Satisfied, Paula took two steps backward, her gaze never leaving her husband's face.

"Ask him again, Agent Powell," Lizzie said.

There was a note of desperation in Powell's tone when she repeated her question. Karl Woodley ignored her, his eyes glued to the television.

"Ask him something else, Agent Powell. I want you to go away from here knowing there is no point in tormenting these fine people."

Not about to give up, Erin Powell dropped to her knees and with both hands turned Woodley's face so that he was staring directly into her eyes. "Are you being coerced by these two women, Mr. Woodley?"

Lizzie sucked in her breath, and said, "That will be just about enough of *that,* Agent Powell. You have overstayed your welcome. Do not try to come back here unless I am present. Just to be on the safe side, I'm going to call Director Cummings myself and let him know about this little visit.

There is cruel and then there is *cruel.* You just stepped over the line, and I will not tolerate it. Paula, show Agent Powell to the door."

The moment the door was closed and locked, Paula ran back to the den. She was clearly rattled. "Is it okay? She can't do that, can she? He can communicate with his fingers and by blinking. You can't let that happen."

"Why? All he can say is what happened, and that was a long time ago."

"No! No! I told him the vigilantes are a few doors down. I told him they were going to come over here to see him. I was . . . I was . . . tormenting him the way he used to torment me."

"Damn!" Lizzie felt a momentary flurry of panic. "I guess that means we have to relocate Mr. Woodley. Not to worry. I can have him out of here within minutes.

"That is, *I hope,*" she muttered under her breath.

Paula ran to the front window. "She's just sitting out there staring at the house. She thinks we pulled a fast one on her. I saw it in her eyes. Damn, she's on her cell phone now." Paula turned around to see Lizzie whispering on her own cell. She strained to hear what Lizzie was saying.

"Like right now, Harry. A medical van. We'll do our best to walk through the backyards and dump him with the Sisters. I'll call you back to tell you where to meet us. Call Charles."

Lizzie turned to Paula. "What are the backyards like?"

"Not good for a wheelchair. The second house up has a tall fence. Why?"

"Powell is going to get a warrant. We have to get him out of here. How much does he weigh?"

"Around a hundred and ten pounds. Why?"

"I know how to do a fireman's carry. You need to go out there to distract Powell, and I'll carry him over to 11063. Stay with her until you see me coming out your front door. The house with the fence, how do I get past it?"

"There's a gate on the side, outside latch. Just open it. The Brants live there. They sit in the living room all day watching television, their kitchen overlooks the back, so I don't think either one of them will see you. The people next door are at work, the house is empty. Do you need any help?"

Lizzie thought that was funny. She laughed. "No. Go out and keep Agent Powell busy. Get as angry as you want and make it good. Threaten anything you feel like threatening. Throw my name around as much as you want. Hurry, Paula."

Lizzie sucked in her breath and approached the wheelchair. Before she could change her mind, she swooped down and threw Woodley over her shoulder. Paula was right, he was a featherweight, all bones.

Woodley's fingers clawed at Lizzie's neck. "Do that again, and I'll tell your wife. I don't think you'll like that. I'm taking you to the vigilantes, so pay attention, you bastard."

CHAPTER 17

The kitchen door at 11063 burst open with a loud bang, the door hitting the wall with tremendous force. The Sisters came on the run, gaping at what they were seeing. Speechless, they could only stare. They all started to babble at once.

"Where do you want this guy?" Lizzie gasped.

They all continued to talk on top of each other until Annie whistled sharply and was rewarded with instant silence.

Unable to sustain Woodley's weight on her slim shoulders, Lizzie dropped him onto one of the kitchen chairs. His legs swung crazily for a second, then he slid off to the floor. Lizzie shrugged. Yoko poked at his leg to be sure he was alive.

"Where are your shoes, dear? Your feet are full of mud," Myra asked inanely.

"Myra, dear heart that you are, I couldn't carry that piece of scum over here through the soggy ground wearing four-inch heels. Listen, as much as I would like to stay here and chat, I have to get back. Call Harry. I would have called Jack, but he's due in court. I saw his name on the court schedule yesterday. He knows what to do. You don't have a lot of time, ladies. I know Powell is sitting out there waiting for one of her guys to show up with a warrant. I'll send Paula over here as soon as I get back. Look, I really have to go. Call me."

The kitchen door opened and closed.

Lightning couldn't have moved faster than the Sisters at that moment. They worked as one, with Nikki and Alexis carrying Woodley to the den, where they tossed him on the couch.

In the blink of an eye, Nikki and Alexis changed into their airline outfits. Their cosmetic transformation took all of eight minutes once they were dressed.

Five cell phones started to ring at the same time, but nothing deterred the women. If anything, they worked faster to hasten their departure.

"Wrap the guy in a blanket and dump him in the airline van," Nikki shouted as she ran to the window in time to see Lizzie's Porsche racing down the street. It was obvious she wasn't obeying the posted twenty-five miles per hour speed limit. "Paula should be here in a minute. Someone call Charles so he can tell us where to take the two of them."

"Pack up all the files, load them in the van," Yoko screeched, as she tossed papers and files any which way into the cardboard boxes.

Karl Woodley's eyes followed the scurrying women. His breathing was labored, but no one paid any attention. His eyes rolled back in his head when he saw his wife entering the room. He tried to bury himself into the thickness of the sofa, but Paula jerked him into a sitting position. "This is all your fault, Mr. Woodley. But don't you worry, I have some wonderful plans for you. Right now I have other things to do, but I will get back to you, and that's a promise."

Paula dropped to her haunches to help the women pack up the boxes, which she then helped carry out to the van.

"Ten minutes and counting," Nikki shrilled. "Who has a permanent Magic Marker?" Three different-colored markers sailed through the air and she caught them deftly. She raced to the garage and made the 6 on the license plates into an 8. The 9 became another 8.

Myra and Annie were working feverishly

with Clorox Wipes, trying to wipe down everything any of them might have touched since their arrival.

"Two minutes!" Yoko called out.

"Done!" Myra and Annie shouted breathlessly.

"Then let's do it!" someone shouted.

"We'll take him, Paula," Nikki said, as she grabbed Woodley's feet and Alexis held him under his arms. Paula held open the door leading into the garage, and they barreled through. Woodley's arms flapped every which way.

"Go! Go!" Yoko shouted. A minute later she shouted again. "We're clear and locked and loaded. Did I say that right, Annie?" she asked fretfully.

"Not exactly, but we get the message that it's time to hustle our asses, dear. Does anyone know where we're going?" she asked as she clambered into the van with the darkly tinted windows. "We should have just taken out Ms. Powell. It would have been so much easier," she grumbled.

"She's a federal agent," Alexis said.

"And Mitchell Riley wasn't the acting director of the FBI when we took him on? We didn't worry about it back then. Powell is just a lowly agent. We should have just taken her out and worried about it later.

Now she's going to cause us trouble. I rest my case," Annie snorted.

"She has a point," Yoko said. "We still have time. I can render Ms. Powell unconscious in a matter of seconds."

The momentary silence was palpable, then everyone was talking at once. Where to stash her car? What to do with her? Agents will be crawling all over the neighborhood asking questions.

"No, we made the right decision. The minute we start to second-guess ourselves is when we'll run into trouble," Nikki said. The others agreed. The remainder of the trip to Tysons Corner was made in silence.

Nikki spotted the ambulance at the far end of the mall lot. It was still early enough in the day that for the most part the lot held only workers' cars. Even the hardiest of shoppers didn't venture forth until late morning or early afternoon. She thought she'd read that somewhere once.

Nikki pulled the airline van alongside the ambulance and waited for Harry and two of his people to get out and walk over to where she was waiting.

The transfer was slick, fast, and efficient. As far as Nikki could tell, no one was paying the least bit of attention to any of them.

Paula Woodley was wringing her hands. "This is all my fault. I'm so sorry, Nikki. Sometimes I just get so bitter and look at all the empty years to come staring at me, and I just lose it. If there's anything I can do, just call me."

Nikki patted her hand, remembering what the woman had been through at her sick husband's hands. "We didn't get caught, so that's a plus. I'll call you. Be careful, Paula."

The women waited until the ambulance was out of sight before they all relaxed.

"Now what?" the ever-impatient Annie asked.

"We sit here and wait for further instructions," Nikki said.

Maggie Spritzer looked at the gaggle of people who made the *Post* run effectively as they waited for her to say something. Once she had been one of them. Now, in her new glorified position, she could see the envy and the animosity in some of their faces. She risked a glance at Ted, who was in the second row, towering over everyone else even though he was sitting down.

Maggie read off the notes in her hand. She'd worked all night on this little speech. Finally, she decided the hell with it, and said whatever popped into her head, which was pretty much, *"Do your job and you won't have time to resent me. If you don't like your assignments, tell someone who cares. That means do not come whining to me, or you'll be outside this building so fast your head will spin off your shoulders."*

"This is your ninety-day trial period. My own as well. I was told by the powers that be that if we don't cut it, we're all out. I urge each of you to think about your family, your 401k, your health insurance, and your expense account if you have one. If we all work together, we can make this paper stand out like a beacon. To that end, I want all of you to get me whatever you can on Martine Connor. I want mentions every day in this paper. I want op-ed pieces that show her in a good light. The new owners of this paper are behind her one hundred percent. That's it for now. Go on, get out of here and get to work. Ted, I need to talk to you."

Ted Robinson remained seated, his heart pounding in his chest. He tried to find something witty or even charming to say, but his tongue was glued to the roof of his mouth. He waited.

Maggie sensed her ex-lover's discomfort and reveled in it. Not that she was exactly a woman scorned, but she was damn close to it. She felt nervous standing in front of him, knowing she had the power to fire him if she wanted to. Not that she would ever be that unprofessional. She corrected the thought. Maybe she would be that unprofessional under the right circumstances.

"Ted, did you just hear what I said about Martine Connor and the new owners of this paper?"

Ted nodded. His tongue was still glued to the roof of his mouth. He tried to bring up some spit from under his tongue, but it wasn't working.

"Okay, because I believe you are the best reporter in the business, I am turning Connor over to you. I want you to be on her 24/7. You will be the go-to guy if any of your colleagues come up with something. I want every word to be glowing. I want to see Connor in the White House, and so do the new owners. The first time you step off the track and start that vigilante crap, your ass is out of here. As far as you're concerned, those women no longer exist. Are you still with me?"

Ted nodded again.

"I want you to pick Pam Lock's brain. Then I want you to play her off against the GOP's guy, what's his name? Yeah, yeah, Baron Russell, that's it. I think there's something funny going on where those two are concerned. Call it my gut instinct or a woman's intuition, whatever feels right to you. Figure it out for me, Teddy."

Teddy? The only time Maggie had ever called him Teddy was in the throes of passion. He blinked. He nodded again.

"One more thing, *Teddy.* The first time I call you on your cell for whatever reason, and you don't answer, will be the last time I call you. I know how slick you are, so don't say you weren't forewarned."

He got it then. Maggie was being sarcastic. He thought about the lyrics to that old song they both liked so much. Maggie was definitely back in town. He knew she was waiting for him to say something, either to tell her to go to hell or to make some smart-ass remark or maybe even say something endearing. He finally got his tongue unstuck enough to say, "Okay, boss." He thought she looked upset that he wasn't going to give her a fight. He untangled his long legs and stood up. As he walked out of the conference room, he turned, and said, "Mickey and Minnie miss you. They sleep on an old shirt you left in the hamper."

Maggie stared at Ted's retreating back. Whatever she thought he was going to say, that definitely wasn't it. A lump the size of a golf ball formed in her throat. She sat for a long time, thinking about the way it had been when she and Ted were together. They were some of the happiest times of her life. But he'd gone and ruined it. She wanted to cry so bad she had to bite down on her lower lip.

Maggie knew she had to snap out of her mood, or she'd start wailing like a banshee. It was almost time to leave to meet Jack Emery for lunch. He'd specifically asked her to get to the restaurant early if she could because he had only ninety minutes for lunch and had to be back in court in plenty of time.

Liam Sullivan, her old boss, never left the building for lunch. Well, she wasn't Liam Sullivan, and she was going to go out to lunch every single day, even if it was just to walk around the block or grab a hot dog from a street vendor.

Maggie shuffled off to her private bathroom to repair her makeup and comb her hair. When she exited the room, she called ahead for the car service made available to the new EIC. She liked the perk. She liked everything about her new job. Well, almost everything. She sighed as she walked to the elevator. As she was riding down, she wondered what she should order for lunch.

Should she go heavy and not have to worry about a good dinner and just have a sandwich later in the evening? Eating on the paper's expense account would save a lot of money on her food bill, since she loved to eat. Or should she go light so she wasn't sluggish all afternoon? She finally decided she'd make up her mind when she opened the menu. Doggy bags were good.

Just as Maggie was stepping into the town car waiting for her at the curb, across town Jack Emery was opening the door for Judge Cornelia Easter, who had reached it seconds before he did. They entered together and sat down together, even though that wasn't the plan. *Screw the plan,* Jack thought. At the moment his thoughts were on Nikki sitting in a van at Tysons Corner.

Gabe's Café wasn't exactly a café. At one time it had been a diner. Then it was turned into a café and later a family bistro if there was such a thing. To Jack it would always be Gabe's Café even though it was currently called Gabriel's. The food was good and plentiful, with always enough left over to fill a good-size doggy bag. Nikki had always called Gabe's fare stick-to-your-ribs food, but she loved it. He knew what was on the menu the moment he opened the door.

Gabe's specialty; bratwurst, sauerkraut, and some kind of dumplings. Homemade black bread with fresh-churned butter and a side order of mashed potatoes for anyone who didn't want the dumplings. Most people took both, including him. No one was ever able to eat a whole slice of Chocolate Thunder Cake, which Gabe made himself. It always went into the doggy bag in a separate container for late-night sugar treats.

The judge sat down first and looked at Jack. "Is this wise, meeting like this and eating together?" She looked up at the waiter, and said, "I'll have a double bourbon on the rocks."

Jack ordered a mineral water. "I'm not even sure why we're meeting. I think Maggie has something for us, or else she wants us to do something for her. Lean in closer, Your Honor, so I can tell you what just happened." Nellie leaned closer to the table, and he filled her in. He finished up by saying, "The girls are sitting in the parking lot at Tysons Corner waiting for orders. This is not going according to plan, or at least what I was told was the plan."

"It never does," Nellie said as she tossed down her bourbon.

Back on Benton Street in Kalorama, Erin

Powell watched the Woodley house. She was mad enough to chew nails and spit rust. She should have hauled Lizzie Fox's ass down to the Hoover Building just for the fun of it. God, how she hated that woman, with her smirking, know-it-all attitude. There wasn't a doubt in her mind that Fox would call the director, and she'd probably be out on the curb on her rear end by the end of the day. Maybe.

Where the hell were the guys with the warrants and the subpoenas? How long did it take a judge to sign off on one or the other? There was probable cause. What the hell more would he need?

Erin stared at the house until her eyes watered. Her gut told her something was wrong, but she didn't know what it was. On impulse, she got out of the car and marched up to the door. She rang the bell, then hit the knocker just in case the Woodleys had the television on and couldn't hear her.

She hadn't expected Paula Woodley to be such a spitfire. Paula had stood next to Erin's car and reamed her up one side and down the other. And while she was doing that, what the hell was Lizzie Fox doing inside the house? All alone.

Erin held her finger on the bell and listened to it peal inside. She gave the door knocker a couple more whacks. Nothing happened. She pressed her ear to the door and couldn't hear anything. It didn't sound like the TV was on. Why would they turn it off since that seemed to be the only thing Mr. Woodley could do other than sit in a chair? Probably his only enjoyment, if you could call it that, came from the huge plasma screen.

Erin looked up and down the street. It was a nice neighborhood, with lots of trees and pretty homes. The whole time she'd sat in her car she'd seen only one other, a rickety bucket of rust, driven by two pimply youths and Lizzie's Porsche. She corrected the thought. She'd seen three vehicles. The kids, Lizzie, and the van. An airline van of some kind. She wished now she'd paid attention to the logo on the side. Definitely some kind of airline, she remembered that much.

It hit her then like a freight train. The Woodley house was empty. She'd bet a day's pay on it. And they'd made their getaway in the white van with the red lettering. They must have gone out the backyard and across the neighbor's lawn. There was no doubt in her mind that Lizzie Fox had engineered the whole thing. Paula Woodley was just a distraction. "Bitch!" she seethed. *Whose garage did that van come from?*

Her cell phone was in her hand a second later, and she barked an order. "I want another warrant for 11063 Benton. No, I don't know who lives there. Make it a Jane Doe. I want it five minutes ago." Erin was so angry she threw the cell phone at her own government-issued car. She watched in dismay as the cover flew off the phone and sailed across the street, the batteries running down the slight incline.

That was one less worry. Director Cummings no longer had a way to reach her in the field.

Chapter 18

Nikki nibbled on her lower lip as her gaze swept the parking lot. They had to get out of here, and the sooner the better. She was contemplating putting the van in gear when a dark SUV pulled alongside and two hulking men got out and walked around to the driver's side of the van. One of the men motioned for Nikki to lower the window, but she didn't comply until he mouthed the words, "Charles sent me." She quickly lowered the window. "What?"

He handed a slip of paper through the open window, then backed away to help his partner. They quickly removed the airline logo and slapped on new, larger colorful signs on both side panels that said the van belonged to Martucci's Produce. The license plate was removed and a Virginia plate installed. The burly man jacked the screwdriver into his pocket, offered a thumbs-up, and both men climbed into the SUV.

"Where are we going?" Myra asked Nikki.

"To Alexandria. Old Town. Charles said he hasn't been able to reach Kathryn and Isabelle. He wants us to keep trying. He wants them out of there . . . like right now. I have to pay attention to the traffic, so someone call them. Yoko, call Harry and ask him to track Jack down."

"What happened, dear?" Myra asked.

Nikki shrugged. "If I had to take a wild guess, I'd say Erin Powell figured it out. She probably remembered there was no traffic on the street except for this van. Ergo, that's why the Woodley house is vacant. Five will get you ten they're breaking down the door to both houses as we speak."

"But why does Charles want Kathryn and Isabelle to leave? They just got there. No one knows about them. That was the plan. I don't understand," Alexis fretted.

"That was before Erin Powell got wise to us," Nikki said as she waited impatiently for the traffic light to turn green. "A lot seems to be happening suddenly. All that the local news is talking about concerns the new ownership of the *Post.* I wish I could remember what it is that I'm missing. If I could just remember . . ."

"It will come to you, dear," Myra said soothingly. "Don't force it."

"Easy for you to say, Myra. We're going to get ambushed. If I could only remember . . ."

Myra sighed. "Perhaps we should play that word game I used to play with you and Barbara when you were children. I would say a word and you say whatever comes into your mind. Shall we try, dear?"

"Why not? I can talk and drive. I don't think it's a thing or a place but more a person. Something a person said."

They went at it then, the Sisters throwing out names and places, then they doubled up with a name and a place. Nothing happened until Nikki slowed to a stop at a four-way intersection in Old Town. It was when Yoko said two names, Bert Navarro and Elias Cummings in succession that Nikki stomped on the gas pedal. "That's it! That's it, Yoko! I love you!

"I remember now. Sometimes I am so stupid I can't stand myself. What's been bugging me is what Charles told us about how Bert was assigned to the task force. And what called it to my attention was when Jack told me that Bert had called him for something or other and was complaining about Cummings assigning him to Erin Powell. Bert was really ticked off. He thought it was a comedown from being

Cummings's number one.

"Then Bert said that he should have figured out something was going on when Cummings went to the White House without him, without even telling him that a meeting there was scheduled. He said anytime a visit to the White House is on the schedule, they get a notice beforehand, and there are always two people at the meeting. You know how sneaky the administration can be.

"And Charles, you'll remember, revealed that Bert only found out about the meeting by accident and soon after he asked Cummings about it, he was transferred to the task force."

"But what does it mean, Nikki?" Annie asked.

"I'm not sure, but I think if we all let our imaginations run wild, we can figure it out. We're women, we're supposed to be smart, so let's figure it out. First, though, let me get my bearings here. Everyone, keep thinking but hold your thoughts until we get inside wherever it is we're going."

Their destination turned out to be what Charles called a "safe house," where operatives in the spook business could hole up until it was safe and time to move on. Safe houses were on no one's radar and came sparsely furnished with packaged staples and hygiene bags in the bathrooms. Safety, not comfort, was what anyone locating to a safe house required.

Nikki pulled the van off the dirt road and onto a gravel driveway at 207 Beaumonde Road. She cut the engine, and they all trooped out of the van to look around at their new digs.

They were in the country, with only one other house on the road, and it appeared to be vacant. The safe house itself looked decent enough, with a fireplace jutting out high and wide on the side of the house. Even without an education in architecture, it was easy to figure out that the house was a preassembled log cabin.

"The key is supposed to be over the ledge. I'll go in and open the garage. Alexis, drive the van in when I open the garage door," Nikki said.

"Turn the heat up," Myra said, a few minutes later as they walked into the refrigerator-like atmosphere of the log cabin. "There is heat, isn't there?"

Her tone was so anxious, Nikki looked around until she saw a thermostat on the wall next to a small kitchen. She cranked it up to 80 degrees before opening the garage door for Alexis.

The inside of the cabin was pretty much like the outside, plain, with no personal touches of any kind. There were no pictures on the walls, nothing on the wide mantel. The kitchen had two pots and an assortment of disposable dishes and cutlery. The cabinets held canned goods and assorted crackers, and there was one bag of cookies. There was nothing in the refrigerator except bottles of water. There was a linen closet that held towels, soaps, and toothbrushes, all prepackaged.

Alexis looked around. "This is depressing. I hope we aren't going to be here too long. We'll be overcrowded once Kathryn and Isabelle get here."

Never one to let something simmer if she could bring it to a boil, Annie sat down cross-legged on the floor and motioned for the others to join her. "Put us out of our misery, Nikki, and tell us what you think this business might mean."

"Maybe we should wait for Kathryn and Isabelle," Yoko said, "so we don't have to go through this all again."

"Maybe we shouldn't," Annie snapped. "We can always give them a summary. It's not like they need to hear all the ifs, ands, and buts."

It was Nikki's cue to speak. "Okay, okay. Let's ask ourselves why would Director Cummings suddenly start up a new task force to find us? We know why, but why right now? And why Erin Powell? Because we were friends once upon a time? If you want my opinion, that's pretty suspicious in and of itself. Why assign Bert to Erin, where he could assume she would make him her number one, and why not take him to the White House or tell him what took place? Bert is or was Cummings's number one. Perhaps the director's thinking is along the lines of Erin's, and he, too, thinks Bert is the mole. I'm saying perhaps. Now, why did the director go to the White House? Bert said the request to go to the White House always comes through in writing first so all involved can clear their schedules. Unless this was a covert meeting and no one was supposed to know about it, not even Bert, would be my guess. As Bert said, he found out only by accident.

"The meeting at the White House was only days after the request from the Republicans came through the message board to ask for our help."

Yoko picked up on Nikki's rundown. "The director appoints Erin to head up the task force, dumps Bert on her to get him out of his hair, knowing full well she isn't going to get anywhere. He's already had one showdown with her. Today, if Lizzie calls him, will make two dressing-downs. Bert is in Chicago by now and out of everyone's hair. So, if Bert's away from Washington, nothing that goes down can be blamed on him."

"Remember what Charles said? He said that Pam Lock and Baron Russell had a midnight, or at least a middle-of-the-night, meeting. What was that all about?" Myra asked.

"Pam Lock, according to Lizzie, is golden. She's on our side even though she doesn't know it. Russell is a Republican, so that means he's involved in whatever went on at that White House meeting. This is a wild guess on my part, but I don't think any donor lists were stolen on either side. I think that's all one big lie," Nikki said. The anger in her voice was so pronounced, the others knew she was on a roll.

As one they all bellowed, "Why?"

Nikki shrugged. "The only thing I can come up with is they're trying to trap us, set up an ambush. We almost walked into it, too. Call Kathryn and see if they're on their way."

Yoko flipped open her cell phone and punched in a number. She identified herself and listened. She clicked it shut after eight minutes.

"They're fifteen minutes away. Kathryn said someone was following her in a maroon-colored Saab. She called Harry, and he ran interference with the ambulance, which he has since ditched at some chop shop he knows, in case we need it at some point later on. He's on his way here on his motorcycle. Actually, he's directly behind Kathryn so he can watch her back. By the way, the Woodleys are safe and sound, and will be leaving the country by midafternoon on a private jet. Charles got on it like white on rice," Yoko said, using everyone's favorite expression.

"That's a relief," Nikki said. "Let's get back to our discussion. Who is responsible for what was to be our impending ambush and capture? The FBI or the White House? C'mon, c'mon, girls, I need feedback here. Throw it out here and let's kick it to death. We aren't leaving this house until I know it's safe to do so."

They all jabbered at the same time, throwing out wild ideas and scenarios that were impossible to comprehend.

When they ran out of steam with no solutions, Nikki said, "I keep going back to that promised pardon. At least we were smart enough at the beginning to know that wasn't going to happen. But, girls, what if . . . ?"

Whatever it was Nikki was about to say was cut off when they heard the sound of a car and the roar of Harry's motorcycle. Yoko raced to the door and leaped into Harry's arms as Kathryn and Isabelle flew into the room.

"What the hell happened?" Kathryn asked bluntly as she whipped off her wig and shook out her hair.

Isabelle sat down, leaned back, and closed her eyes.

"This is a dump," Kathryn said as she looked around. "Tell us what happened."

Annie summed it up quickly. "What excuse did you give Pam Lock for . . . uh . . . bugging out?"

"Said I cracked a tooth and was in pain, and Isabelle had to drive me to the dentist. She bought it. I liked the lady. I can tell you this, within minutes I figured out there was no way anyone could have gotten hold of her donor lists. The lady has it going on, let me tell you that. It all smelled of a setup, and she thinks so, too."

Annie's jaw dropped. "And you figured all this out in, what, an hour?"

"Well, yeah, Annie. I was there to spy. So

I spied. Plus, Pam likes to chatter. We got on right away. And here's a second plus for you. When a woman hates a man the way Lock hates Baron Russell, it was all a greased slide. Aside from all the claptrap and the bullshit, Pam Lock and her family are very patriotic and political."

"What about that middle-of-the-night meeting?" Myra asked.

"Sorry, Myra, I didn't get that far. Yoko called, and Isabelle and I flew out of there like we had wings. Then we picked up that tail. Has anyone heard from Bert?"

"No, dear, he hasn't called in," Myra said. "He's probably just arrived in Chicago. Even if they suspect that Bert is their mole, they have no proof."

"People have been convicted on less," Kathryn said. She was worried, and the Sisters could tell, so they tried to reassure her. But Kathryn wasn't buying false hopes. "Bert put his neck and reputation on the line for us. We need to do something to protect him."

Harry and Yoko joined the group sitting on the floor. Harry dropped down and said, "I know I don't have a voting voice with all of you, but this is one time I'd like to make a suggestion. They're going to hang Bert out to dry unless you can switch it around.

My suggestion is you make Erin Powell the mole."

Annie was on her feet, gesturing wildly with both arms. "See! I told you we should have taken her out! I just didn't get far enough in my thinking that we should frame her. I think that's a stupendous idea, Harry."

"Then let's do it," Kathryn said, a dangerous glint in her eyes. "Nikki, if you're right, and Powell is still at the Woodley house, call and talk to her. Arrange a one-on-one meeting. We'll be your lookouts to make sure she doesn't have her people watching her back. We take her out right then and there. Charles can clean up after us. Yeah, yeah, we have to call him first. I think it will be better if it comes from Myra." The others agreed. "Charles should have foreseen this."

Myra immediately went on the defensive. "How could Charles possibly know something like that ahead of time, Kathryn?"

But Kathryn was in a fighting mood. "He knows everything else, doesn't he? If he didn't know, he should have anticipated something like this happening. We've been flying blind since we got here. Our intel was sloppy at best. Our intel comes straight from Charles, so there is no one else to blame, and someone needs to take blame here or Bert is going to get caught, and where does that leave us? We owe it to Bert."

"You're absolutely right, Kathryn. We do owe it to Bert to step in." Nikki looked around at the others, who were nodding in agreement.

Nikki's cell phone seemingly materialized out of thin air. She jabbed in Paula Woodley's home phone number while Myra contacted Charles. Nikki wasn't surprised when a deep male voice answered Paula's phone and asked who she was.

"This is Carol Maloney from the *Post.* I'd like to speak to Special Agent Powell. I have something urgent to tell her about a case she's working on."

"Hold on. What'd you say your name was again?"

"Carol Maloney."

Nikki listened as the agent bellowed for Erin to take the call. Myra was off the phone before Erin Powell came on the line. She whispered instructions to Nikki, who nodded.

A moment later Nikki heard her old friend identify herself. Erin followed up with, "How did you get this number, and how did you know I was here? I don't know anyone named Carol Maloney. What do you want?"

"Hello, Erin. Is that any way to talk to a

member of the press? This is Nikki Quinn. To answer your question I watched you all morning. I was right under your nose, to be exact. If you're trying to trace this call, don't bother. I'm willing to meet you one-on-one. I have people watching you. Not only do I know exactly where you are right this moment, I can actually see you. If you want to confide in your fellow agents, my proposed deal is off. So, do you want the meet or not?"

"Why should I meet with you? For God's sake, Nikki, you're a felon. I have orders to find you and bring you in. The FBI does not make deals. You know that."

"I am a felon, and so are the others. I don't deny it. Don't give me that bullshit that you fibs don't make deals. You do it all the time as long as it benefits you. Listen to me, I want to help you. You're being set up by Director Cummings. He thinks you're the mole. That's why he gave you Navarro, and you fell right into his trap by making him your number one. You were always smart, Erin. I'm surprised you didn't figure it out. You're going to be twisting in the wind unless you chop them off at the knees. There goes your career. Meet me somewhere, alone, and I'll turn over the information I have so you can save your skin and at the same time turn the tables on them. This is just between us, Erin. If you try anything funny, I won't like it, and the vigilantes will have to retaliate. Are we clear on that?"

"How do I know . . . ?"

Anticipating the question, Nikki jumped in with, "You don't. You'll just have to trust an old friend and know she'd never do anything to harm you. It's your call, Erin."

Erin's voice was hesitant when she said, "Where and when do you want to meet?"

"Right now, within the hour. The British Embassy. I'll be waiting. One wrong move on your part, and it will be the last one you ever make. Do you understand what I just said?"

"Yes, I do. How accurate is your intel?"

Nikki knew by the whispered voice that she had her. Her fist shot in the air, a signal to the others that Erin would play ball.

"We haven't survived this long by sharing information. Suffice it to say we're never wrong. One hour." Nikki slapped the encrypted cell phone shut and looked around at the small group. "She went for it. I told you all along she's a smart cookie. She's already seeing the handwriting on the wall.

"Myra, call Charles and have him call the British Embassy and make sure they invite her in when she gets there. Harry and his people will be right behind her. They'll do the snatch and grab, and it's over and done with."

"Then what?" Harry asked.

"Then we have Judge Easter call the director, since the two of them have a history, and tell him his mole was Erin Powell. Not to worry, we'll make sure Erin has a good life someplace quite distant from here. I suspect Charles will find her a very good job at Interpol or maybe even MI6, and give her a new identity.

"Kathryn, call Bert and tell him to catch the next plane home from Chicago. He can always say Erin called him back. We're going to need Bert."

Annie clapped her hands. "I love it. We're smokin' now."

"Harry, move it," Nikki said. "We'll have Charles call you once you're at the embassy. Okay now, ladies, let's get down to business. We need the guy who set this all up. I'm thinking it's the president's chief of staff."

"So how are we going to get to him?" Myra asked.

"We aren't. You're going to call Justice Pearl Barnes and have her arrange a meeting. He won't dare turn down someone like her. We swoop in and make him regret this little charade. I think it might be a good idea to include Director Cummings, too, if we can prove he's implicated — along with Baron Russell."

"Girls, we are on fire!" Annie chortled.

Chapter 19

The Sisters huddled after Harry's departure. They worked in sync, Myra and Annie working the phones as they cheerfully blackmailed the seamier side of Wall Street. Annie was especially adept at finding incriminating information in the dossiers they'd confiscated from Mitchell Riley, before he'd been sent to the federal pen to live out his life. She ended each phone call with the same words, "I absolutely will not take no for an answer. Wire the money to this account. I'm so happy for you that now you will have a ten-thousand-dollar stake in the election of the next president." For those who wanted to balk, she offered to fax them a list of their extracurricular deeds. Two hours into their gig, Myra had it down pat and was even more vicious than Annie. Neither took any prisoners.

With Charles's help, the Sovereign Bank of Virginia was now the recipient of a fund designated as the proceeds for seating at Martine Connor's upcoming soirée at the Waldorf-Astoria. The date of the soirée was to be announced by Pam Lock in the campaign's next press release.

Isabelle spent the major part of the morning conferring with Maggie Spritzer, dictating articles and editorials the Sisters wanted to run in the paper. At the same time Alexis was glued to the phone with Lizzie Fox, tying off all the legal loose ends.

Nikki sat at the computer as she talked to Charles hour after hour, working out the final details on wrapping up a mission that had smelled like a dead fish from the beginning.

Kathryn spent her time talking to Bert by phone until he had to board his flight home. From time to time the others would look at her and smile. They'd never seen Kathryn so happy.

Cold-as-ice, hard-nosed, kick-ass, take-names-later Kathryn Lucas was in love.

Yoko tapped away at her computer, backing up everything Nikki sent her way. When Nikki finished a call to Charles, she'd hop on the phone with Alexis's help to order materials for the Red Bag.

It was totally dark outside, almost eight o'clock, when all the women stopped what they were doing, as if some ultrasonic signal only they could hear had gone off.

The signal, as it turned out, was the roar of Harry's Ducati, and Jack and Bert arriving in separate cars. The women ran to the door and turned on the outside light. Their sighs of relief could be heard all the way to the vacant house down the road.

Kathryn's eyes devoured the tall, strapping federal agent. Always a gentleman, Bert just dropped his arm around her shoulders. Not caring about appearances, Harry picked up Yoko and headed outside in the darkness. Jack simply reached for Nikki, drew her close, and kissed her till her teeth rattled. The Sisters clapped when the couple came up for air.

A devilish grin on his face, Jack bowed low and Nikki did a full curtsy. The Sisters clapped a second time. Then they applauded a third time when Bert held up a huge shopping bag.

"Chinese and Italian!"

"Oh, you dear, sweet man," Annie gushed. Then she whispered in Kathryn's ear. "See, dear, one cannot live on love. One must have sustenance. How wonderful that Bert recognized that little fact."

Kathryn gave her a playful swat on her rear end as Annie danced away with the aromatic bag.

An hour later all of the food and the beer was gone. Alexis bagged up the trash and carried it out to a garbage can at the side of the house. She made sure to clamp the lid on tightly so that raccoons couldn't get into it. As she walked back to the cabin, she thought about her life as it was before and what it had become. She missed Grady and she felt sad that there was no one in her life to hold hands with, no one to tell her she looked pretty once in a while. When she reached the steps leading to the front porch, she sat down and hugged her knees.

If she was back in the real world, what would she be doing right now? Probably just getting home from work and heating up a can of soup because she was too tired to do anything else. A warm bath, then bed, so she could get up at four thirty, walk Grady, and still be at the office by six thirty so the powers that be could see what a dedicated worker she was.

She couldn't help but wonder what she would do if she was suddenly given a pardon and was able to go back to her own life. *What would I do?* Tears gathered in her eyes when she had to admit to herself that she truly didn't know. Could she handle being thrust into the mainstream of life after all she'd been through? Did she even want to go back to that old life?

Maybe she could open a small office and be a one-woman financial planner. She grimaced at the thought. She got up from the steps and winced. Her knees felt stiff and sore. Maybe she was getting the arth-a-ritis, as her old grandmother used to say. She laughed, then sobered instantly. Arthritis would be the least of her problems at this stage in her life.

She looked up at the star-spangled sky and the half moon that lit up the straggly front yard. *What day is it?* She couldn't remember. Earlier Myra had said something about Thanksgiving fast approaching.

Shaking her head to clear her thoughts, Alexis walked between the cars and Harry's motorcycle out to the end of the road. She looked right and left, wondering, if she walked either way where the dirt road would take her. For one split second she was tempted to turn right and start walking, but she didn't. She looked back at the yellow light spilling out of the cabin's windows and knew she'd committed to the people inside. She couldn't walk away any more than she could stop breathing. This was her life. She turned around and walked back up the driveway and onto the little front porch. She opened the door and was greeted with a warm hug from Yoko, who was about to go out into the night to look for her.

"I thought something might have happened to you," Yoko whispered. "We were all worried."

Alexis felt warm all over. This, then, was her family. "Silly. It's a beautiful evening. I sat down on the steps to look up at the stars. It's been a while since I wished on one. I saw the Big Dipper and the Little Dipper." Realizing Yoko had no clue what she was talking about, she said, "I wished us all good luck and good fortune. *After* I wished for good health and happiness. Is something happening?"

"Not yet, but any minute now. Justice Barnes and Judge Easter are on the phones with Annie and Myra."

"What about Erin Powell?"

Yoko laughed, a delightful sound in the quiet evening. "She's on her way to Merry Old England as we speak. She's probably at thirty thousand feet in Annie's private plane. According to Charles, Ms. Powell didn't kick up a fuss or anything. She just accepted the situation and gave in gracefully. She did leave a message for Nikki, which said in essence she wished Nikki had trusted her a little more and known she would have found a way to fix things."

Alexis looked dumbfounded. "Do you all believe it?"

"Nikki said no, not in a million years. No, none of us believed it, especially Myra."

"I'm relieved. That's another thorn out of our sides, at least for now."

Yoko led Alexis to the wide circle on the floor, and they promptly sat. Alexis licked her lips, wondering if the others knew what she was feeling. She rather thought they did and understood by the way they all smiled at her. When you loved and cared about someone, it showed. It was showing now.

"So, what wonderful things happened while I was taking out the trash and looking at the stars?" Alexis asked.

Annie laughed and waved a yellow sheet of paper over her head. "Myra and I could turn into first-class blackmailers at this point. However, we lowered our estimate of the ten million for the soirée to seven. Charles seems to think he can get Elton John to perform, and possibly Paul McCartney. I also think Pam said she might be able to get Hootie and the Blowfish if we donate to some education fund they endorse. Maggie Spritzer is going to allude to all that in tomorrow's paper. It's going to be a sellout event. I feel it in my bones. People will be begging to be allowed to attend. I engaged the services of a very fine printing firm for specially engraved invitations, and they will follow through with Pam Lock. I think we're good to go."

The women cheered.

"And while you've been busy doing all that, what have the guys done?" Alexis asked, a devilish glint in her eye as she pointed to Bert, Harry, and Jack.

Bert went first since it looked to him like Alexis directed her question to him. "I have to head back and dismantle the task force. I received a call from Director Cummings on the way here. I'm back to being his number one, but he didn't tell me why. He said he will meet me at six in the morning. We're to have coffee together. He sounded, for want of a better word, stressed. He didn't say I was to dismantle the task force, I'm just assuming that's what he will want me to do. I don't think he knows yet what all went down today. He told me he was going out to see Judge Easter for a late dinner. Which," Bert said, looking down at his watch, "should be getting under way just about now."

"But what about what went down at the Woodley house?" Jack asked.

"I tried calling Mangello, Akers, and Landos. They wouldn't tell me a damn thing. I guess someone convinced them that I'm a mole. At least that's the impression I walked away with. If they know about Erin's being spirited away, they sure as hell are keeping it a secret. I think I played it cool when I told all three of them that Erin recalled me from Chicago but wouldn't tell me why. They said they didn't know anything about it. I couldn't very well ask what went down on Benton Street because I'm not supposed to know. In the morning, when the dark stuff hits the fan, I should have more news to report."

Bert stood up. "Much as I'd like to stay here this evening, I have to get back. I'll call the moment I know something."

"I'll walk you out, Bert," Kathryn said.

Nikki looked over at Myra. "Please tell me Justice Barnes is on board."

"Oh, she's not only on board, she's driving the train," Myra laughed. "She can't wait to get her hands on the COS over at the White House. She told me what she thought of him in no uncertain terms. She called him a . . . Well, what she said was, he was . . . a dickweed. I don't think I ever heard that term before, but I'm sure it's not complimentary." Myra's face turned a rosy hue as she fingered the pearls around her neck.

"Pearl also said the president is an idiot and relies way too much on Daniel Winters. She said Winters was a bigger idiot . . . among other nonflattering names . . . than the president. She said Winters stays at the White House until eleven at night to make sure he doesn't miss anything, so she's calling him this evening. She also told me she has the president's residence phone number. It still has to go through the switchboard, but not too many people have that number, so she seemed confident the operator would put her through if Winters doesn't cooperate."

"Has anyone talked to Lizzie since this afternoon?" Nikki asked. The women shook their heads. "Okay, I'll call her. She needs to be brought up-to-date. We can't afford to leave her out of the loop at this point. Jack, how did it go with Maggie and Judge Easter at lunch?"

"Very well. Maggie's on it. Maggie, in my opinion, finally found her true calling. She'll do everything you want her to do, maybe more. The paper will be so pro–Martine Connor that as long as she gets the nomination, she's a shoo-in come next November. As for Judge Easter, she was a little schizo, but that's who she is. She had *two* double bourbons. She loosened up after that. Not to worry, she'll have Elias Cummings on his knees before she's finished this evening. Trust me on that. Look, it's time for me to go. I should have left when Bert left but . . . I'm still here. I have to be in court to plead a motion at nine. I'll be in the office after that if any of you need me. I'll make some calls on my way back into town and call if I find out anything. Mark Lane might have some news," he said, referring to his old friend from the FBI who was now in private practice but freelanced for the fibbies.

Nikki uncurled herself and stood up. "I'll walk you out."

Harry looked down at Yoko. "I have to leave, too. I have an ambulance I need to make disappear before the night is over."

"Well, ladies, it seems we're all alone," Annie said. "I think we did exceptionally well today. And the best is yet to come. Too bad we don't have something to celebrate with."

"We didn't drink the wine Bert brought. We just drank the beer," Alexis said. "The wine was for the Italian food, and the beer was for the Chinese."

"Who knew?" Annie quipped. "Do the honors, dear, and don't skimp. Fill those glasses to the brim. As for the others," she said, pointing to the door, "you snooze, you lose."

"Yes, ma'am," Alexis said smartly as she headed to the little kitchen to do the honors.

Chapter 20

Elias Cummings walked through the underground garage to where his car was parked. He tried to remember the last time he'd actually driven himself anywhere, but he couldn't come up with a time or a date. He hoped the five-year-old Chrysler would start. More to the point, would there be enough gas in the car to get him to McLean? He tried to remember when he'd last filled the tank. Once again he couldn't come up with a time or a date.

A fine layer of dust was all over the black Chrysler, which told him it had been many moons since he'd driven it. The car chirped twice when he clicked the remote.

He settled himself behind the wheel, turned on the engine, then the windshield washers to clear the grimy windshield. He looked down at the gas gauge and saw that it was one line below full. He was good to go. The only problem was he didn't want to go. What he wanted to do was go home and go to bed. He was sick and tired of the demands, the pressures, the agents. He was just damn sick and tired of everything.

He hadn't wanted the damn job as director of the FBI to begin with. He'd been pressured into taking it on when the vigilantes came down on Mitch Riley. He struggled to remember how many times he'd trooped to the White House, how many times he'd respectfully declined the appointment. Until . . . Well, he wasn't going to think about the *until* part, and if he was lucky, he'd never have to think about it ever again. The *until* part was why he was sitting here right now and why he *was* the director of the FBI.

He'd stepped up to the plate with gusto and done a damn fine job, with one exception: the vigilantes. Cummings could feel his shoulders tense up. The *Post* and every other damn paper in the District, and even the outlying papers, had had a field day with the Bureau's unsuccessful attempts to apprehend the fugitives. Hell, the Bureau had been reduced to a laughingstock worldwide. There was no point in denying it, even to himself. Now, with new ownership at the *Post,* it was a whole new ball game.

Cummings swung the Chrysler out of the

garage, flicked on the GPS, and roared down the street. His thoughts came back, darker and more ominous than before. He really didn't want to think about the call that had come through on his private cell phone at six o'clock on the dot. Most telephone conversations were two-way calls, but this one was meant for him just to listen. He hadn't said a word and when he closed his cell phone, his hand was shaking.

Cummings tried to slouch down in his seat, but his legs were too long. He wanted to close his eyes and recall the words he'd heard. But if he did that, they would be carrying him away in a body bag. Everyone knew you had to keep your eyes on the road in order to get where you were going. Not that he wanted to go there. He didn't.

According to the voice on the phone, tomorrow's paper was going to be devoted to editorials, op-ed pieces, columns, and articles — showing the paper had swung toward Martine Connor as the next nominee of the Democratic Party. And once she got the nomination, the paper would go all-out to get her elected president. Then the voice had given him a direct order: "Find out exactly who the new owner of the paper is. Sift through the mysterious corporations, the equally mysterious holding companies, and get back to me with the results." The call had ended with the voice saying, "You're the fucking FBI, so start acting like it."

It wasn't as if he hadn't tried. He'd had a whole division of agents working on just that the moment the rumor hit the street that the paper was being bought up. He'd even sweated Lizzie Fox, who handled the final sign-off. For all the good it did him. He hated to admit it, but Lizzie Fox was almost as powerful as he was. So were the judges she was on a first-name basis with. On top of that, Lizzie Fox was a sexpot who looked hot as a firecracker, and he just looked like a grizzly old grandfather with watery eyes and two bad hips that needed to be replaced.

His worst nightmare was that somehow, some way, it would come to light that those crazy women owned the paper. He couldn't conceive of how that could possibly be, but in this new world, anything was possible. Especially when it came to the vigilantes. He gritted his teeth as he tried to figure out how it could have been done. It couldn't. It was that simple. He'd been assured by a hundred-plus lawyers that it could never happen. Did he believe those hundred-plus lawyers? Hell no, he didn't. The minute he knew Lizzie Fox was involved, he'd tossed in the towel.

It suddenly dawned on Cummings that he was sitting in bumper-to-bumper traffic. How the hell did that happen? He didn't stop to think about it, simply reached over for the magnetic flashing strobe, powered down the window, reached out, and stuck the flashing light on the roof of the Chrysler. A second later he activated the device, and it shrilled with the shriek of the siren. He inched his way out of the traffic and roared down the road, his hand on the horn for good measure. He was finally able to slow down once he passed what looked like a rear-end accident. He didn't see an ambulance. A group of people were standing next to three state troopers gesturing wildly, no doubt each blaming the other. To his practiced eye it looked like, aside from the traffic pileup, the troopers had the situation in hand.

Still, Cummings kept the strobe flashing and siren wailing until he got to the turnoff that led to Nellie's farm. He wondered, and not for the first time, how a federal judge managed to afford such a luxurious spread in McLean, where the prices were over the moon.

He drove up the long road that had to be at

least a mile and a half before he came to the stout iron security gates. Nellie had done all right for herself. As long as you didn't count losing a daughter in a terrible car accident. And yet, somehow, she'd managed to survive that mortal blow and go on. Just like Myra Rutledge had gone on after losing her daughter. Nellie had been a damn fine judge and had proven to be a good friend to his now-deceased wife and him over the years. He owed her, it was that simple.

He knew, just knew, Nellie Easter was involved in the mess confronting him, and he also knew there wasn't a damn thing he could do about it. He could threaten till he turned blue, and she'd never admit to anything but her name and possibly her Social Security number.

The big question facing him was why she had invited him out to the farm for dinner. Now that he thought about the phone conversation he'd had with her earlier, it hadn't been so much an invitation but an order. Where the hell did she get off ordering him around? The fact that he'd accepted and was now just feet from her front door made him wonder why all the more. For a home-cooked meal? He hadn't had one of those in months and months. A couple of stiff bourbons? Playtime with all her cats? *What am I doing here? Well, I'll find out soon enough,* he thought, as he climbed out of the car and headed up to the wide front porch.

The lights were on, even the spotlights at all the corners of the big farmhouse. A bale of hay with a stuffed scarecrow sat underneath the porch light. Pumpkins, all sizes, were lined up, along with pots and pots of colorful fall flowers. His wife used to do the same thing, God rest her soul. Even when the children went off to college, then married, she'd continued to decorate the porch for every single holiday because they *might* come home. They rarely did because they were too busy with their own lives. He wondered what his wife would have thought if she'd known their two sons hadn't made it home for her funeral. They came afterward, and he'd asked them why they had bothered. Ever since, they'd been estranged. His daughters were no better. They'd left right after the service, saying they had things to do. He just stood alone and shook his head. Ungrateful bunch of shits was his final assessment of his children.

They called on Father's Day and, if he was lucky, maybe Christmas. He never called them, it was too painful to be told by whoever answered the phone that they weren't there or couldn't come to the phone.

A year ago he'd changed his will and left his sizable portfolio, his house, everything else he owned, thanks to his wife's expert management, to the hospice that took care of her at the end.

He thought about the day he'd marched his ass into Lizzie Fox's office and told her what he wanted her to do. When she'd looked at him with tears in her eyes and asked him why he was doing what he was doing, he'd said, "Just call me a wild and crazy guy, and let it go at that." Then he did something even wilder and crazier when he appointed Lizzie Fox executrix of his estate. He'd walked away from her office with lighter shoulders knowing that his four children would never go up against Lizzie Fox.

Lizzie was up to her eyeballs in this mess, as he referred to it, just the way Nellie was.

Cummings banged on the door a moment after he spotted the doorbell. Normally, when he came out, he drove around to the back and entered through the kitchen. He took a moment to wonder why he'd come to the front door instead.

The door opened. "I have a doorbell, Elias. My cats are used to the doorbell. When you banged on the door, you scared them half to death. And, you're late. My roast chicken is going to be all dried out, and you're going to complain. Well, come in. Why are you still standing out there?" she asked briskly.

"I was admiring your décor and reminiscing. Marian always used to do up our porch like this. We're getting old, Nellie. Do you remember the trick-or-treaters and how much fun it was on Halloween night?"

"I remember," Nellie said with a catch in her voice. "It was a lifetime ago. I don't think this is the time for either one of us to stroll down Memory Lane."

"You're right. Do you want to tell me why I'm here, or should we wait till after we eat the dried-out chicken?"

"I lied. The chicken isn't dried out. I knew you'd be late because you're always late, so I put the chicken in an hour later. Come along now. I have your drink all ready."

It was a pleasant kitchen, almost like his own when Marian was still alive. She'd change the color scheme every so often. It was homey and cozy. He'd always liked eating in the kitchen. For some reason he now felt calm, relaxed, as he waited for whatever shoe Nellie was going to drop.

"Does anyone know you came out here, Elias?" Nellie asked coolly, looking him straight in the eye.

"No, Nellie, no one knows. I gave my driver the evening off. He's going to come back to the Bureau at midnight to pick me up and take me home. I told him I had to work late on something important. Why am I here, Nellie? Off the record, okay?"

Nellie casually stuck her hand in her pocket to bring out her cigarettes and lighter before she turned the miniature cassette player to the ON position. She offered her guest a cigarette that he refused. She lit up and puffed away.

"You really need to give those things up, Nellie."

"I'm working on it, Elias. One of these days. We should make small talk now. Tell me how life is treating you. How did all those clowns you have working at the Bureau fare over Halloween?"

Elias bristled. "That was very unkind, Nellie, and so unworthy of you."

"You think?"

Nellie got up and started to put the warming dishes on the table. She'd carved the chicken right before Elias arrived. In some ways it was like a Thanksgiving dinner, with all the same vegetables and stuffing. "Just eat, Elias. Tell me how good it is, and we'll go from there. I can even make up a plate for you when you leave. We're also having pie, but I didn't make it. There's this lovely lady who lives in Kalorama who makes the most delectable pies in the whole world. Today I was one of the grateful recipients," Nellie lied with a straight face. There was no need for Elias to know that she'd picked up the pie from a Safeway bakery in town earlier in the day. "I'm sure you know her, perhaps not personally, but I'm sure you've heard of her, Paula Woodley, she's the wife of the former national security advisor."

The fork halfway to his mouth, Elias stared across the table at his old friend, who was chewing contentedly and slipping slivers of chicken to the cats lined up at her feet. He forked the stuffing into his mouth, chewed, swallowed, and said, "This is every bit as good as Marian's recipe. If you have something to say to me, Nellie, say it. I hate this dancing around things. I know what went on out there today. Why does it not surprise me that you know? Let's hear it. I really am capable of eating, thinking, and talking at the same time. It's called multitasking. I'd really like to know how you know what went down at the Woodley home?"

"Talking while you eat is not good for the digestion," Nellie snapped. "I just know things," she added as an afterthought.

"Then be so kind as to tell me what else you know before I haul your butt back to town."

"That's an idle threat, and you know it, Elias. Shame on you for even saying it. I know that Erin Powell was your mole and not Bert Navarro. I know that you set her up to fail. I know she sent a handwritten letter to your office saying exactly what I just told you before she skedaddled to parts unknown. That's another way of saying she was undercover for the vigilantes."

This was the shoe that dropped. Nellie's bomb. Elias stopped eating. Suddenly he felt sick to his stomach. "And you know this . . . how?"

Nellie waved her arms around. "I just know things," she said again vaguely.

Elias finished off his bourbon, then looked surprised when he saw that the glass was empty. He got up to refill it, and he didn't stint. He looked down at Nellie's glass, and she nodded. "Tell me what else you know."

"No. You tell me what you know. I went

first. Don't even think about lying to me, Elias."

"You're one of *them,* aren't you?" Elias asked. It was a statement of fact, not really a question.

Nellie surprised herself when she said, "Yes, Elias, I am. The only reason I'm telling you this is because I know those bastards on the hill have you by the short hairs. They're blackmailing you. Don't deny it. I saw Riley's dossier on you. If it's any consolation to you, I would have done the same thing you did and let the Devil take my soul for doing it. Now, it really is your turn. By the way, I know all about that weasel Winters."

Elias looked at the food on his plate. He moved the fork through it several times, stirring it this way and that way before he answered. "That weasel, as you call him, Dan Winters, called me one day recently and asked me to come alone to the White House. It wasn't really a request but an order. So I went. Alone. I didn't tell anyone where I was going but somehow it leaked out. Not that it was important at the time. I go to the White House on a regular basis, but Navarro is always with me. When they told me he was the mole that was helping the vigilantes, I lost it. I didn't want to believe it, but they had all this . . . evidence. Winters is the one who wanted me to set up the task force to trap him. He said the vigilantes would come to his rescue. Winters cooked up this scheme with Baron Russell about the donor lists being stolen, the Connor campaign's, too, and how all those rich donors were screaming for blood.

"He said the Bureau couldn't take any more bashing or black eyes because it was reflecting badly on the administration. That part was true enough. Then he said he had a way to get the vigilantes back in town. I'm not wise in the ways of message boards and blogs and all that computer stuff. I let my people handle that. Anyway, they, and when I say *they,* I mean the White House, sent out feelers to see if the women would take the bait. Look, I'm not sure the president knew about this. I did ask but didn't get an answer."

"What was the bait, Elias?" Nellie asked coldly.

"A presidential pardon. They didn't bite on it, Nellie. Even I knew they were too smart for that, but Winters is your typical power-hungry asshole. With everything going on in the world, the administration's polling numbers are in the toilet. Donations have dried up. The country was about to turn to the Democrats, and Martine Connor seemed the likely candidate. It wasn't pretty for Winters or his boss. They did their best to dig into Connor's background, but she's so squeaky clean it was a disaster. So they had to make up something to destroy her credibility. Who better than the vigilantes to help their cause? The one thing they didn't count on was Lizzie Fox and her impressive Rolodex. That set them back, I can tell you that. Then they made Lizzie mad, and you know what happens when Lizzie gets her knickers in a knot.

"At that point they still didn't have any confirmation from the vigilantes because the women wanted to see proof and a guarantee about the pardon, and Winters couldn't come up with that. They ordered me, through Erin Powell, to sweat you all. For all the good it did us. That didn't work, either. Then Winters hauled out my file and hit me between the eyes. He said he was going to go public with what was in the file unless I went along with what he wanted. You're right, Nellie, he had me by the short hairs. Either way, my ass was fried. Tell me, how did you get Powell to take the hit?"

Nellie shrugged. "It's a woman thing, something you wouldn't understand. In case you're worried about what you all tried to do to her, don't be. She's got the world by the tail now. You'll never see or hear from her again."

"And the Woodleys?"

"You'll never see or hear from them again, either. Elias, you really have to get over the idea that this is a Mickey Mouse operation. Everyone is happy, happy, happy." Nellie fired up another cigarette she didn't want or need, but it was something to do with her hands, and stared through a plume of smoke at her dinner guest.

"Was it just the polling numbers or is there more to it?" Nellie asked as she watched a perfect smoke ring sail upward.

"Winters likes the power. He wants four more years. And, he doesn't want a few things to become known, which could very well happen if the Dems unseat them. If Connor gets in, Nellie, she's going to make a fine president. I know Marian would have voted for her. I will, too, if I'm not in jail. Look, that's all I know. What is it you want from me, Nellie? You already have my silence. I never ratted you out, even though I knew and have known for quite some time that you've aided and abetted the vigilantes, just like I know about all the others — Lizzie Fox, Emery, Wong, and, yes, Bert. For Christ's sake, Nellie, I'm the director of the Goddamn FBI. I'm supposed to know these things. What I do with what I know is something else entirely.

"You know what, Nellie, I'm tired, so I'm going to go home and try to get some sleep before the world caves in on me. I'm sorry I didn't do justice to your dinner."

Nellie got up and walked her guest to the door. "I'm going to need your help very shortly, Elias. Tell me I can count on you. We might be able to make this work for you and for the vigilantes. I want your word."

"For whatever it's worth, Nellie, you have it." Elias reached down and wrapped Nellie in his arms. "Would you really have done the same thing?"

"In a New York minute. You want that pie to take home with you?" Nellie asked to lighten the moment.

"No, but thanks for asking. Where'd you buy it?"

Nellie laughed. "Safeway bakery."

Nellie could hear the director chuckling all the way to his car.

Chapter 21

The Sisters watched Myra as she did a little jig the moment she clicked off her cell phone. They waited impatiently as she called Charles to report in before she said, "Nellie did it! She stepped up to the plate and by the time the director left, she had him eating out of her hand. Nellie was . . . She was . . . *giddy.* Cummings is on our side, girls. I don't think it gets any better than that."

"That's not wishful thinking on Nellie's part, is it Myra?" Kathryn asked, suspicion ringing in her voice.

"No, dear, it's not. Elias is from the old school and a dear friend to Nellie. But he's also director of the FBI. He doesn't like the capital's politics any better than we do. It goes without saying he will protect the institution at all costs, but he will close his eyes to . . . certain things. At least for now. I think I recall Nellie telling me a while ago that he would be retiring next year. Shortly after the election, if I'm not mistaken."

"Just tell me Bert's safe," Kathryn said.

"As safe as if he was in his mother's womb, dear." Myra smiled.

Kathryn grinned from ear to ear. The others smiled indulgently.

"What did Charles say, Myra?" Nikki asked.

"Actually, dear, he's said quite a bit. We've kept him hopping with all our moves, then Erin's departure, not to mention the Woodleys. He's very happy that Nellie was able to, as he put it, pull our buns out of the fire. Right now it seems that messages are coming in by the dozen on that . . . that board or blog or whatever it is. He said he now has confirmation on something called the IP about who the person is. It's just who he thought it was, Daniel Winters, the president's chief of staff. We now know his agenda, thanks to Nellie and the information she got out of Elias Cummings. Winters, who still thinks he's anonymous, wants a meeting with the vigilantes. An eyeball-to-eyeball meeting before he commits to the pardon. If we were stupid enough to agree to something like that, that's when he would have Cummings and all his agents swoop in and arrest us. That isn't going to happen,"

Myra said.

"As we sit here talking, Justice Barnes is on the phone with Winters trying to set up a private meeting with him and Baron Russell. I think it goes without saying that Pearl will do everything in her power to make it happen. It will be her way of thanking us for getting her out of that sticky mess she found herself in a while back. She said she misses Maggie and Lizzie but understands that her way of life is not for them. They were invaluable to her when she made the transition from the Supreme Court to . . . uh . . . to shoring up her underground railroad to save women and children.

"She promised to call, no matter the hour and no matter the outcome. She can be very persuasive, and she is extremely well connected in town. I'm certain Winters will agree to meet with her. Pearl can be every bit as tenacious as Nellie when she puts her mind to it."

Nikki's cell phone rang. She looked down at the name appearing on the small screen. Maggie Spritzer. As Nikki listened, she motioned to the others to power up their laptops. She hung up a moment later. "The *Post* is online now. The paper was just put to bed a little while ago. Maggie said she wants a gold star and to please let her know

Martine Connor's reaction."

Nikki booted up her own laptop and started to read. She smiled, she grinned, she laughed out loud, as did the others who were reading over her shoulder. Finally, she sat back and hugged her knees as she looked around at the Sisters. "Tell a woman what to do, and she damn well does it. Think about what we did today, girls. Nellie reeled in Director Cummings. Pearl Barnes is going to give us Daniel Winters and Baron Russell on a gold plate. Maggie and the *Post* just endorsed the woman who is going to be the most powerful woman in the land. Lizzie Fox is our secret weapon. Do you see one single man in this scenario? No, you do not. I'm not discounting Jack, Harry, or Bert. But *they* didn't make this happen. Even Charles didn't make it happen. *We* made it happen. Us. Women."

"And we take no prisoners," Annie shouted as she smacked her hands together and whooped with pleasure at what they'd accomplished.

Nikki looked over at Kathryn, who was laughing as hard as she was.

"You're thinking about the punishment we're going to visit on those men, aren't you?" Myra asked as she joined in the laughter.

"You know it," Kathryn said.

"I think we need to start planning our departure, girls," Myra said. "Charles said he would get back to us by first light. It's late now, so I think this might be a good time to call it a night so we can be up and ready to leave on a moment's notice. Our new vehicles will be arriving sometime soon, but we don't have to worry about that. If Pearl calls, I'll hear it, since I'm a light sleeper. Then I'll wake you all up."

The girls headed for the loft of the cabin while Annie and Myra stayed to tidy up and pack everything into their cases and the boxes.

They chatted quietly so their voices wouldn't carry to the loft overhead.

"A lot can happen in a six-hour ride, Annie. I admit I'm a bit jittery."

"Don't be. Bert, Jack, and Harry have our backs. Think about it, Myra, we're going to be doing this right under the noses of the CIA. Look, Charles sent us a map of the terrain, we rehearsed, right down to the last nanosecond. I know, I know, what can go wrong will go wrong, but the guys will be there, too. Great Dismal Swamp, here we come," Annie said.

"Charles is the one who came up with the location, so I guess . . . Sometimes I think he is more daring than we are. He said the CIA used to do all their advance paramilitary operations there. They call it The Point. We have to trust him that even though the CIA is there, practically in our faces, that it's the way to go. He said Winters won't think twice about meeting us there and will be able to convince Russell to go along with it."

"Harry and Bert are going to be tailing Pearl, so if it turns out to be a setup, they'll spot it, and we abort and go on to Plan B," Myra said. "Timing is going to be everything." Myra looked around the cabin. Everything was neat and tidy, all their gear piled up by the front door.

Annie sat down on the sofa, leaned back, and closed her eyes. "The nights are the worst, aren't they, Myra?"

Myra joined Annie on the sofa. "Yes, dear, the nights are the worst. When the girls were little, you listened to their prayers, all those God blesses, then you tucked them in and thanked God for another good day. As they got older you sat up and waited until they came home. Motherhood is such a joy and such a challenge. I'm sad, Annie, that our girls are past the childbearing stage. Well, they aren't, really, women have babies today when they're over forty, but I don't know if that's going to happen to our chicks."

"C'mon, Mom, don't be sad."

Myra and Annie both bolted upright. Annie looked around, her eyes wider than a Frisbee. "Myra, did you just hear that?"

Myra smiled. "Hello, darling girl! I'm not sad. Well, I am a little. Is everything all right? Are you here to tell me . . . something?"

"Yes and no. I brought someone with me tonight. Aunt Annie . . . Elena is here."

Annie looked wild when she whirled and twirled, her gaze sweeping the room to find where the voices were coming from.

"Mom, it's me, Elena."

"Oh, dear God!" was all Annie could say. "Am I dreaming? Myra, do you . . . Where . . . is your brother . . . your father . . . ?"

"Everyone is fine, Mom. Daddy said to tell you he's proud of you. Jonathan said mothers can do anything. He said he remembers you telling him that a thousand times."

Myra moved off, hoping Barbara would continue to converse with her while allowing for Annie to talk to her own spirit daughter. "Darling girl, is this going to work out all right?"

"Mom, you have to stop worrying so much. I'll be right there with you tomorrow. Stay alert

and do your share." A tinkling laugh erupted and seemed to ricochet around the room. *"How does it feel being a Democrat?"*

In spite of herself, Myra laughed. "Don't tell anyone."

"Your secret is safe with me. Gotta go, Mom. I want to say good night to Nikki."

Myra nodded as she wiped the tears from her eyes.

In the loft, the Sisters stood at the railing as they tried to figure out what was going on down below. Nikki winked. "Someone stopped in to say good night and to ease a few doubts. That's all." She turned, and whispered, "Thanks, Barb."

"No problem. Be careful, Nik. Those guys have a lot at stake. My money is on you, though."

Nikki smiled as her hand batted the air, her way of signing off with her spirit sister.

Down below, Annie fell back onto the sofa, her breathing ragged. "Tell me that wasn't a dream, Myra. Tell me we . . . talked to our spirit daughters."

"We did, Annie. Shhh. We don't talk about it afterward. Elena will come to you now that she's broken through. But, only when you need her the most. That's usually how it works. At first I was just like you are now. I thought I was crazy. Then I switched up to believing that I was dreaming because I needed . . . Oh, God, I needed her so badly. I guess . . . I want to believe she knew that and came to me. We don't ever have to talk about it again, Annie, if that will make you feel better. It's such a deep, personal thing, I like to go off by myself to just think about it. I feel better for weeks after a little chat with my darling daughter."

Annie struggled for words. "I don't want to talk about this right now. Perhaps later. Elena said my husband is proud of me. Oh, God, Myra, I am so . . . I don't know what I am right now."

"Let's go with happy and go to sleep. I'll take the recliner, and you stretch out there on the sofa. Sweet dreams, Annie." Myra looked over at her old friend, but she was already asleep. She sighed as she stretched out on the recliner and closed her eyes. "Thank you, God, for what you just did for Annie and me." A second later, she, too, was asleep.

Retired Supreme Court Justice Pearl Barnes dressed carefully for her early-morning breakfast meeting. She wore a copper-colored Vera Wang suit. Lustrous pearls, much like the kind Myra Rutledge wore, adorned her neck, with matching pearl studs in her ears. At the last second she'd slipped on several magnificent diamond rings. She carried a Prada purse that held more junk than her kitchen drawer did, but it was junk she was never without. She teetered a bit on her heels, but once she got the hang of them, she was okay. These days she didn't get dressed up very often and had given up heels for Birkenstocks.

Pearl looked down at her watch. The sun would be up in another hour. If she left for the District, she could make it in forty-five minutes. She smiled, but it wasn't a smile that reached her eyes. Actually, it was a grim, angry smile, if there was such a thing.

She marched out to the powerful black Hummer that sat in her driveway. She loved the vehicle, and it was perfect for transporting people to places they weren't supposed to be. She particularly loved the blackened windows. By driving it, she was making a statement, and it had all been Lizzie Fox's suggestion.

She'd called Daniel Winters at two minutes past five, the moment she finished dressing. He'd answered on the first ring. She'd stated her business quickly and concisely, ending with, "I'll be in the back booth at the Hound and Hare at six thirty, I will wait exactly five minutes, not one minute longer. I owe it to the president to pass along what I know." This last was said so virtuously, Pearl felt herself cringe at the lie she was telling. "If you aren't there, I will leave, and you'll regret missing out on the information I have for you concerning the vigilantes. I'll go to the *Post* instead."

As Pearl tooled along in the Hummer, her thoughts were all over the map. While she was clear on her part and what she was to do, she had no idea how or where Baron Russell was going to come into play. Myra and Annie had said she wasn't to worry. How could she not worry? While she'd been fooling people for a good many years and covering her tracks while working at being an associate justice on the United States Supreme Court, somehow it didn't compare to what she was about to do.

Back then, it had been her own skin she'd had to protect. This was another can of worms — one that she had almost no control over. All she could do was her best, and if that wasn't good enough, then the vigilantes would have to step up to the plate and take over. She started to talk to herself to ease the stress building between her shoulders. "I can do this. I can do this. I can really do this. I have to do this. If I don't do this, terrible things are going to happen.

I *can* do this."

Pearl sucked in her breath. She didn't feel one damn bit better. Her foot pressed down on the accelerator, and the Hummer plowed forward.

The sky was just growing light on the horizon when Pearl parked the Hummer, taking up two parking spaces. She dropped money in both meters to cover herself. Her government license plate should do the rest in case an aggressive traffic cop decided to ticket her.

The early bird gets the worm, Pearl told herself as she yanked at the door and walked into the Hound and Hare. When she was sitting on the bench, she'd been a regular here. Twice a week she'd have breakfast with Nellie or other judges to talk over legal matters or just to shoot the breeze. She wished she was here to have a shoot-the-breeze breakfast with Nellie. She wished it so bad she wanted to cry.

She was greeted warmly by the staff and shown to her favorite table. A cup of coffee appeared as if by magic. Then a crystal decanter of freshly squeezed orange juice was set in the middle of the table, along with a covered basket of warm croissants. A perky waitress rushed up to Pearl's table and poured the juice into a small goblet.

Pearl drained it in one long swallow. The waitress poured a second glass. Pearl was sipping it when Daniel Winters waltzed through the door with a minute to spare. He strode purposely to the table, made a point of looking at his watch. Pearl looked down at her own Patek Phillippe and nodded, her features cold and controlled. "Sit," she said.

Winters frowned but did as he was told.

Daniel Winters wasn't a good-looking man. He wasn't ugly or homely, either. He was just ordinary, with the bad combover that so many Washington men favored. He wore glasses that did nothing for his appearance. He was weak-jawed, thin, but not in any way athletic. His complexion was ruddy, his nose pink. *A drinker,* Pearl thought to herself. He was dressed in a charcoal-colored suit, power tie, and gleaming white shirt. His clothing wasn't custom-made. Nor was it of designer quality, but he still looked put together. His wing tips were spit shined. She was reminded again of how ordinary-looking he was despite being so power-hungry. Everyone in the District knew about the man's ambitions.

Pearl watched Daniel Winters's manicured nails as he poured his own juice and snapped his fingers for coffee. She smiled inwardly. The staff, well-known for anticipating its guests' needs, did not respond well to snapped fingers. Pearl knew she would be done with her coffee before Winters even got close to getting his. She could do this. She would do it. She owed Myra and the others her very life, so she would do what she had to do.

Since she was the one who'd issued the invitation, it was up to her to initiate the conversation and pick up the check. She didn't bother clearing her throat or thinking twice. Instead she reached into her handbag and withdrew a folded envelope that held a single piece of paper inside. "I received this in my mailbox yesterday. At first I thought it was a trick of some kind or just a random . . . thing. But the more I thought about it, the more I realized it was probably real because of my friendship with Myra Rutledge and Anna de Silva even though we haven't seen each other in over twenty-five years." Pearl wondered when she'd become such an accomplished liar.

"Whoever sent this . . . this letter must be under the impression I am in contact with those women. Now, what do you want me to do? The letter specifically says they will contact me promptly at seven o'clock. That's eight minutes from now. I have no idea how they would know my private cell phone number, since it was issued to me by the Court, and I can count on one hand the number of people who have the number."

The dapper man sitting across from Pearl withdrew the letter from the envelope and read it slowly.

Pearl watched as Winters read the letter. She came to the conclusion he must be a poker player because there was no expression on his face as he read slowly, line by line, as though he was committing to memory the letter signed by the vigilantes.

Winters folded the letter with one hand and picked up his coffee cup with his other hand. When he saw the cup was still empty, his expression changed, reflecting his anger. He snapped his fingers, then snapped them a second time. None of the waitstaff paid him the slightest attention.

"And how did you come by this . . . this . . . letter?"

"It was in my mailbox," Pearl said. "I told you that."

"Why?" Winters asked. He looked down at his coffee cup again and saw that it was still empty. This time he turned around and shouted. "I'd like some coffee here."

Pearl decided the man was rattled. The first thing a lawyer learns in law school is you never ask a question if you don't know the answer. Winters was a lawyer and should have known better.

"I asked myself the same question aside from the obvious. I was just the means to be sure this letter was hand-delivered. I did that. Now, I'm to wait for a phone call. I think you're the one who should be answering questions, not me. You're the president's chief of staff, Baron Russell is the GOP's top fund-raiser. Why do the vigilantes want to meet with you two men? It goes without saying you're free to leave if you don't want to stay for the phone call." Pearl finished the coffee in her cup. An attentive waiter refilled her cup immediately.

The waiter was about to move off when Winters reached up and grabbed his arm. "I've been sitting here for ten Goddamn minutes. I'd like some coffee, please."

The waiter raised his eyebrows and pointed to the pot in his hand. "I'm sorry, sir, but I have to get a fresh pot."

Pearl took a deep breath so she wouldn't burst out laughing at the expression on Winters's face.

"Well?" Pearl asked.

"I'm not at liberty to discuss presidential business with you, Justice Barnes."

Somehow or other Pearl managed to act

surprised. "Are you saying the vigilantes are *presidential* business?"

Winters looked confused for a second. "No, that's not what I'm saying. Yes, it sounded like that, but what I meant was I cannot discuss anything pertaining to the White House. I work there. Anything I do or say reflects on the White House."

"That's political speak, Mr. Winters. Why did you even bother to take my phone call and agree to meet me if this has nothing to do with you or your . . . employers? You could have just told me to go paddle my canoe in some other lake. You're here." She leaned back and sipped at her delicious coffee. She risked a glance at her watch. Not enough time had gone by. How much longer could she keep this up? Maybe her watch was running slow. Or else this was the longest eight minutes of her life.

Winters's mind raced. He felt a small flurry of panic as he, too, waited for the phone call to come through. How did those stupid women know he was the one who wanted to hire them? Maybe they weren't that stupid after all. He never should have agreed to this meeting. When he got hold of Cummings, he was personally going to strangle him — very slowly. Everyone in the damn town knew the FBI leaked like a sieve. Now he had a bad feeling. He was about to get up to leave when Justice Barnes's phone chirped. Pearl looked at it, and so did Winters. It looked to her like Winters was going to snatch it, but she beat him to it. She picked it up, flipped it open, and said, "Pearl Barnes."

The voice on the other end was clipped and professional sounding. "If you would be so kind, Justice Barnes, please put your guest on the phone." It was Nikki Quinn, she recognized her voice. Pearl handed over the phone to her breakfast companion.

Winters looked like the phone was a snake poised to strike, but he reached for it and brought it to his ear. Even though the heat was on in the restaurant, Winters shivered when the voice on the other end of the line spoke. "Do you have the pardons in hand, Mr. Winters? That was really a foolish question on my part. But, I did want to give you the benefit of the doubt, knowing you were lying all along. There was no donor identity theft. We both know that. What am I going to do with you, Mr. Winters?" the voice asked playfully.

"What's this all about? You're fugitives, and I shouldn't even be talking to you. In fact, I'm going to call the FBI right now. They'll be able to trace this call."

"You think?" the voice teased.

Winters's blood ran cold. He forced himself to say, "Yes, I think they can."

The playful voice erupted in laughter. "It's not nice to fool with the vigilantes, Mr. Winters. We have long memories, and we have a . . . history. Shame on you!"

Out of the corner of his eye, Winters saw a tall man bearing down on his table. He looked up, stunned to see Elias Cummings. Cummings, a phone to his own ear got as close to Winters as he could, and whispered, "Keep her talking, we have a fix on the location."

The relief on Winters's face was just short of comical as he blustered on about not knowing what Nikki was talking about.

Pearl thought it might be a good time to take a trip to the ladies' room. After all, she'd had two cups of coffee and obviously was not adding anything to the situation. On her way to the restroom she passed a handsome man she recognized — Baron Russell. She smiled to herself.

"End of the road, gentlemen," she said, as the door to the restroom closed behind her. She knew that when she returned to the table, all three men would be gone. Within a matter of hours Winters and Russell would be in the vigilantes' clutches.

CHAPTER 22

Outside the Hound and Hare, Cummings ushered Winters and Russell to a dark sedan double-parked at the curb. Winters looked at the sedan, then at Cummings. "What? I can't go with you. I have to get back to the White House. Take Russell with you. I told you, Cummings, I can't be implicated. What part of that didn't you understand?"

"The part where the vigilantes told you to be there. There's someone close by, I can guarantee it, who is watching us right this minute. If you don't get in this damn car right now, you'll never make it to the White House. Make up your mind."

Winters looked around, his breathing ragged. "Where are your people?"

"You don't need to know that. We're covered. You said you wanted to be in at the kill. The only way that's going to happen is if you get in the car. Being as important as you are at the White House, I'm sure you can delegate what has to be done for the day. This will get global coverage. Your picture will be seen around the world. Who knows what the future holds for you once that happens. The same thing goes for Mr. Russell here. We're wasting time, gentlemen."

The RNC fund-raiser and Winters looked at each other. Russell glared at Winters and whipped out a copy of the *Post* he'd been carrying under his arm. He shook it open and said, "Read it and weep. Get in the car, Daniel. You promised me a rose garden, and I damn well want to pick a few blooms. Even I can see there are no options here," he declared, pointing to the paper in his hands.

"But . . . POTUS . . ." Winters said, referring to the president of the United States.

The immaculately pressed and creased Russell fought to protect his blow-dried hair as the icy November wind whipped across the street. Around his ankles, he could feel warm air seeping out from the open car door. The bone-chilling cold was almost as lethal as his voice when he said, "Screw POTUS." To prove his point, he gave Winters a shove, and the chief of staff sprawled facedown across the backseat. Russell slammed the door and climbed into the front seat next to Cummings.

Elias Cummings looked into the rearview mirror and liked what he saw, the frightened face of the disheveled chief of staff, who was struggling to get his cell phone out of his pocket, skim the morning paper, and straighten his tie all at once. He hadn't even buckled up.

As the FBI sedan roared down Connecticut Avenue, Winters finally managed to get his seat belt fastened and talk to someone on the other end of the line at the same time. None of it sounded important to Cummings. The presidential pardon for a turkey, a group of seniors who were protesting something concerning Medicare that had already been settled and just wanted a photo op with POTUS. He listened as Winters mumbled something about an energy file that had gone missing and to get the damn fax machine fixed. Just another important day in the White House. Cummings smirked to himself as he raced out of the city.

"Where the hell are we going, Elias? What time will we be back? I have a dinner engagement with some very important people. I cannot cancel it, the president is expecting me to be there."

"In that case you better call in your regrets

now. There's no way you're going to be back in time." *In fact, you pip-squeak, you're not coming back at all.* "But to answer your question, we're going to Dismal Swamp in North Carolina. Six hours going, six hours for the return, if we're lucky, and my foot holds out, plus time for whatever happens in between: traffic, bottle-necks, a little road rage, photo ops, interviews, the whole ball of wax. It's what you told me to do, Daniel. I'm doing it, so shut up and enjoy the ride. That goes for you, too, Russell. I drive better without conversation."

"Dismal Swamp! North Carolina!" Winters sputtered. "Why the hell are we going to a swamp in North Carolina?"

"You are a dipshit, Daniel. The vigilantes are in North Carolina. But then so is Harvey Point. It's near Elizabeth City. You know, the CIA uses The Point these days as an advanced training center for its operatives. Don't tell me you expected those women to come up to you at the Hound and Hare and beg you to arrest them. They want to see you and me sweat. I'm sweating, and you're a damn fool if you aren't drenched in your own juice right now."

"Wait just a Goddamn minute, Elias. The deal was your agents were going to swoop in and make the arrest. I'm just on the sidelines."

Cummings thought about Winters's words for a few minutes. He sounded like he was discussing the menu at a less-than-upscale restaurant when he spoke. "I suppose it could turn out that way. Unlikely, but a possibility. I'm thinking those women want something more . . . up close and personal where you and Russell are concerned."

Russell finally opened his mouth. "I don't think I like the way this all sounds. Dismal Swamp? I know I've heard of it. The CIA? The vigilantes! Something isn't working for me right now."

Cummings was enjoying himself. "Let me guess, you thought the way Winters thought — that this was going to be a walk in the park. It's not. We're dealing with seven very, very savvy women who have a hate on for you like no other. They don't like me much, either, but that's beside the point right now. You're their focus. I'm just here to round them up and cart them off to a federal prison."

"How . . . how many agents do you have assigned to this takedown?" Russell demanded. His voice sounded so jittery it was all Cummings could do not to laugh out loud.

"Twelve," Cummings said succinctly.

"Twelve? You need a hundred and twelve to take on those women. Twelve! How stupid is that?"

Cummings tilted his head to the side. "So, okay, I make thirteen. I know that's an unlucky number, but you go with what you've got. If you don't like that number, go with fifteen and include yourselves. You might have to get down and dirty. Your call, gentlemen. Remember now, this whole mess was your idea to begin with. You made a promise to those women, and you done them dirty. Now, both of you shut up and let me pay attention to the road."

Two hours later, Cummings spoke. "I think we've picked up a tail. Don't be so damn obvious and stare. Just trust me. I told you this would happen. Those women have their eyes on us and have been watching us since we were all at the Hound and Hare."

"Well, then, do something for Chrissakes," Winters sputtered. "Stop the car, pull them over, and arrest them."

"On what charge? This isn't a game, Winters. They're driving on a road, so are we. For all I know they could be headed for the same place we are and end up claiming to be lookie-loos. There's no probable cause here."

"You just said a car was following us," Russell squealed as he envisioned a shoot-out on I-95 and his dead body going back to the District in a black body bag with a zipper down the front. His face was ashen.

"What I said, Mr. Russell, was, I thought we picked up a tail. Do I know that for a fact? No, I do not, and I'm not going to risk a possible lawsuit to make you two happy. Just sit there and be quiet, and the first one who turns around to look at the car behind us is going to get tossed into the swamp when we get there. Are we clear on what I just said?"

Both men looked like they were rooted to their seats, prompting Cummings to mumble something about being spared from people whose brains were in their asses.

Two cars behind the FBI sedan, a black Chevy Suburban kept pace. Bert Navarro, Jack Emery, and Harry Wong were dressed in camouflage outfits. Their footwear was referred to as swamp boots.

"Who the hell thinks up this crap?" Harry asked, referring to the boots that adorned his normally sandaled feet.

"Some stupid advertising agency, for big bucks," Bert volunteered.

"You're both whining," Jack said. "I'm not feeling any love here. We need warm and fuzzy before we go into battle."

"Screw you, Jack," Harry shot back. "I don't like swamps. I hate the slimy things that live in them. What the hell are they thinking?" he asked, referring to the Sisters. "We're going right into the CIA's nest. That's making me a tad nervous."

It was making Jack nervous, too, but he wouldn't admit it. Bert just looked openly worried. He wished he could think of something witty to say, but nothing came to mind. He concentrated on watching the road.

"A sing-along might be good right now," Bert chimed in.

"Is that what you FBI guys do when crunch time comes?" Harry snorted to show what he thought about *that.*

Bert Navarro had excelled at the FBI Academy in the endurance and defensive driving course. He was driving the black SUV with the blackened windows that Charles had somehow commandeered from the Secret Service. What that meant was it was not your normal SUV — more horsepower, bulletproof, with special weapons built into the sides of the doors. Harry had turned white when he saw the rocket launcher in the back cargo hold. Even Bert and Jack had a bad moment. It was Bert who had the temerity to ask if any of them knew how to work it. He'd shrugged and climbed into the driver's seat. Grenades — now those with pins intact, would have given him a problem.

"What the hell are we waiting for?" Jack asked an hour later.

"For a break in traffic," Bert said. "I thought I was calling the shots on this one."

"You are. You are. We're still two hours out. We need to make our move. Traffic is steady. I don't see it lightening up anytime soon."

Fifteen minutes later, Bert spotted a wide shoulder. He slowed the SUV and told Jack to call Cummings. "Get your face gear on. Remember now, no English. Jack, just Spanish if you can remember it. Harry, only Japanese, and I'm pretty damn good in Arabic. Even if we screw it up, they aren't going to know the difference."

Jack punched in Cummings's number. "Drive one mile and pull over to the shoulder of the road. But first, confiscate Russell and Winters's cell phones." Jack grinned as he slipped his own phone into his pocket. He knew all of about thirty words in Spanish. He wondered if either one of the jerks in the car would notice if he kept saying them over and over. Probably not, he decided, and if they did, who cared? They were never going back to the District.

"Showtime!" Bert grinned when he pulled the SUV behind the FBI sedan.

"What? What's going on?" Russell bellowed as he watched the three camouflaged men striding toward their car. "Jesus H. Christ, will you call 911? Where's your damn gun? Get it the hell out, Cummings. I don't like this."

"Look, just do what they say and let me handle it. I think it would be a good idea for both of you to keep your mouths shut," Cummings said.

"Up to now you haven't done a fucking thing," Winters said. "Good Christ, they look like mercenaries. Fuck you, Cummings! Will you fucking do something already?"

"I detest profanity. You need soap in your mouth. Do not ever speak that way again in my presence."

"Fuck you," Winters squealed. "Oh, Jesus, they're opening the door! Will you fucking call 911?"

Cummings reached over the seat and with the butt of his gun cracked Winters alongside his jaw. "I told you no more profanity. I never say anything I don't mean. In case you don't realize it yet, we're being kidnapped. You always play along and hope you get out alive. Now shut up!"

Bert Navarro swung open the passenger-side door and pushed Russell to the floor as he jabbered a mile a minute. Jack and Harry were busy pulling Winters out of the backseat and had him on the ground, leaving the door open so no one in the passing vehicles would see what was going on. Harry rattled off an impressive stream of Japanese that Jack couldn't hope to duplicate with his limited Spanish, so he kept his mouth shut.

Winters, even though he was on the ground, was proving to have more guts than his friend Russell as he shouted to him that the big guy was speaking Arabic and he knew it was Arabic because he'd sat in on hundreds of Arabic translations. "You can't trust those sneaky bastards."

Director Cummings opened the door and slid out the driver's side, but not before he slid his gun and the three cell phones across the seat. Jack jammed them into a black mesh bag that hung from his utility belt as he waited for the head of the FBI to walk around to the side of the car. Jack spoke a few halting words in Spanish to Bert and waited. A long string of guttural words ensued.

Cummings translated for his two passengers. “Mr. Russell and Mr. Winters, you are to go with these men. If I understand what this big man is telling me, he is saying he doesn’t want me because I am with the FBI, and he wants no trouble with my people. He just wants you two. I’d do what he says if I were you.”

“Well, you aren’t me, you asshole,” Winters tried to snarl, but it came out as a whimpering whine.

Harry clamped one of his swamp boots down on the man’s back. Russell remained cowering on the floor with his eyes closed.

Bert let loose with another string of words.

Cummings rolled his eyes as he attempted to translate. Finally, he gave up and said in English, “Either you get up, get your asses in that black SUV, or they’re going to shoot your dicks off.”

Russell and Winters hustled.

Director Cummings climbed back in his car and waited a moment until Jack tossed in the mesh bag. “Drive carefully, Director. Don’t lose those cell phones. They’re going to be worth their weight in gold when this shit goes down tomorrow. By the way, good job.”

Cummings laughed. "What was your language of choice?"

"Pure Bronx, with about thirty words of Pidgin Spanish."

"Good thing you didn't say much, then."

"Yeah, yeah, that's what I thought. See ya."

"No, you won't. I'm taking early retirement starting next week. By the way, what are those things on your feet?"

"Swamp boots. I'll send you a pair for Christmas, Director."

Jack could hear the director laughing as he clipped his strobe light to the top of his car, hit the siren, crossed the median, and drove back the way he'd come.

Back in the SUV, Jack slipped into the passenger side and ripped off his knit face mask. He tossed it on the floor. He turned around to see Harry doing the same thing. He was sitting between the two men but he'd handcuffed each of them to a door handle with stout FlexiCuffs.

It was obvious to all three men that Russell was scared out of his wits. The consensus was that Winters was too stupid to be scared. A string of obscenities spewed from Winters's mouth about it all being a setup, and he knew the three sons of bitches were in on the heist and he was going to make sure they went to a federal prison.

"Well, damn! See! See! Now we're having fun." Jack cackled uproariously; Bert and Harry joined in. "I love it when the good guys catch the bad guys. Just luv, luv it! Being up close and personal is so important. I just feel warm and fuzzy all over. How about you guys?"

Winters started to explode again, but Harry whacked him full in the mouth. One of Winters's front teeth flew out of his mouth and landed on the dashboard. Jack laughed harder. "If he opens his mouth again, take off one of those swamp boots and shove it in. Then shove the other one up his ass. That should shut him up until we get where we're going."

"I hear you, boss."

CHAPTER 23

It was late afternoon when Bert steered the armor-plated SUV to the rendezvous point. He pulled into a gas station that looked like it had gone out of business a hundred years ago. He drove around to the back, where a huge Dumpster was leaning against the ramshackle building that had once been a minimart, so they would be invisible from the road.

The two black Hummers with their blackened windows, engines running, looked frightening in the gray afternoon light. "Why do I feel like I'm in a Stephen King movie?" Jack asked under his breath.

"What's going on? Where is this place? I want out of here right now. This is God-damn kidnapping. I'll have your asses for this, all three of you. Russell, do something," Daniel Winters bellowed.

The fund-raiser stared straight ahead but remained silent.

"Shut up," Bert said. "I can't stand that whiny voice of yours. How the hell did you ever get to be the president's chief of staff, anyway?"

Russell finally spoke. "He probably blackmailed him. That little shit isn't even good at what he does. The rumor in town is that he's going to get his walking papers if the president gets in for a second term. Didn't you figure out yet that this is what it's all about?"

"Well, yeah, I did figure it out. I just like hearing that little squirt make himself sound important. Loser," Jack snarled.

"You're going to regret this. Russell is just a greedy bastard who tries to seduce every woman in town. Sex is all he thinks about," Winters sniped.

Russell rose to the bait and squawked. "Yeah, well me and everyone else in town heard about you and that intern and how you couldn't get it up. Then you wrote a disparaging letter, and she was terminated."

"Boys, boys, boys! Enough of this pettiness. You're giving me a headache. Just sit there and worry about what's going to happen to you at the hands of the vigilantes," Jack said.

"It will be dark in fifteen minutes," Harry said. "You sure you have the route down pat, Bert?"

"Got it. I take the lead. I've been at The Point before, so I pretty much know my way around. It's not like we're going to drive up to the gate or anything. This is clandestine. I came here with Cummings about two years ago, and we got the royal tour. He wasn't the director back then. Contrary to what the media says, the CIA and the FBI do get along. Most of the time. Relax, Harry."

"I see snow flurries," Jack said. "Temperature must be dropping." He craned his neck to look at the impressive dash with all its bells and whistles. "I'd say 34 degrees is a bit nippy. Too bad our guests are wearing Wall Street attire. Those wing tips are not going to do well in a swamp."

"Where are you taking us?" Winters bellowed so loud, Jack clamped his hands over his ears.

"All right, all right, if you really need to know, we're taking you to the vigilantes. They are going to take you into the swamp. Now, are you happy that you know where you're going?"

Winters sounded like a petulant schoolboy when he said, "I'm not going into any swamp in the dark. You can't make me."

Bert turned around and glared at Winters.

"You know, for an asshole, you're one cocky little bastard. You messed with the wrong people, and now they're going to make you pay for what you did. Get it through that thick head of yours, the life you had before this morning . . . gone."

Russell tried to lean forward, but Harry slapped him back into place. "Please, I'll tell you everything I know, and it isn't much. All this was Winters's idea. For God's sake, I'm just a professional fund-raiser who believes in his president. That little shit doesn't even like the president. All he does is bad-mouth him."

"Save it for someone who cares. We're just the transportation guys. The vigilantes are the ones you need to tell that sob story to," Bert said.

"Okay, it's dark," Harry said. "Time to get this show on the road."

Bert turned on the headlights and backed up one car length. He gave a light tap to the horn so the Hummers would follow him.

The caravan drove forward on what looked like a normal country road but was actually government property. Bert turned on his signal and made a left turn into a deeply rutted road that looked like it led to nowhere. Minutes later, he pulled off to the side and parked the SUV. Bert ran around to the back and opened the cargo hold's door. He started tossing out gear left and right. Night vision goggles, infrared binoculars, an infrared-equipped handheld video camera, weapons, and a length of steel cable.

The women were busy doing the same thing.

"We look like a pack of space aliens," Jack said as he opened the door and yanked at Russell.

Harry pulled a protesting Winters from the backseat.

"Gag them!" Jack recognized Nikki's voice.

"With what?" Jack demanded.

"Who cares?" Nikki shot back. "This place is quiet as a tomb. If they start yelling, the whole damn complex will come on the run."

She had a point. Jack peeled off his swamp boots and ripped off his socks. He stuffed them into Russell and Winters's mouths and used some duct tape he took from his pocket to keep the gags in place.

"How far, Bert?" Myra asked.

"A half hour's walk, maybe a little less. From here on in we have to be quiet. We use hand signals to do our talking. If anyone has anything to say, now is the time to say it."

"Actions speak louder than words," Kathryn said, leaning in close to Daniel Winters to make sure he got the message. He cringed, and Kathryn grinned.

"This is so exciting, isn't it, Myra?" Annie asked. "I can't believe I'm walking through a swamp in the dark, and the CIA doesn't even know I'm here. This is like a dream."

"It's a nightmare, Annie. My heart is pumping so hard it might leap right out of my chest."

"That's what I mean. Our adrenaline is telling us we're alive, and the world is ours for the taking."

"I hope you still think that when the CIA catches up with us. Didn't you hear Bert? We have to keep quiet now."

"You're such a poop sometimes, Myra."

What was supposed to be a thirty-minute hike to their destination turned into a fifty-minute slog, with Winters dragging his feet, falling down, and having to be dragged. Finally, in frustration, Harry slung him over his shoulder and joined the parade.

Bert stopped suddenly and raised his arm. He turned to Jack, and hissed, "Did you hear something?"

Jack shook his head. The others waited until Bert raised his arm again to continue. Five minutes later they came to a small clearing surrounded by old oaks and maples. To the left of the clearing was a fenced-off area. Razor wire was stretched all along the top of the six-foot-high chain-link fence.

Harry dumped Winters into a heap on the ground and pointed to the fenced-off area. He grinned down at the man groveling at his feet.

Kathryn minced her way over to Winters, dropped to her haunches, and whispered, "Do you know what's inside that fence? C'mon, take a guess, you piece of shit. No? Okay, I'm going to tell you. It's *QUICK-SAND!*" Winters's eyes rolled back in his head, and the tears flowed. Russell sank to his knees, shaking from head to toe.

A strong gust of wind whipped through the clearing, bringing a swirl of snowflakes that temporarily blinded the group. Winters opened his eyes to see ten sets of green eyes staring at him. His eyes rolled back in his head a second time. Russell, to all appearances, had given up and was just sitting propped up against a tree with his head between his knees.

The rest were a team then, working in sync as Bert lashed the length of cable to a stout oak limb that was bigger than his waist. The end dangled down over the quicksand pond. Jack and Harry were snapping at the razor wire with bolt cutters and tossing it into the underbrush. When they finished, they hauled both men to their feet and slipped the cable under their arms and tightened it. Standing at the big oak, Bert reached up to see how much slack he had. Satisfied, he gave two tugs, and Winters sailed up and over the quicksand pond. Jack did the same thing with Russell.

Annie, who was standing beneath the tree, looked up, and said, "Hey, Mister Chief of Staff, look at this!" She pulled up one of the signs with bold red letters that said, STAY CLEAR. QUICKSAND. She threw the sign into the dark, muddy pond, and they all watched as it disappeared with a gurgling sound. "That was quick," she said, her voice full of awe.

"Serves you right, you . . . you . . . you *Republican!*" Myra said.

"Oh, Myra, I'm so happy for you. You've accepted being a Democrat!" Annie gushed.

"Jack, bring Winters down and take out his gag," Nikki said. "We need to have a little talk. If he opens his mouth except to answer my questions, just drop him in the quicksand."

Jack eased back on the cable, and Winters dropped to the ground three feet from the edge of the deadly pool.

"It's too late to lie, Mr. Winters. Just tell us why you tried to set us up," Nikki demanded.

Annie directed the beam of a high-intensity light at his face while Jack stood behind Winters and propped up a screen, which had been unfolded to shield the light directed at Winters from prying eyes. Once the interrogation began, Kathryn stood a ways behind Nikki and operated the handheld video camera, recording Winters's answers for later use just in case it ever became necessary.

"If I tell you, will you let me go?"

Nikki and the others had to strain to hear what he was saying. "Of course. This is all about truth and the American way. I don't want little bits and pieces, I want it all. Whose idea was all of this? Speak up so we can all hear you," Nikki said.

With his eyes focused on Nikki, Winters did not know he was being taped, which no doubt contributed to his speaking freely. "It was my idea, but POTUS had told me to find a solution to our problem. He said he didn't want to know the details. I did nothing but eat, sleep, and drink this crisis, and it *was* a crisis to the president. We kept dropping in the polls. Those in the know said he was toast unless a miracle occurred. Catching you was supposed to be that miracle. I went to the director of the FBI, told him Navarro was a mole. Told him to set up that task force to flush you out. I really did try to get you a pardon, but the president laughed in my face. That's the truth, I swear it.

"I went to Russell and asked him to help. He was getting nowhere, all his donors were stepping back and taking a second look at the administration. The funds were drying up fast. We came up with the idea of the stolen donor lists together, but I was really the one who thought it up. Can I go now? I'm freezing."

"What about Martine Connor and Pam Lock?"

"Connor is as pure as the driven snow. Aside from sleeping around, Pam Lock has a good political reputation and is a great fund-raiser. She hit the roof when she was told the lists were stolen. She blamed Russell right off the bat. She didn't want to hide it. She wanted to go to the press right away. We had a clandestine meeting, and I convinced her — in the interests of national security — to keep quiet. She gave me a time limit. She actually had the gall to give *me* a time limit. I've told you all I know.

Ask Russell if you don't believe me."

"Oh, I believe you, Mr. Winters. That's not my problem right now. My problem is that you blackmailed Elias Cummings. You threatened Pam Lock, and by threatening her, you were threatening Martine Connor. You were going to destroy a very fine federal agent with your lies, and you were going to try, I stress the word, *try,* to send us all to a federal prison. Well, look where you are, and look at who put you there!"

"Kathryn, you can stop taping now. Jack, stuff that gag back in his mouth," Nikki ordered.

Nikki waved her arms, and Daniel Winters sailed through the air once again. Jack let him dangle over the quicksand pond for a good three minutes before he loosened the cable and let the man slide down, down, down. The quicksand made sucking, gurgling sounds as it swallowed his body. When Winters was up to his nose, Jack hauled him out, then Bert lowered Russell and did the same thing. They did it to each of the men six times and had to stop when the pain in their arms got unbearable.

The wind kicked up as it whistled through the trees. The snow had a bite to it by the time Jack and Bert pulled up, then lowered the two men like yo-yos one last time. When a second gust of wind roared across the clearing, the group could hear voices.

The women froze. Bert looked at Jack, who looked at Harry. "Shit!" Bert said succinctly. "Somebody better think of something really quick. It might be some kind of night maneuvers."

Kathryn stepped forward. "Yank them all the way to the top and let them dangle among the tree limbs. Everyone, take off your goggles. Get down, and don't even breathe."

No one had to be told twice. They all skittered toward the underbrush, where they burrowed in as deep as they could. Without the eerie green glow of the night vision goggles, the night was totally black. Unless the new arrivals were wearing the same kind of gear, the vigilantes would be invisible.

Jack, Bert, and Harry hunkered close to the base of the old oak as they waited, hardly daring to breathe.

The minutes ticked by as the wind picked up yet again. The voices sounded closer, or was it a trick of the wind? They continued to wait until suddenly they saw two sets of green eyes. The men were tall, extremely muscular, and dressed for the weather.

"Do you see this? Do you? Son of a bitch!" one of the men said. "We'll be out here all night trying to put that damn fence back up. Goddamn kids. They keep coming around here doing whatever the hell they don't want their parents to know about, and we have to clean up after them. Jesus, for all we know they might have . . . Now we're going to have to get the equipment out here and plumb the quicksand. Okay, here's the drill. Dzbinsky, go back to headquarters and bring a team along with the equipment. Don't drag your ass, either, it's cold out here."

The Sisters waited ten full minutes before they crawled forward until they were surrounding the man who had been giving the orders to his partner. As one they clamped on their night vision goggles and stood up.

"Hey, good-lookin', you looking for us?" Alexis asked as she sashayed front and center.

"What the hell!"

"Shhh. Voices carry in the wind," Alexis said, wagging her finger under the man's nose while Kathryn pulled the gun from his holster.

Nikki made a motion with her hand for Jack, Harry, and Bert to stay out of sight. The three men stepped back into the darkness behind the tree.

"Allow me to introduce ourselves. However, you go first since we're trespassing."

"I think I know who you are. Chuck Dalton."

"And what do you do, Chuck Dalton?" Isabelle asked. "Besides repair fences."

"A little of this and a little of that. What I'm told, mostly."

"CIA speak," Annie said. "We need to make some decisions here and we need to make them quickly. For starters, Alexis, take his goggles."

Alexis reached up and removed the man's goggles. She swallowed hard when she looked into his eyes. Nice eyes. Kind eyes. Warm eyes. She licked at her lips. "I'm . . . I'm sorry, Chuck," she whispered.

"I know."

Alexis blinked.

"You women are all my mother talks about. Her sisters, too. And all their friends. What's the game plan here? You're beautiful."

Kathryn was on him like white on rice as she yanked at his arms and twisted them behind his back. Annie, right behind her, kicked out, and he went to his knees. "Hey, Alexis, look alive here. One more second, and he would have had you in a neck lock."

Still, Alexis didn't move. She looked down at the man on the ground. "Is that true?"

"Yes. But everything else I said was also true."

Alexis didn't know what she was going to do next but she moved — just in time to dodge Yoko, who appeared out of nowhere, arms and legs flying. Then suddenly Chuck Dalton was unconscious.

"Now what?" Annie asked. "How long will he be out?"

"How long do you want him out?" Yoko asked.

"At least thirty minutes."

Yoko bent over and pressed a spot on Dalton's neck. "You have your thirty minutes."

"Let's huddle, girls," Nikki said. "We need to make some fast decisions. Either we take Russell and Winters with us and follow through on Charles's plan, or we leave them for the CIA. C'mon, girls, think fast. Our clock is ticking. I think we should leave them for Mr. Dalton to deal with. And, do we care if they mention our names? Absolutely not. Jack, Harry, and Bert will be given airtight alibis for this evening."

"I'll call Charles to arrange it as soon as we get back to our vehicles," Myra said. "But now, Nikki, why don't you give Winters and Russell the word on their future lives."

Nikki walked to the edge of the quicksand

pool and addressed the two men still dangling high above the swamp. “Listen up, gentlemen. Here’s the way it’s gonna be. When we leave here, the CIA will be showing up to clean up after us, and that’s when they’ll find you. You’re free to say whatever you want about the lovely women you spent your evening with, but say a word about the men, and *we* will be back. And, know this, by the time you are rescued and out of here, the men will have ironclad alibis for today and tonight, so saying anything will get you nowhere except back in our clutches.

“When the CIA finally believes you and lets you go, you will *not* return to Washington. You will go wherever you intend to spend the rest of your lives and submit your resignations immediately. You will drop out of political activity altogether and lead quiet lives from now on. And the reason you will do this? Because if you do not, the tape we made of your confession, Mr. Winters, which implicates you as a coconspirator, Mr. Russell, will be released on every cable channel and show up on the *Post*’s Web site. After that, I doubt that either of you could get a job mucking out stables for GOP bigwigs, much less working in the political arena.

“Are we clear, gentlemen? Nod if you

understand."

After the two men indicated that they understood, the women all agreed that it was time to go.

"Okay, we're outta here," Annie said.

Bert walked out to the clearing. "Since we're leaving them, do you want to make this easy for the spooks? Or do you want to make it hard?"

The women laughed. "Hard."

"You got it!"

Bert ran back to the tree, lowered the two men so that they could be seen, and cut the cable wire with his bolt cutters. Only twelve inches of slack remained, which meant Dalton's crew would have to find a way to rescue the two men dangling from the tree.

Then they were gone, and the night turned even darker as the snow thickened and fell, coating the quicksand pond with a fine layer of glistening white flakes. Suspended above the pond, the two men twirled around and around every time the wind blew in their direction, quite literally twisting in the wind.

Chuck Dalton slept peacefully, the snow covering him like a fine cashmere blanket.

Six hours later, sirens and strobes flashing all the way, the two Hummers and the armored-plated SUV roared onto the tarmac at Dulles Airport. On orders from Charles, they ran toward Annie's sixty-million-dollar Gulfstream 5, which now belonged to the *Post,* and climbed on board.

Myra, first aboard, yelped her pleasure when she saw Charles opening a bottle of champagne.

"Where are we going, Charles?"

"To an island no one ever heard of, where the people who live there will give Bert, Jack, and Harry the alibi they need. Buckle up now, and as soon as we're airborne, I will dispense this fine bubbly. Think in terms of three weeks. We'll be back on the mountain well before Christmas. Not to worry, Bert and Jack are covered. You're all safe. By the way, Harry, I closed your *dojo* and had a sign put on the door that said you went fishing."

Harry, who was snuggling with Yoko at the back of the plane, ignored him.

The women looked at one another. They were grinning from ear to ear as the Gulfstream lifted off the runway and headed to the island no one had ever heard of.

Epilogue

It was the third snowfall since the Sisters' return to Big Pine Mountain.

"It's so beautiful," Annie said wistfully. "And peaceful. It makes me feel . . . I don't know, kind of ethereal. And sad."

Myra draped her arm around her friend's shoulder. "I think a lot of it has to do with Christmas being right around the corner. We, you and I, tend to get a little maudlin at this time of year. We had a very good year, Annie. And the best thing of all is you got to speak to Elena."

"I know, I know. I think I'm going to get dressed and go for a walk in the snow. Do you want to come along, Myra? We could take the dogs out."

"Of course. I thought you'd never ask." She leaned over and whispered in Annie's ear.

"What a wonderful idea."

■ ■ ■ ■

Five minutes later, the front door of the Big House opened, then closed. The Sisters, and Charles, too, ran to the window and watched the two women walk out to the center of the compound and drop to the ground. A moment later they were both moving their arms and legs. Two glorious snow angels appeared in the deep snow as Myra pulled Annie to her feet.

"What are they doing?" Alexis whispered.

"I don't know," Nikki whispered in return.

"Look!" Charles said.

Was it a trick of the light? Was it the swirling snow? Or was there someone else out there with Myra and Annie?

"There are four snow angels out there," Yoko said, her nose pressed to the window. "Who made the other two?"

Charles smiled as Nikki sent off a little salute. The others, their eyes moist, moved away from the window.

Charles dabbed at his eyes as he poked at the fire. The Sisters sat down, Indian style, and stared into the dancing fire.

They were waiting for "the boys," as Charles put it, and their other guests.

"They're an hour late," Kathryn fretted.

"Do you think it's the snow?"

Charles's voice was soothing when he said, "They'll be here, dear, just be patient. Jack said he had to make a stop before he picked up the others. He didn't say what it was about, though."

Earlier, seven hundred miles away, Jack Emery had trudged through the snow to the gates of the Angel of Peace Cemetery. It was dark, but he knew exactly where he was going. He'd done a test run a few days earlier.

He saw her, snow covering her silvery hair. She was bundled up in a fur coat with a bunch of flowers that were frozen in her hands. If she knew he was there, she gave no sign. She didn't protest when he reached down and picked her up under her arms. "It's time to say good-bye, Lizzie." He took the flowers from her hands and laid them down on top of the stone.

"Not yet, Jack."

Jack scooped her up in his arms and carried her back to the Hummer. She sobbed against his chest. He stroked her snow-filled hair and kissed her cheek. "C'mon, it's going to be Christmas in a little while. I'm taking you home to our family. They're all waiting. This is a new beginning for you,

Lizzie. Don't blow it, okay?"

"Did . . . did you tell anyone?"

"No, Lizzie, I didn't. No one is going to ask you any questions. You okay?"

"No, Jack, I'm not okay."

"That was the right answer, but guess what, you will be. Will you trust me?"

"Yeah, Jack, you earned my trust. How long is the trip?"

"With this weather, we should get there around ten o'clock."

"I don't have any clothes or presents."

"Nellie took care of that. She did a little breaking and entering when you left to come out here. She said you had presents under your tree, and she packed some things for you. Hey, we had it going on. In case you don't know it, Lizzie, you got the best damn family in the world looking out for you. Merry Christmas, Counselor."

"Merry Christmas, Jack. And thanks. Is everyone really going to be there?"

"Yep. It's Christmas, and all is right with our world."

"The eternal optimist," Lizzie said.

"Thanks for everything, Lizzie."

"Cut it out, Jack, or you'll make me blush. Let's just go join that family of ours, okay?"

"You got it, Lizzie."

ABOUT THE AUTHOR

Fern Michaels is the *USA Today* and *New York Times* bestselling author of *Up Close and Personal, Fool Me Once, Sweet Revenge, The Jury, Payback, Weekend Warriors, The Nosy Neighbor, Pretty Woman,* and dozens of other novels and novellas. There are over seventy million copies of her books in print.

Fern Michaels has built and funded several large daycare centers in her hometown, and is a passionate animal lover who has outfitted police dogs across the country with special bulletproof vests. She shares her home in South Carolina with her five dogs and a resident ghost named Mary Margaret. Visit her website at www.fernmichaels.com.

The employees of Thorndike Press hope you have enjoyed this Large Print book. All our Thorndike and Wheeler Large Print titles are designed for easy reading, and all our books are made to last. Other Thorndike Press Large Print books are available at your library, through selected bookstores, or directly from us.

For information about titles, please call:

(800) 223-1244

or visit our Web site at:

http://gale.cengage.com/thorndike

To share your comments, please write:

Publisher
Thorndike Press
295 Kennedy Memorial Drive
Waterville, ME 04901